Praise For Amanda Robson

'I absolutely loved it and raced through it. Thrilling, un-putdownable, a fabulous rollercoaster of a read – I was obsessed by this book.'
B.A. Paris, bestselling author of
Behind Closed Doors and *Bring Me Back*

'*Obsession* is a welcome addition to the domestic noir book-shelf. Robson explores marriage, jealousy and lust with brutal clarity, making for a taut thriller full of page-turning suspense.'
Emma Flint, author of *Little Deaths*

'What a page turner! Desperately flawed characters. Bad behaviour. Drugs. Sex. Murder. It's all in there, on every page, pulling you to the next chapter until you find out where it will all end. I was compelled not only to see what every one of them would do, but also how they would describe their actions - they are brutally honest and stripped bare. This is one highly addictive novel!'
Wendy Walker, author of *All Is Not Forgotten*

'A compelling page-turner on the dark underbelly of marriage, friendship & lust. (If you're considering an affair, you might want a rethink.)'
Fiona Cummins, author of *Rattle*

'Very pacy and twisted – a seemingly harmless conversation between husband and wife spins out into a twisted web of lies and deceit with devastating consequences.'
Colette McBeth, author of *The Life I Left Behind*

About the author

After graduating, Amanda Robson worked in medical research at The London School of Hygiene and Tropical Medicine, and at the Poisons Unit at Guy's Hospital where she became a co-author of a book on cyanide poisoning. Amanda attended the Faber novel writing course and writes full-time. Her debut novel, *Obsession*, became a bestseller in 2017 and has received widespread acclaim from authors and press alike. *Guilt* is her second novel.

By the same author:

Obsession

AMANDA ROBSON

GUILT

avon.

This novel is entirely a work of fiction.
The names, characters and incidents portrayed in it are
the work of the author's imagination. Any resemblance to
actual persons, living or dead, events or localities is
entirely coincidental.

AVON

A division of HarperCollins*Publishers*
1 London Bridge Street,
London SE1 9GF

www.harpercollins.co.uk

A Paperback Original 2018

3

First published in Great Britain by
HarperCollins*Publishers* 2018

A catalogue record for this book is
available from the British Library

ISBN-13 PB: 978-0-00-821224-7
ISBN-13 TPB: 978-0-00-824814-7

Set in Bembo by Palimpsest Book Production Limited,
Falkirk, Stirlingshire

Printed and bound by CPI Group (UK) Ltd, Croydon CR0 4YY

To Richard, Peter and Mark.
Love you all, too much.

THE PRESENT

1

She presses a tea towel to her wound to try to stem the blood, but it is gushing, insistent. The harder she presses the more it pushes back. She cannot look at her sister, at her clammy, staring eyes. A siren grinds into her mind. Louder. Louder. Her eyes are transfixed by repetitive flashing lights. The doorbell rings and she feels as if she is moving through mercury as she steps to answer it. To open the door with a trembling hand – a hand that smells like a butcher's shop. Three police officers stand in front of her: two men, one woman.

The woman asks her name softly.

She gives it.

'Can we come in?' the female officer asks.

She nods her head.

Two steps and they are out of the tiny hallway. Two steps and her entourage follow her into the living room of their shiny modern flat: stainless steel and travertine, brown IKEA furniture. Two more steps and three police officers stand looking at her sister's blood-mangled body. At hair splayed across the white floor. At alabaster stiffness.

The larger male police officer barks into his phone, demanding backup, forensics, a police photographer. And someone who sounds like a robot talks back to him.

'Backup on the way.'

The policewoman turns towards her, puts her hand on her arm. She has soft blue eyes that remind her of a carpet of bluebells hovering like mist on the floor of the woods back home in springtime. Woods where they used to play.

'You said on the phone that you'd killed your sister. Is that what happened?' the policewoman asks.

'I thought she was going to kill me. So I . . . So I . . .'

She cannot continue. She cannot speak. She opens her mouth but no words come out. She hears a howl like a feral animal in the distance, and then as the policewoman puts her arm around her shoulders and guides her towards the sofa, she realises that she is the one making the noise.

The policewoman sits next to her on the sofa, smelling of the outside world. Of smoggy city air. Soft blue eyes melt towards her.

'What happened?' the policewoman asks.

'My sister was angry. So angry. I've never seen her like that. Never.'

Her words die in the air, like her sister has died. They just stop breathing, without the blood. She moves towards bluebell eyes. The police officer puts her arm around her and she clings to her, sobbing. The woman strokes her back, whispers in her ear, rocks her back and forth, like a baby.

She sits for a while. She does not know for how long. Time has abandoned her. Somewhere in the distance of time that she is no longer part of, her neck stops bleeding. Somewhere in the distance of time her flat is invaded. By people in cellophane suits wearing plastic caps and rubber gloves. By a photographer. By an army of dark-suited people with no uniforms.

Somebody is moving towards her. She cannot see him properly; everything is blurred — nothing in tight focus. He is speaking to her, but she cannot hear him. He looks so concerned, so insistent. Some of his words begin to pierce through the silence that is pushing against her eardrums.

'Arrest. Suspicion of murder. Something which you later rely on in court.'

And he is pulling her up to standing and cuffing her. The gentle bluebell woman has melted away. As he leads her out of her flat, she cannot bear to turn to say goodbye to her sister. She cannot bear to take a last look.

Into the custody suite. Plastic bags taped to her hands and feet. When did that happen? In her flat? Before she got into the police car? The custody suite is a state-of-the-art tiled rabbit warren. No windows. No corners. No edges. It doesn't seem real, just as what has happened doesn't seem real. Voices don't speak, they reverberate. It smells of stale air and antiseptic.

A police officer wearing rubber gloves and carrying a pile of paper bags escorts her to a cell. The cell is so modern it doesn't even have a traditional lock on the door. Everything is electronic. Space age.

'I'm just going to take a picture of your neck wound,' the police officer says.

A small camera appears from her pocket and the officer takes a string of snaps.

'And now I need to remove your clothes and bag them. They will be sent for forensic analysis. Is that OK?'

The prisoner nods her head. The police officer removes her clothes, so gently. Folds them and puts them in individual paper bags. Gives her a paper jumpsuit and instructs her to put it on.

'Forensics will be here soon to examine your hands.'

Hours later, hands inspected, plastic bags removed, a silent police officer is escorting her to the interview room in the custody suite. She looks at the wall clock. Eleven p.m. The officer opens the door of the interview room to reveal her family solicitor, Richard Mimms, sitting behind a plastic table, the skin around his overtired eyes pushed together too much, framed by black-rimmed glasses.

She has only seen him once before, when they went to his office with her mother, many years ago. She thought his eyes were strange then. They're even stranger now. She sits down next to him on a plastic chair, the grey table in front of them. The officer leaves the room, locking the door behind him.

'Your mother has instructed me to act for you. Is that acceptable?' Richard Mimms asks.

The word *mother* causes nausea to percolate in her stomach. She pictures her being told the news. Home doorbell slicing through canned TV laughter. Mother putting her teacup down on the coffee table and walking across the sitting room, into the hallway to answer the door, silently begging whoever is disturbing her evening peace to go away.

But the voice she doesn't recognise in the hallway isn't going away. It pushes its way into her quiet evening, tumbling towards her, becoming louder, more insistent. Mother is pale, moving like a wraith. For she has seen the foreboding in the police officer's face.

'Please sit down, I've something to tell you,' he says.

'Your mother has instructed me to act for you. Is that acceptable?' Richard Mimms repeats, jolting her back into the room. She looks at him and nods her head.

'Yes. Please.'

'So,' Richard Mimms continues, 'we're allowed a short time on our own together before your interview.' There is a pause.

'I want you to say as little as possible about what happened. Too much detail can be twisted against you.'

'How?' she asks, confused.

'Stick to the basic outline of what happened – don't tell the police anything personal. Anything they might be able to use against you.'

She can only just follow what Richard Mimms is saying. Her head aches and she isn't concentrating properly. All she can see is her sister's face contorting in her mind, from the face she loved, to the face that moved towards her in the kitchen.

'Did you hear what I said?' Richard Mimms is asking. 'Leave the detail to us. Your brief and me. The professionals.'

Words solidify in her mind.

'My brief? Already?' she asks.

'I've got someone in mind. Very thorough. Never lost a case.'

She tries to smile and say thank you but her lips don't seem to move.

Richard Mimms leans towards her and puts his hand on her arm.

'Keep strong until Monday. I'm sure we'll sail through this and be granted bail.'

But his manner seems artificial. Overconfident. She wants him to go away.

They are interrupted by a senior officer arriving, filling the room with his broad-shouldered presence and understated importance.

'Detective Inspector Irvine,' he says, shaking her hand. He sits down opposite her. 'My colleague Sergeant Hawkins will be here soon so that we can start the interview. Can I get you anything: tea, coffee, water, before we start?'

'No thanks.'

A difficult silence settles between them. He is appraising her with his eyes in a way that is making her feel uncomfortable.

She is relieved when the Sergeant arrives. He doesn't introduce himself. He just sits down next to DI Irvine and nods across at her. She is too traumatised to nod back.

The DI presses a button on the tape recorder.

He leans towards it, announces today's date, and the names of those present in the room. He leans back in his chair, and folds his arms.

'So,' he starts. 'You called 999 and told the operator that you'd killed your sister. Is that what happened?'

'It all happened so quickly. My sister stabbed me . . . and then I . . .'

She stammers. She stops.

'Has the medical officer seen your injury?'

'No. Not yet.' She pauses. 'An officer has taken a picture of it.'

'So it can hardly have been that serious if you've not requested a doctor.'

He stands up to have a closer look.

'We'll need forensics and medical to check it properly,' he says, without an ounce of sympathy. 'So your sister stabbed you – what did you do to defend yourself?' he asks as he sits down again.

Her insides tremble as she recollects. Her sister's eyes coagulate towards her.

'We were . . .' She pauses. 'We were in the kitchen.' Another pause. She bites her lips. She begins to sob.

She feels the slippage of skin. The resistance. The wetness.

'We need to know precisely what happened. Where you were standing. Step by step. Movement by movement. Can you remember?'

She doesn't reply.

'Can you remember?' he repeats.

She stirs in her chair. 'I was standing by the sink.'

'What did your sister say to you?'

'She was angry.'

'Why was she angry?'

'I don't know. I can't think.'

'Please think,' the DI insists.

'My sister never got angry. Not like that. I had never seen her like that.'

His words rotate in her head.

'Detective Inspector, my client is extremely distressed. Mentally incapable of continuing this interview. I request she is allowed some sleep and that we continue this tomorrow, when everyone is a bit fresher,' Richard Mimms demands.

DI Irvine presses the tape recorder button again.

'Request allowed,' he says. Richard Mimms collects his papers, crinkling his eyes at her as he leaves.

Back in her cell, all she can think about is her sister's cold, dead, fish-like eyes. She lies awake all night on the hard trundle bed, shivering and trembling.

In the morning, breakfast is a piece of dry toast, and luke-warm coffee in a disposable cup. She feels as if someone has punched her in the stomach, so she cannot touch the toast. One sip of the metallic-tasting coffee and she pours it down the sink. Then Sergeant Hawkins appears, to take her back to the interview room.

Once there, she begins to hear her sister's voice screaming in her head. A hysterical scream becoming louder and louder. Trying to push her sister's scream away she sits down next to Richard Mimms. She can smell his aftershave. Herbal. Overpowering. DI Irvine and Sergeant Hawkins are opposite, their accusing eyes pushing towards her. She watches a finger pressing the button of the recording machine. The date is announced. The names of all present. And the interview begins again.

'Tell me, when did you first see your sister yesterday evening?' DI Irvine asks.

Her words stagnate in her mouth. The screaming is overpowering her. And somewhere through the tears and the darkness and the scream, she answers DI Irvine's questions. And somewhere through the tears and the darkness and the scream, she hears the words.

'You are charged with the murder of your sister.'

Charged. Murder. Sister. Sister. Murder. Charged.

Words slipping through her brain as she is escorted back to her cell.

THE PAST

2

Miranda

'Zara, you need to go to Tesco to buy something for supper,' I say as I sink exhausted into my brown leather sofa after yet another day selling my soul as an accountant with Harrison Goddard.

You sigh impatiently and raise your eyes to the ceiling. You've been living with me for two weeks and it is only the second time I've asked you to do anything.

'Isn't there something in the fridge?' You pout.

'Why don't you take a look? It's your turn to cook.'

You open the fridge door to inspect the contents. I know only too well what you will see. Cans of lager and the garlic dips from our takeaway pizza last time it was your responsibility.

'Mmm delicious, lager and garlic – what's wrong with that?' you announce.

So hopelessly undomesticated, and yet I can't berate you. Sometimes your incompetency, your vulnerability, make me love you more than ever – my unidentical twin sister, who I feel so responsible for. Your eyes smile into mine and we both start to laugh. You lift your arms in the air in surrender.

'All right. All right. See what you mean. I'll go.'

You are gone a long time. So long I begin to worry. Mother and I, we always worry when you move off radar. You've been living with Mother for years, doing a filing job in our hometown. It has taken over ten years since leaving school for you to find the confidence to apply for a degree course. Now you've moved to Bristol, a mature photography student at UWE, it's my turn to look out for you. And I need to look out for you. Because you're a cutter.

And twice you have cut too deep.

Once, a very long time ago when we were at school. I still remember that winter afternoon so clearly. Walking to meet you from your netball session, after my hockey had finished. A perfect winter afternoon. Sunny, with a nip in the air. The sort of afternoon that fooled for a second, making me believe I was walking through a ski resort. But something was wrong. People were staring at me. Whispers on the wind.

'Zara. Zara Cunningham.'

'They called the ambulance and the police.'

The PE teacher told me what had happened.

'Your sister slit her wrists.'

A slow creeping numbness seeped through me.

'The PE assistant found her unconscious covered in blood. This afternoon, just before netball.'

'Is she all right?' I asked with a tremor in my voice.

The PE teacher put her hand on my shoulder. 'We found her in time. I am sure she'll have regained consciousness by now.'

In time. Regained consciousness. The PE teacher's words jumped in my mind. Zara, I wanted to know how you could do this to yourself. How could you try to take your own life? You whose life always seemed so much more interesting, so much more carefree than mine.

But it wasn't like that, was it? You hadn't tried to kill yourself. Cutting seems to give you some sort of euphoria.

'I cut to take the pain away,' you told me later. 'And to stop the panic attacks.'

'What pain?' I asked. 'How can more pain take pain away?' I paused. 'And what panic attacks?'

The second time you cut too deep by mistake was only six months ago. Just when Mother and I thought that maybe at thirty years old, after so many years of antidepressants and CBT, maybe you had stopped doing it. A phone call to Harrison Goddard to inform me. Just as I was tidying my desk, about to go for lunch. Mother's voice on the line, riddled with panic, only just recognisable.

'Come quickly Miranda. She's slit her wrists again. Deeper this time. The paramedic said it's touch and go whether she'll survive.'

I left work immediately. I drove up the motorway to our hometown, the world passing me in a blur. When I arrived at the hospital I scrambled out of the car and allowed the place's sprawling bowels to swallow me up. I felt as if I was floating. The hospital seemed to move around me. People being triaged. The reception desk protected by an armoury of glass, with only a thin slit for conversation. The receptionist was busy. Tapping a computer keyboard with her long blue tapered fingernails. No time to look up. The phone on her desk rang. She picked up, frowning as she listened.

'OK, OK. Will do.'

She put the phone down. At last she looked up and noticed me. 'Can I help?' she asked.

'I'm looking for my sister, Zara Cunningham. She was admitted earlier. My mother is with her.'

Blue fingernails stabbed at the computer keyboard again. 'She's in Critical Care. I'll get a nurse to take you to her. Wait by the door to A&E.'

'Thanks.'

I stood by the door, as requested. Bracing myself to wait for a long time. But no sooner had I arrived than a plump, blonde nurse wearing a pink uniform was putting her head around the door asking me whether I was Ms Cunningham. No sooner had I said yes than I was escorted into the unknown depths of A&E.

'I'll take you to find your mother,' the nurse said.

'Can't I see Zara?' I asked.

'Not right now.'

The panic that had been simmering inside me for hours became volcanic. 'Why not?' I asked.

'A team of doctors are assessing her at the moment.'

A team of doctors assessing my sister who's slit her wrists. A team of doctors assessing my sister, who was laughing and joking with me on the phone the previous evening. Just under twenty-four hours ago. The nurse and I walked past cubicles containing people in distress. A man lying on his back with a protruding stomach, his mouth covered by an oxygen mask. A young child giving a bloodcurdling scream. A woman with a black eye and a bloodied nose.

Through A&E.

Right and right again. Along a corridor with windows to a small garden with pebbles, ferns, and rubbery plants. The pink nurse stopped by a soap dispenser at the entrance to Critical Care. I washed my hands with something that looked like cuckoo spit. And then finally she led me to a small seated area where my mother was waiting.

My mother, but not my mother. A woman wearing a facial expression that my mother never wears. She stood up. She walked towards me. She held me against her. Holding me so tight as if she wanted to engulf me. She felt like my mother. She smelt like my mother. Of love. Of despair.

Deborah Cunningham of Heathfield Close, Tidebury, Lancs.

Heathfield Close, an oxbow lake of modern housing, at the right end of town. Wide pavements. Leafy streets. Divorced from my father when we were toddlers. He moved to the States. We never saw him again. Mother working her socks off as a teacher, to support us. Always responsible for us alone.

'How is she?' I ask.

'No news yet.'

'Can I get you anything? Tea, coffee, anything?' the nurse asks.

'My daughter back,' Mother said.

'We're doing our best.'

The nurse evaporated, I don't know where. Mother turned on the small TV mounted on the wall in the corner. But I did not watch it, figures just moved about on the screen in front of me, and I thought of you, Zara. Of holding you, touching you. Asking you why you had done this again after so much help, so much therapy. You always said you cut to feel better. But was it true? Or did you really want to kill yourself?

The previous time this happened, so many years ago, you denied that suicide was your motive. But it is hard for someone who doesn't understand cutting to really grasp the significance of its euphoria.

This time, the second time, somehow, I don't know how, Mother and I managed to contain ourselves, as hours and hours passed. I felt as if I was sitting in a vacuum. My life had stopped and I would only feel better if I got you back. At last a doctor was walking towards us, stethoscope around his neck. We did not stand up to greet him or walk towards him. We did not have the strength. We sat and watched him approach, transfixed, waiting for news. He stood in front of us, a half smile in his ice-blue eyes.

'Zara is stable. She has regained consciousness. All the neuro-logical tests are positive.'

Stable. Positive. Neurological. Words tumbled in my head and for the first time in hours I stopped having to concentrate to breathe.

My stomach tightens with worry. What are you doing now, Zara? Why have you been gone so long?

You finally return to my flat after your trip to Tesco, over an hour later, looking flustered.

'What's the matter?' I ask, unable to disguise the anxiety in my tone, as you waltz through the door, placing two microwaveable boxes of chicken tikka masala on the kitchen table and sighing noisily. You are wearing your Doc Marten boots and a floral skirt with a creamy background that always looks a bit grubby. I do not like your nasal piercing. I do not like the way you have sliced into your hair, just on one side, above your ear, with a razor. I don't think it suits a woman of your age.

'I've met someone,' you say.

The word *someone* hovers in the air. A word of importance. You are always meeting people, laughing with them, talking to them, dating them. But never someone. Not until now.

'Someone?' I ask.

'Yes. Sebastian Templeton. I met him in Tesco. Just now!' You are trying to look nonchalant, but not managing. 'He's moving to Bristol from London. He's got an interview at your firm.' A deep, overegged sigh. 'He's really handsome.'

All your boyfriends are handsome. Nothing unusual about that. Not that their looks help them keep your attention. None of them ever last more than a few months.

'He has a lovely voice,' you continue.

'A posh southerner perhaps?' I ask.

'Give me a chance to find out where he comes from. All I know so far is that his eyes are electric.'

Instead of eating the chicken tikka ready meal you have just bought, you inform me that you are going out to a restaurant with him. One of the expensive ones on the front. A restaurant that reeks of interior design. Plated food, pretty enough to be used as wallpaper. Edible flowers. Colour coordinated. You spruce yourself up by putting on an extra layer of make-up, run your fingers through your already carefully tousled hair, and leave.

3

Sebastian

Jude, I was sitting on the bench outside Tesco when I first saw Zara. She walked past with a jaunty step like you used to have; shiny-eyed, as if she was about to do something far more interesting than visit Tesco. Feeling sociable after the E I had taken, I followed her in. With her tousled hair and creamy skin, she reminds me of you. There is an edginess about her that makes me feel invigorated, as if, after all my problems, one day I will feel alive again. One day my life will work out.

'Have you eaten here before?' Zara asks, as I sit opposite her at Chez Luigi's.

'Once or twice, on special occasions,' I reply.

'So being here with me is special?' she asks, flicking her hair from her face. 'I bet you say that to all the girls.'

'I don't usually pick people up in supermarkets.'

'Neither do I,' she replies.

'When I met you in the supermarket, you said you were a twin,' I remind her. 'Are you identical?'

'No.' She pouts a little. 'I can assure you that I am one hundred per cent individual.'

Zara Cunningham. Not defined by being a twin. Zany.

Interesting. Button nose. Perfect cheekbones. So spontaneous, so free flowing. Someone I so want to fuck.

4

Miranda

The chicken tikka meal you brought back from Tesco tastes weird: a mix of canned tomatoes, anchovy paste, ground coriander and additives. After I have forced myself to finish it, I download the latest series of *Game of Thrones* from Amazon – my latest addiction. This evening, its strange world engulfs me as usual, then spews me out, as my favourite character dies. She is decapitated, which distresses me. There is something about decapitation that seems so much more brutal than other sudden deaths.

I am contemplating why this is when you float through the front door at midnight humming to yourself, looking ethereal and strange. You seem overfriendly, elated, holding me against you and hugging me before you go to bed, as if I am long lost, and you haven't seen me for years, not just a few hours.

And the next morning, over orange juice and Dorset Cereal, your Sebastian Templeton monologue starts.

Sebastian. Sebastian. Sebastian. A eulogy to a modern-day god.

'He's from Bristol,' you say as we sit cramped together at our veneer table. 'Attended Bristol Grammar School and then went to Cambridge to study maths. Stellar CV. Like yours. His parents are doctors. His dad's a consultant in obs and gynae. His mother's in community medicine. A lot of medical women do that. Go into community medicine because it's more nine to five, easier if you have children, or so Sebastian says.' Silence for a second as you take a spoonful of muesli and sip your orange juice. 'He's so empathetic because he's so close to his mother.'

Zara, you talk about Sebastian all the time. I know more about him than anyone else in Bristol, even though you've only known him for five minutes and I've lived here for years. He doesn't drive a car because of its effects on the environment. His chest size is forty-four. He votes for the Green Party. He supports Chelsea FC. He isn't religious. He isn't superstitious. An Aidan Turner lookalike. A dark-eyed cavalier of a man, whose hairy arms turn you on. His favourite film is *Love Actually*, which always makes him cry. Thirty-two years old.

He knows how to find the G-spot and tells you you are the first person he has ever been in love with. He told you he loves you, two days after he met you. A real romantic - big time. You love him back. You know I will appreciate him when I meet him. What's not to like, about a man like that?

THE PRESENT

5

Her mother is visiting her at the custody suite, allowed to see her in the visit area. Waiting, surrounded by grey sterility. Shell-shocked by what has happened. By what she has done. Exhausted by her long drive from the Lancashire coast.

She is being escorted to the visiting area, along the corridor, not knowing at first that her mother is here. She hasn't been told. She assumes she's being interviewed again. When the door is opened and she is brought in, the sight of her diminished mother greets her. She inhales sharply and struggles for breath.

Mother and surviving daughter are standing opposite one another, eyes locked. Her mother sees a bedraggled young woman standing in front of her, panda-eyed from lack of sleep, hair tangled, hands trembling. She smells her other daughter's blood. Her daughter sees the earthy fragility of her mother's grief. The damage it has done. Grief more virulent than disease.

Her mother steps towards her. They clamp together. At first, touch replaces words. For a while neither can speak. The more her mother holds her, the more the screaming in her head begins to decrease. Then, slowly, slowly, pushing back the tears, she tells her mother what happened. What her sister did.

The day of the bail application arrives. She is escorted from her cell by a police officer with friendly eyes and a sympathetic smile. The sympathy cuts into her. She shrugs it away, too emotionally closed down to cope with it. She pulls her eyes away from the officer as they step out into the yard and he hands her to the guard.

For the first time in days, fresh air assaults her face. She inhales greedily, drinking it like champagne, but before she is satiated, she is shunted into the van – a cattle van. Or at least that is what it looks like. The sort that takes sheep and bullocks to be slaughtered. The sort she has seen so many times rattling up and down the motorway, making her think how awful it must be to be inside.

Inside such a thing now, in her own pen, which has a seat and a high window. All she can see through the window is sky. She looks up intently. A mackerel sky. Pale blue. White feathers. Beautiful white feathers. She would like to be up there with them, flying and floating, inhaling fresh air. The van sets off, jostling her from side to side. Making her feel sick. Look at the horizon, look at the distance, she tells herself. Her mind rotates towards the feathers in the sky, but still she feels sick. She feels sick as she remembers.

The van finally judders to a halt in a car park at the back of the crown court. Now her experience becomes surreal. She cannot believe it is happening to her. She feels as if it is happening to someone else and she is looking down upon it from above. Someone else being cuffed to a middle-aged guard with grey hair and dandruff. Being taken in a small lift to a holding cell beneath the court. Sitting on a wooden slatted bench, head in her hands, waiting to be called into court. Someone else turning her mind in on itself to close it down and allow time to pass in a mist.

After a while, the grey middle-aged guard is standing in front of her again. 'You've got a legal visit. Your brief.'

She is ushered along a winding corridor, through two metal gates, and escorted into a legal visit room. A man is sitting waiting for her. A man who looks about her age. He stands up when she enters the room. He has golden amber eyes and auburn hair with a wave in it that caresses the top of his shoulders. The shoulders of a rugby player. Smiling at her with a wide dimpled smile. He moves around the plastic table he was sitting at to stand in front of her.

'Hi, I'm Theo Gregson, your brief.' His voice is strong and deep.

He takes her hand in his and squeezes it lightly. Her eyes are caught in his. He doesn't look like a barrister. He looks like the front man in a sexually pumped-up rock band. Springy and virile. About to go on stage to play a riff.

He removes his hand from hers. 'Let's sit down and talk about the bail application.'

He sits back down at the other side of the table; she sits opposite him. He pushes his hair back from his eyes.

'I've read the papers so far. Bail isn't normally granted for the defendant in a murder trial, but you have made it quite clear from the moment the police arrived that you acted in self-defence so I am going to give it a go.'

She looks into his amber eyes.

'Thanks.'

Time has melted away. She is sitting in the dock, behind a wall of glass, next to a rotund guard with a red face. She looks across at her mother in the front row of the public gallery, head turned anxiously towards her. She smiles at her across the courtroom.

A whisper of a smile, tangled by grief. Her mother is wearing her best black trouser suit and a baggy frilly blouse, which disguises her love handles. Her heart shreds as she looks at her, eyes stinging with tears.

She searches the courtroom for Sebastian. He is not here.

The lawyers are sitting at the rows of wooden workbenches in the middle of the court. Richard Mimms and the rock star brief, heads together in deep discussion. Her heart leaps for a second. Are they really going to get her out? Then the heavy leaden feeling in her stomach expands and takes over. Wherever she goes from now on her sister won't be there. Will going home help? Will her memories of her sister assuage the guilt or make it worse?

In the distance of her mind, she sees lawyers on the other side of the court. A tall thin brief, talking to a small pretty Asian woman with a neat face. Lawyers from the Crown Prosecution Service. Must be. She can't bear to look at them. She looks at the floor. At her feet, clad in the sensible flat pumps her mother brought into the custody suite for her to wear. Then she raises her head to check for Sebastian again. He still isn't there.

The guard nudges her. The court is rising for the judge's entrance. A judge with a leonine face, wearing blood-red robes. He enters slowly, gracefully, like a swan or a king. He bows to the court and they sit. He asks her barrister to present his case.

Theo Gregson stands. Bull-like shoulders. Strong hair escaping beneath his wig, making his wig balance awkwardly on his head, like a small hat. He coughs a little before he speaks. The judge is watching him like a hawk.

'I request bail for my client, the defendant, a responsible citizen. No previous brush with the law of any kind. She has stabbed and killed her sister in self-defence. She made that point quite clear from the initial point of contact with the emergency services. She presents no flight risk or danger to the public.' He pauses. 'I request bail in these circumstances as my client's emotional vulnerability after losing her sister means she should be at home, not in prison.'

'Thank you, Mr Gregson,' the judge says. His voice is long-vowelled. Almost ecclesiastical.

Mr Gregson sits down.

'Have the Crown Prosecution Service any comments on this?' the judge asks.

A barrister from the other side of the benches stands up. The one she noticed earlier with a long thin back.

'We oppose bail. She is so emotionally vulnerable that she has stabbed and killed her sister. We believe it is safer for all concerned, including the defendant herself, if she remains in custody.'

The judge frowns for a second.

'Bail denied.'

THE PAST

6
Miranda

The doorbell rings. I open the door. You step into our box of a hallway holding his hand, eyes stuck to his like plaster. Reluctantly your eyes separate and you introduce him to me. Sebastian.

'Hi,' he says and fixes his eyes into mine for a second too long.

'Hi.'

I think he needs a shave. He is wearing designer jeans: pale blue, with carefully placed rips. Well-worn brown suede boots. Black cashmere round-neck sweater. He has a black stud in his left ear – subtle but quirky. I feel his almost-designer stubble as he leans forward to kiss me. He smells of mint. He must have just cleaned his teeth. We move two steps into our sitting room-cum-kitchen.

'Good to meet you, Sis,' he says.

'Please call me Miranda,' I reply with a smile.

'Of course, Miranda. Far more glamorous than Sis.'

'Not as glamorous as Sebastian.'

He grins. His grin is a major weapon in the artillery of his attractiveness.

'I suppose my name is a little flowery.' He pauses. 'Not as compact as Jude.'

'What's Jude got to do with it?' I ask.

'Nothing.' He grins again. 'Just the name of someone I once knew.'

Zara, you and your lover follow me towards the sofa, wrapped together like a pair of climbing plants. I pour you a glass of wine each, which you untangle yourselves to accept, and then we all sit in a row: Sebastian in the middle on our large brown sofa, my left thigh pressed against his right. I shift away a little. He turns to me and gives me another shot of his grin. I hold steady, lowering my eyes. I don't grin back.

He takes a sip of wine and asks, 'How's your job going?'

'Hard work. Heavy hours but it's rewarding all the same.'

'Did Zara tell you I had an interview with Harrison Goddard?'

I try to suppress a grin. 'She might have mentioned it; she does sometimes talk about you,' I say.

'They've just offered. Today.' There is a pause. 'I've already accepted.'

My stomach tightens. So. My sister's boyfriend is coming to work in my office. A man with dangerous eyes and an over-exuberant grin.

'When do you start?' I ask.

'Next week.'

'Be prepared. They like to take their pound of flesh.'

'That's why I love photography,' you chip in. 'It gives me freedom and range.'

My stomach curdles as you say that. It sounds so pseudy. But it's true, you have always loved photography, ever since you were a young girl.

'I'm used to it. The firm I came from in London were just the same,' Sebastian continues.

'What made you leave London?' I ask for the sake of something to say. 'Isn't London the Metropolis? The place to be?'

26

'I was brought up here in Bristol. My parents still live here. I just wanted to move back to where I grew up. It's so much smaller, so much more charming than London.'

Sebastian suddenly loses interest in conversation with me. He leans across and kisses you. You melt together on the sofa like an octopus. When you have finished exploring each other's mouths, Sebastian retrieves his wine glass from the floor. He looks straight at me, wanting to talk to me once again.

'Any chance of coming to mine for a drink some time, to give me a run-down on the organisation before I start?' he asks with a smile and a flash of his eyes.

A few days later, walking to work, pulling my way up Park Street with a heavy file in my bag, I feel my phone vibrate in my pocket. I pick up.

'Miranda.' His voice is in my ear.

'Sebastian.'

I hear him breathing down the phone.

'Can you come to mine tonight, like you promised? I really could do with a Harrison Goddard run-down.'

Promised? Did I? I don't remember saying that exactly. But he must have got my mobile number from you, Zara, so how can I refuse?

'Tonight OK?'

'I suppose so, yes.'

'No need to sound so enthusiastic.'

'No, I mean it's fine. I'll look forward to seeing you.'

So, after a long day at work, I am visiting his Edwardian house in Clifton. He answers the door, treating me to a swashbuckling grin. There is something maverick about him. Modern-day pirate. Modern-day Errol Flynn.

'Come in,' he says, welcoming me into a bland magnolia entrance hall, containing nothing but an umbrella stand and a mirror.

'Follow me,' he commands.

Out of the entrance hall, into the sitting room of this fine house. A room with patio doors onto the perfectly kept garden. But the room is spiky and cold. No photographs of people. No clutter. No trinkets.

'How long have your family lived here?'

'My mother grew up in this house.'

Silence for a while. Then: 'Can I get you a drink? A glass of wine? Whisky? G&T?'

Leaning towards me, a smile in his eyes. The corner of his mouth curling, as though he is about to laugh.

'A cup of tea please.'

The laugh. Overegged and resonant.

'Zara said you were a cup of tea kind of girl.'

I bristle. 'What's that meant to mean?'

'Nothing. It was just a joke.' There is a pause. 'OK, OK, what would you like? Orange pekoe? Lapsang souchong?'

'Builder's please.'

Another laugh. Head back. Raucous. 'I didn't have you down as a builder's girl.'

'I don't want you to have me down as anything.'

'Make yourself at home. I'll go and get the tea.'

He leaves the room. I sink into one of the creamy leather sofas. Pale and elegant. Colourless. I occupy myself by looking around the room. The painting above the fireplace looks like an imitation Rothko – pale rectangles, no subject. There is an unnervingly tidy bookcase: authors filed alphabetically as in a bookshop or library. Bret Easton Ellis, James Joyce, Franz Kafka, Vladimir Nabokov, John Updike.

Sebastian pads back into the room, carrying a cup of tea for me and a glass of whisky for himself. He hands me the tea and sits next to me on the sofa. I edge away.

'I hear that Zara tells you everything, so you know I've been away at university and working in London?'

'I know you have a first-class CV.'

'I understand you do too. Do you think we're two of a kind?'

He pushes his eyes into mine. I edge a little further away, and sip my tea.

'What would you like to know about Harrison Goddard?' I ask.

'Who to avoid. Who to network with.'

'I work in Tax; you're going to be in Acquisitions. Our departments only overlap sometimes.'

'Pity.'

He moves closer to me and takes a gulp of his whisky. A greedy gulp. More like a slug. He pats my knee. 'Come on. You must have dirt on someone?'

I bristle. 'Dirt? Is that what this is about?'

'Yes please.'

'Well, I'm afraid I haven't got any. And even if I had, do you think I'd spill the beans to someone who hasn't even joined the firm yet?'

'Maybe.'

'You don't know me very well then.'

'For heaven's sake, Miranda, you're so defensive. I'm only being friendly, trying to get to know you better.'

I smile at him and raise my shoulders. 'So, dirt, or friendship?'

'Both.' He pauses. His eyes are trying to play with mine. 'Or perhaps you could just tell me how come you're an accountant, and Zara's an artist?'

'I'm interested in numbers; she's interested in photography. What's odd about that?'

'Twins usually like the same things.' He puts his hand on my arm. 'Don't you find?'

I remove his hand. 'Not necessarily.'

His eyes darken. 'You're in denial.'

'What am I in denial about?' I snap.

'I don't know yet. I'd like to find out. You're a very pretty girl, Miranda. You and your sister cut quite a swathe. But which one of you is the more passionate?' There is a pause. 'You are the first-born twin. Tell me, is it you, do you think?'

I put my cup of tea on the glass table in front of me and stand up. 'I don't want to get involved in a conversation like this.'

'What do you want to get involved in?'

'Nothing.'

A Machiavellian grin. 'Adventurous, aren't you?'

How has Zara managed to find this man? I suppose good character judgement was never her strong point. So many boyfriends. Never the right one. I've never met the right one either, but I've not tried so many in the process. At least the men I have had relationships with have been reliable. And polite.

I leave without saying goodbye. He doesn't try to stop me. He doesn't come after me.

Out through the icing-sugar hallway. Out onto a street, once architecturally pretty, now invaded by multi-coloured recycle bins. Pushing my way through light drizzle. Was he hitting on me? Or just being friendly? Like most women, I have a special gift that helps me to look after myself. A gift that deciphers friendly. I'll be careful with this man from now on.

Back at the flat, Zara, I find you rummaging through your portfolio.

'How'd you get on?' you ask, face lighting up as soon as you see me. Golden-brown eyes toasty and warm. 'His house is nice, isn't it?' You pause. 'Although his parents drive him mad apparently.'

'I'm going to send him a brochure about the firm,' I say as pleasantly as possible.

'I'm just finishing something off for college then I'm off to see him later.'

'And are you eating with him or with me?' I ask.

'What's on offer?'

'Superfood salad. There's enough for you if you want.'

You wrinkle your nose. 'No thanks.'

The way you disparage my cooking annoys me. But tonight I do not want to eat with you anyway. I want to be alone. I am not in the mood for small talk. I don't want to let slip my concern that your boyfriend was flirting with me. I leave you sorting out your portfolio, help myself to a portion of superfood, and retire to my bedroom for some peace.

7

Sebastian

Jude, do you remember the time we went walking in the Brecon Beacons, after we'd finished our A levels? Three days walking and camping in the Welsh mountains; not seeing another soul. No shops. No music. Sharp morning light on purple heather. Watching the sun melt across the horizon at the end of the day, leaving us cloaked in the intimate privacy of darkness. Dark, eerie peace.

Do you remember the night we camped at Pen-y-Fan? Singeing fingers and faces as we hugged the campfire, circled by its light. That night, that moment, the world stopped moving around us. Jude and Sebastian. Nothing and no one else. A complete life. A complete universe.

I feel like that when I hold my body against Zara's. Just for a moment, the whole world stops.

8

Miranda

Sebastian started at Harrison Goddard this morning, already there when I arrived, sitting at the opposite corner to me in our open-plan office. At eleven o'clock I watched him weaving between workstations on the way to the coffee machine. His suit tightly cut. Italian. His shirt made of silk. Highly polished, pointy shoes.

He looked up when I was staring across at him and winked. I didn't wink back. I just lowered my head and carried on reading the balance sheet I was checking. Later on in the day he came up behind my desk and put his hands on my shoulders. People don't usually touch me at work. I jumped a mile. I turned around and he was standing looking down at me, brandishing his smile.

'Oh it's you,' I said. 'Hi.'

He laughed. 'Didn't mean to scare you, just thought I ought to make contact.'

He smelt of sandalwood and cigarettes.

'Welcome to Harrison Goddard,' I said, trying to sound as if I meant it.

'Thank you,' he replied, pushing his eyes into mine. 'Do you have time for a coffee?'

'No thanks, I'm trying to get on.'

'Please, Miranda. It's important *we* get on – for Zara's sake.'

I soften. 'OK, OK, I'll make time then.'

I get up from my desk and we walk together to the coffee machine area.

'How's it going?' I ask.

'Never better.'

His voice seems artificially loud. Bombastic. I know that even if he was finding settling in difficult he wouldn't admit it. I smile a saccharine smile.

'Good.'

'I glanced across the office; I saw you sitting there, looking bored. So I thought you needed a breather. A chance to cheer up.'

'Coffee with you, the perfect mood enhancer?'

His grin widens. 'Yep,' he replies.

'Thanks.' I pause. 'Still not missing London?' I ask, fumbling for something to say.

'Not at all. Why would I? Bristol is the perfect city.'

Not the sort of person to concede that there are many different ways to live your life.

'What can I get you?' he asks.

'Espresso please.'

He starts to press buttons on the coffee machine. I sit down. The Harrison Goddard relaxation area. A cross between Costa Coffee and John Lewis. Comfortable but sterile. Too much green. He joins me with our coffee fix in two oversized white porcelain cups. Odd-shaped saucers, a little biscuit to the side. They are overfilled and as he places them down the coffee slops.

I take a sip. The coffee is strong, biting my tongue. It leaves an edge on my teeth.

'What is it with you, Miranda?' He pauses. 'Even though

you've welcomed me into your flat, I can't help feel that your attitude to me is a little . . . abrasive.'

I put my coffee cup on the table. I take a deep breath. He has asked so I will tell him the truth.

'I'm worried about my sister. She's vulnerable.'

'Vulnerable? Why?'

'Didn't she tell you?'

He raises his eyebrows a little and shakes his head. 'No.'

'Well ask her.' I pause. 'But please don't hurt her. She wouldn't cope with it.'

He sips his coffee, dark eyes watching me, considering. 'What makes you think I'd do anything to hurt her?'

Silence. Eye contact held too long.

'The way you behaved when I came to your house.'

He shrugs. 'You didn't really think I was flirting with you, did you?'

I flush with embarrassment. 'I did wonder. Yes.'

He puts his head back and laughs. A resonant braying laugh. 'Oh for heaven's sake, Miranda, I was only playing. Surely you realised that? I was just sounding you out.'

'Sounding me out? What am I? A pitchfork?'

Another laugh that eventually morphs into a grin. 'Sounding you out to see whether Zara could trust you.'

'But,' I spluttered, 'she's been able to trust me all her life.'

His eyes slither into mine, making me feel uncomfortable.

'You can trust someone all your life and they can still let you down. I needed to push you outside your comfort zone.'

I pull my eyes away from his and deliberately focus on the wall behind. 'You flatter yourself to think that someone I don't even find attractive trying to flirt with me will push me outside my comfort zone.'

'You're oversensitive. You flatter yourself to think I was flirting with you. Maybe you're one of those women who imagine all

35

men are flirts. Anyway, is telling each other how much we don't fancy each other the best way to make friends?'

'Under the circumstances, it is. We're laying down boundaries. Important in any meaningful friendship. Our boundary is platonic.' I pause. 'Platonic. Platonic. Platonic.'

'OK,' he says now using a contrived but searing smile. 'Platonic it is. You win.' He pauses. 'But for the record, platonic was all I ever meant.'

His eyes coagulate into mine again.

9

Zara

Bristol is a cool city. The perfect city. The smell of salt on the breeze. The craggy squawk of seagulls. The Georgian architecture. Banksy. Quirky bands. Quirky bars. Individual shops that no one outside Bristol has heard of. The soft rolling Bristolian accent that sounds as if people are hiding fudge beneath their tongues.

My photography course is fantastic. What a versatile, intellectual art form photography is. Although I always liked taking photographs, I never realised what an artist I was until I began this course. I have taken four hundred photographs for my extended project, although I haven't told anyone what it is about yet. It is a special secret that I am looking forward to unleashing.

Miranda, you are fantastic too, with your glamorous shiny flat. My sensible, caring sister, a sister like a second mother. But then you have always been there for me.

Most of all, and I want to shout this from every balcony in Bristol, I am on a high because I'm infatuated with my lover Sebastian. His craggy face. His swarthy complexion. The darkness of his stubble that radiates testosterone. It's the first time

I've ever been infatuated with anyone, isn't it, Miranda? You have always teased me about how I suck men in and spit them out.

And I haven't had a panic attack since I arrived.

I will never forget my first one. At school. At the start of my first mock A level. Chemistry. I could hardly breathe. The more I looked at the words on the exam paper in front of me, the less I could read them. They became black wavy lines swimming in front of me. When the result came out I had an E. Not a result to shout about. Not like yours always were, Miranda.

This bad experience made future exams even more nerve-racking. Looking back, for me, moving towards exams was like moving towards the guillotine. It was simple. My life was about to end. No life beyond them. This is not how I feel now on my photography course. My photography course at the University of the West of England is so natural, it feels like an extension of me.

After my first panic attack, a barrage of further attacks hit me regularly, assuaged only by cutting. The panic attacks pulled me down. Cutting lifted me up. So many panic attacks. So much cutting.

The last one was the night before I came to Bristol. Since I came to Bristol, the panic attacks have gone. What has stopped them? The smell of salt on the breeze? The way Sebastian melts into my soul? What will it take to make me throw away my blade? Or will throwing away my blade always be one step too far?

10
Miranda

I watch delicate fingers making the spliff, sprinkling the tobacco, spreading the shaken bud on top of it. Rolling tightly. Licking the edge of the Rizla paper, pressing the paper together with casual but practised insistence. You always roll the perfect spliff, don't you, Zara? I have never been an expert. I don't even know where to buy the stuff. But neither of us smoke much. An evening of you to myself. An evening of best Colombian Gold.

We lie on the rug in front of the TV – on our stomachs, facing each other. Your golden eyes sharpen beneath the electric light of the wintry evening as you light the spliff and take the first drag. You inhale deeply, as if you are sucking the elixir of life into your very being. A passing frown as you concentrate. Holding in. Holding in. Holding in. Release. The musky aroma of cannabis spreads thickly around us. Clinging. Sickly. Sweet. You pass the spliff to me. The same routine: holding, holding, release. The cannabis is making me feel floaty.

'You and Sebastian. Don't you think it's too quick?' I pause. 'Is it lust, or love at first sight? Don't you think it might just be lust?' I ask.

'I thought you'd ask that,' you sigh, looking into the distance beyond me. 'But it isn't lust, it's definitely love,' you continue. 'And when you really love someone you want them to love you back. You want to possess them.' There is a pause. 'I do worry that I love Sebastian too much.'

'What's different about Sebastian?' I ask, handing the spliff back.

'You sound disapproving.'

'No. I'm curious. Just interested. I want to know.'

The spliff is burning down in your hand. Slowly, slowly, you take a drag. Then you say, 'He's volatile. Dark. There's nothing bland about him.'

'Don't you think a bit of bland might be more relaxing?'

'No. Bland is boring.'

'So for you dark and volatile means love?'

'You're twisting my words. I didn't say that.'

'Come on, tell me, really tell me about love.'

'Should I quote the Bible or Shakespeare?'

'No. Tell it for yourself.'

'When I touch him, something jumps inside me.'

'That's sexual.'

'When I'm in a crowded room with him I don't see anyone else.'

'That's antisocial.'

'I think about him all the time when I'm not with him.'

'Try being an accountant, not a photography student.'

'That's condescending.'

You laugh your heady laugh. You raise the spliff in the air, in sudden proclamation.

'Listen Miranda, when you love someone you just know. It's a physical actuality, a certainty that settles in your mind. And from that moment on, the rest of your life swings around it. The love, the certainty, is the pivot from which everything else flows.'

THE PRESENT

11

Bail denied. Back inside the cattle truck. First it rattles along a straight road, presumably the motorway. Now it twists and turns down country lanes. Never-ending sickness. Never-ending discomfort. Even when the truck stops still the ground moves beneath her feet. Still she feels sick as she is escorted from the truck into the prison yard.

The prison building unfolds before her. It looks like a 1960s secondary modern school. Dusty, boxy, low-rise architecture. Surrounded by open countryside. Green upon green. Tree upon tree. Beech and oak, ash and sycamore. Air that tastes fresh. Air that tastes clean. But she will not breathe it for long. Soon she will be incarcerated.

She is the only prisoner to arrive today. No one else to watch. No one else to empathise with as the guard takes her through the yard.

Inside, the registration area looks like a hotel reception. Premier Inn? Travelodge? Almost, but not quite. The receptionist is a prison officer. A prison officer with shiny blonde hair, scraped up in a bun. Looking more like a ballet teacher than a prison officer. The ballet teacher hands her paperwork. So much paperwork. Piles of instructions. About the prison routine. About what will happen to her.

The ballet teacher hands her the suitcase her mother has brought in for her with a label on it announcing it has been checked. The ballet teacher, who is also Little Miss Admin Efficiency, with soft-pink painted fingernails and carefully dyed eyelashes, asks her for details, primly and crisply. Then when she has finished interviewing her, she telephones to request another officer to take her inside. Deepening her voice on the word *inside*, making it sound as sinister as possible.

'Before you go inside you will be searched,' Miss Ballet Admin Efficiency warns.

Her stomach tightens. Her chest burns. She thinks she's about to have a panic attack. She's seen too many films where women are strip-searched. Miss Ballet Admin Efficiency sends her across the vestibule to a doorway on the opposite wall. She knocks on it.

'Come in,' says an elderly voice.

She breathes deeply to prepare herself. But as soon as she steps inside the small, sterile room she sees a female officer of about sixty, smiling at her. She is gently patted down. So gently she's not sure how they ever find anything. How easy it must be to smuggle things in. That worries her too. Her insides tighten again.

'That's fine,' the elderly officer says. 'Is it your first time in prison?'

'First and last.'

A bell-like laugh. 'Good for you. Good luck.'

Back into the vestibule. The next officer is waiting for her. The officer to take her 'inside'. He is a big muscly man with bulging eyes and a bald head. Dragging her large red suitcase, she follows him into the holding room.

'You're the only one coming in this evening,' he says conversationally.

She doesn't reply.

The holding room is long and rectangular. It doesn't have any windows, just doors coming off it. It has scratchy grey woollen sofas set in rows along its middle.

'This is where you wait to go to your cell. Where you are processed.'

The bulgy-eyed man disappears. She sits on one of the scratchy sofas and waits. She tries to read some of the bumf she's been given, but there is a mountain of it. Not a word goes in.

Next stage seems like an attack. More prison officers coming to see her. Handing her more paperwork she can't read. Prison officers approaching her, asking questions, ticking her answers off on tick-box sheets. Questions. So many questions. What are all these questions about? Has she ever been depressed? Does she have any allergies? Has she ever taken drugs? Does she smoke? Is there any possibility she's pregnant?

Somewhere in the middle of all this, a prisoner arrives to see her and asks her if she would like a cup of tea. A cup of tea? How is that going to help? Somewhere in the middle of it all she sees a nurse, who checks her blood pressure and asks her more tick-box questions. Some time after that she sees a doctor. Somewhere in between form filling and medical check-ups she collects a variety of plastic bags. Perforated of course. A plastic bag for the contents of her suitcase. A plastic bag with her bedding: pillows, sheets, duvet. A plastic bag with her allocation of plastic crockery and cutlery. A plastic bag with what are laughingly called luxuries: paper, pen and pre-paid envelope to write a letter home, tea bags and biscuits – rich tea and digestives. Eons of plastic bags.

She is taken to a cubicle where she is allowed to make a phone call. Her heart beats like the wings of a trapped bird as she tries to call her mother. Ten rings and her mother's voice speaks to her from voicemail. She sighs inside. Where is she? This time, why isn't her mother there when she needs her? She has always been there for her before.

Suffocating in paperwork and plastic bags, she waits to be taken to her cell.

A scary-looking prison officer with dark hair pulled back in a ponytail finally arrives and walks towards her.

'Hi, I'm Vanessa. I'm taking you to your room on the induction wing.'

Her voice is very manly. They walk along an empty corridor together. The longest walk of her life, along a corridor crawling with pipes and tubes. The prison officer has a set of keys jangling menacingly on her belt. They move through iron gates. Through another contorted corridor. Another gate. Gates and locks and corridors. Up metal stairs. She struggles with the weight of her four plastic bags. The prison officer doesn't offer to help. It's not her place.

They reach the induction wing.

'It's late. Everyone's already locked up for the night – that's why it's so quiet,' the prison officer explains in her throaty voice.

She looks at her watch: 6:45. So early. She shudders inside. The prison officer is unlocking the door to her cell. They both step inside. She drops her plastic bags to the floor. The cell is small and cramped, not much in it. Just as she imagined. Just as she has seen in so many TV crime dramas.

'You'll have it to yourself for a few days while you settle in because you're a newbie,' the prison officer explains.

She looks around more closely. Bunk beds with flat blue plastic mattresses. Concrete flooring. A hard, spiky chair with wooden arms. A small desk. A sink. A shower. And a toilet with only a shower curtain hanging half-heartedly from the ceiling for privacy. She prays a silent prayer that she never has to share the room. The more she looks, the more she sees that the room is filthy.

Then it dawns on her. They don't have cleaners in prison. The prisoners do the work. The person who had this cell before has left it filthy. Brown marks all around the toilet and some on the walls. Dried bloodstains on the bottom bunk mattress. She looks at the mess and feels sick. The prison officer is watching her.

'I can get you some cleaning materials tomorrow.'

'Yes, please.'

Tears are welling in her eyes. She wants to cry. She wants the release.

The prison officer puts her hand on her arm. 'Take it easy. It's always tough on your first night.'

The prison officer looks at her, kindness burning in her eyes, and then leaves, locking the door behind her.

She pushes the sound of the locking door to the corner of her mind. With a trembling hand she opens the plastic bag with the writing paper and envelope in. She sits at the desk and writes to Sebastian – begging him to come and visit her. She wants to explain.

THE PAST

12
Zara

Early morning, Miranda already clattering about in the kitchen, doubtless making her porridge. Sebastian and I are clamped together, naked, in bed. He knows about my cutting now, so I don't need to hide my scars. He says the thought of me doing it turns him on. I haven't done it in front of him yet, although he keeps asking me to. He says the ultimate experience would be for us to do it together one day. One day. Not yet. I love lying next to him naked. Skin on skin.

'My mother's coming to stay next weekend,' I tell him.

He doesn't reply. His body stiffens a little. I lie, head on his chest, tasting the exhalation of his breath.

'Girls' weekend, is it?' he eventually asks.

'No. Not really. Mother just thought she'd come and see us.'

'Sounds like a girls' thing to me.'

Trying to look casual, I stroke his tattoo with my forefinger.

'I was rather hoping you'd come out for a meal with her. Meet her.'

His eyes hold mine.

'No thanks. Meeting girls' mothers is not something I do.'

There is a pause. 'Not yet.' Another pause, longer this time. 'Maybe never.'

And I've not met his parents yet either. A wave of fear washes through my core. What's all this about avoiding each other's parents? Despite his protestations of love, am I just a fling?

13

Sebastian

Jude, she wants me to meet her mother – already. For obvious reasons I couldn't face it. Don't you think that would have been one step too much?

I've been having nightmares again. The dreams are getting worse. Last night I dreamt we were in the hallway. I saw you all moving in slow motion. First, Mother reaching for her jacket – the soft lambskin she always wore, stretching her arm, stretching, stretching her hand to pull it from the coat hook. Fifty-seven years old. Hands already developing age spots. Dappled like frog-skin. Her three-diamond engagement ring glistening in the light piercing through the leaded window of the hallway.

As she looked across at me and smiled I watched the wrinkles fanning from her eyes deepen into furrows. In my dream I knew I had never loved her as much as I did in that moment. I experienced a sudden realisation of her vulnerability. As if up until then I had always taken her for granted. She always used to say that parents should be taken for granted. That was their role. To provide so much love it became a natural part of life. Love, like air, necessary and always there. A permanent background. I took her in my arms and hugged her. I never wanted to let her go. But I had no choice. Her body dissolved in my arms.

Then Father stepped towards me. Dressed in his favourite outfit, country singer meets accountant. Checked shirt. Carefully pressed Levi jeans.

And you, Jude. In my dream, you were walking down the stairs on constant replay. You never got to the bottom. I tried to put my hand out to reach you, to pull you forwards, but our fingers couldn't touch.

And then suddenly, the tempo of the dream changed. You stepped from the stairs into the hallway. Mother reappeared. Father held her hand, and you too, Jude. All three, holding hands in a line, stepping towards the front door. I stood in the doorway to stop you leaving, but you were marching now, stomping towards me. And when you reached me you stepped right through me, for your bodies were not bodies but shadows.

I woke up talking to your shadows. Shouting. Begging you to come back. Then I realised no one was there. No family. No shadows. I reached across for the jar of pills by my bed and took some diazepam, to calm me down.

14

Miranda

Mother is in town. Zara, you and I are her welcome party at Bristol Temple Meads Station. Pleased to be out of a suit, I am weekend casual, wearing Hugo Boss jeans and a silk polo-neck jumper. You are, as usual, arty-farty funky. You haven't disposed of the skirt or the boots. Mother winces when she sees your hair but she doesn't say anything. Despite your weird attire, she hugs you first, as is her custom.

Sebastian has disappeared. Gone to dust. Every trace of him in my flat has been removed. No tatty toothbrush lying in the bathroom basin. No razor. No aftershave. To make sure Mother is comfortable, you move out of your bedroom and camp on the sofa. Zara, you are heavy this weekend – sultry and pouty. Despite your mood, we plod along together showing her the sights. An art exhibition at the Arnolfini, bold and impressive, followed by tea and cake at the café. A trip round the SS *Great Britain*.

Saturday night. Dinner at the Ribshack on the front. But your mood is thickening, Intensifying. After a rather turgid conversation you stomp to the toilet. Men's eyes follow you. Men's eyes always follow you despite your weird attire. It is your ambiance. Your perfect figure. Your perfect cheekbones.

I try my best to look nice, but I am tall and thin and flat-chested. When I put my eyeliner on carefully you flatter me by telling me I look like a cross between Lily Allen and Keira Knightley. I wish. But when I look at myself in the mirror all I see is a serious woman with large eyes and a prominent nose. The Ancient Egyptian look, verging on clown.

'What's the matter with Zara?' Mother asks as soon as you leave the table.

'She's sulky because she's not seeing her boyfriend this weekend.'

'But we're not stopping her. We invited him to come this evening.'

'That's the problem. She doesn't understand why he didn't want to join us.'

Mother's face furrows in concern. 'Is he just busy doing something else, or didn't he want to meet me?'

'I don't know. And she obviously doesn't know either. That's why she's so scratchy. They spend a lot of time together, but it's early days. They've only known each other a few months. We can't worry about it.'

Mother's worried eyes shine into mine.

'I can.' There is a pause. 'She can't cope with being hurt.'

'I know.' I put my hand on my mother's arm. 'If it gets anywhere near that I'll encourage her to break if off. Come on, Mother, it's OK. Everything's under control. We're adults now.'

'Nothing is ever completely under control. I can't help worrying. I keep remembering six months ago. What if it happens again? What if she really hurts herself?'

I don't tell Mother, but what happened six months ago is constantly haunting me as well. Not just my memory, but what Zara told me it was like. Blood. The rush. The feeling of release. Realising she had cut too deep. Sitting on the toilet at work, trying to stop it. Pressing and pressing against a never-ending fountain of blood. Too weak to panic. Pressing and pressing until her world turned black.

I push the memory away and I am back in the Ribshack in Bristol looking at my mother. Although a bit chubby now, she is still soft and pretty. She looks a bit like you, Zara, with her pale-chestnut eyes and golden hair. I must look more like my father, the man I have never known.

'What if it happens again? What if she really hurts herself?' Mother repeats.

'She still Skypes her therapist regularly. That helps.' Another pause. 'I really think she's all right.'

When did things change? When did I become the one who had to reassure my mother? I squeeze her hand. She squeezes back. Her eyes calm and soften.

Zara is returning from the toilets, weaving between tables, almost smiling through her pout. She bumps into an elderly man who rests his eyes a little too long on her as she apologises.

'Come on. Let's get the bill,' she says to us. 'When we get home I'm going to show you my coursework portfolio.'

She seems a little more relaxed now.

We walk home. Arm in arm along Harbourside. Past the smokers outside the sports pub, heads together chatting conspiratorially as they puff. Past groups of girls in short skirts striding out and giggling, about to go clubbing. A middle-aged man walking a Westie. A man slumped on the pavement strumming a guitar, a cap to collect money by his side. Electric light dappling the water, softening the city, softening the darkness. Into our flat for a nightcap.

Mother and I sit on our sofa, drinking another glass of wine each. Alcohol is softening our edges, helping us to relax. Zara disappears to her bedroom and returns with her photography portfolio.

'This is my extended project,' she announces proudly and places it on the coffee table in front of us.

We lean forward to look at it; Mother opens the folder. First, an A4 blow-up of Sebastian's face. His handsome craggy face, bearing a confident grin. She turns the page. Ten small photographs of Sebastian. Ten different expressions. Each one laughing and smiling. Another page. More photographs of Sebastian. Some straight-faced. One frowning. One raising his eyes. Hundreds of photographs. All of Sebastian. Close-ups of his face. A smile. A grin. Another sultry frown.

Sebastian. Sebastian. Sebastian, everywhere we look.

Mother and I exchange a worried glance. Zara Cunningham. How much are you in love?

THE PRESENT

15

Allowed out of prison for her sister's funeral. Sitting in the back of a police car, siren blasting.

Three hours up the motorway back to her hometown. Three hours sitting in silence watching juggernauts and cars. The back of the driver's head. Flies catching on the windscreen. Three hours remembering the feel of her sister's skin splitting as she stuck the knife in. How her sister's head jerked backwards and her eyes clouded. A sight she will never forget.

The police car pulls off the motorway onto Tidebury bypass, wrapping her in familiarity. It feels as if her sister is here. As if she hasn't gone. She imagines her sister with her. The soft sound of her sister's breath as she rests her head on her shoulder, her tousled hair smelling of musk.

The police car turns left at the roundabout, past Warren Farm onto Southport Road. Right onto Paradise Lane, past their primary school. Tracing the way they used to walk home from school, the wide bend at the corner of the lane, past what was once a private school with sumptuous grounds that has recently evolved into a housing development. Past the end of our close. Her stomach rotates. Left at the crossroads, where in late spring, they always stopped to admire the mass of bluebells. Her stomach is like a stone. Left again at St Peter's Church.

St Peter's Church. Attached to their local C of E primary school. The church they attended every term time Wednesday morning, for six years, from the age of five to eleven. Six long, slow years. Time is distorted in youth. Walking from school to church, hand in hand, along Church Path, beneath the dappled shade of chestnut and sycamore. Entering its hallowed hall. The smell of polish and silence. The thumping voice of the vicar. Boredom ameliorated by respect. Sisters together forever, frozen in memory, still holding hands.

The driver parks outside the church; the hearse and the family car arrive and park in front of them. She sees her sister's mahogany coffin covered in lilies. Her mother unfolds herself from black metal and moves towards the police car. The guard she is cuffed to sidles along the seat and accompanies her out into this cloudy day, the air a cascading mist of dampness, the sky gunmetal black, to match her mood.

Somewhere on the pavement she meets her mother. Her mother manages to take her in her arms without manhandling the guard who stiffly avoids the love-in.

'So pleased they let you come,' Mother says in a weak voice.

Although she could stay like this forever, holding on to her mother for comfort, it starts to rain and they move inside. Past elders of the church handing out service sheets. Past sheaths of white roses and lilies. Past burning eyes. The church is almost full as they move to their reserved seats on the front row. Mother on her left, right hand in hers. Flanked on the right by her guard. Her mother squeezes her hand and turns to look at her, but her eyes seem veiled, concussed.

She turns to glance around the church. It is overflowing with people and restrained emotion. So many people – three lines standing at the back. Some people from school she recognises.

Many people she doesn't. She never realised her sister knew so many people. She supposes young death always attracts a big congregation. A tangle of pity and respect.

The organ begins to trumpet. Everybody stands. The organ continues: deep-throated, regal, majestic. Slowly, slowly, her sister is carried down the aisle, wrapped in her mahogany package of death. Slowly, slowly, balanced on the pallbearers' shoulders, who place her carefully in front of the altar between the choir stalls, and gently move away.

Silence.

The vicar appears like an actor in a surreal play and stands to the left of her sister's coffin.

'First, let us sing,' he announces.

The organ rises with a melodious thumping. They sing her sister's favourite hymn. They kneel. They pray. Attached to the police officer it is uncomfortable. She closes her eyes to join in, but she cannot concentrate and opens them again. She turns around to look at faces, twisted shut in prayer. The church in ecclesiastical overdrive. All thoughts swirling towards eternity and the death of her sister. So much love. So much energy. The emotions of the people in the church press against her and make her feel wretched.

As she turns her head back to the front, back to the floor, she notices a length of gold braiding. A vicar's belt. Nestling in the dust at the end of the pew. Gently, she stretches towards it, carefully pulling as far away as possible from the police officer she is attached to. He doesn't notice. She manages to grab it with her fingers and push it into the pocket of her coat.

Prayers are over. They stand and sing again. They listen to the vicar eulogise. In death, her sister is even more perfect than she was in life. Mother cries. She cries inside. The organ pulsates more grandly than it did at the start and the pallbearers carry her sister away. A sleeping princess, away to the hearse, away to the crematorium where she will burn to ash. Mother will follow and she will be escorted back to Eastwood Park. She's not even allowed to go to the wake. She walks with her mother behind her sister's coffin, still shackled to the guard. Head down, the church's sea of blue carpet drowning her.

Suddenly, she looks up to check her balance. Sebastian. Sitting at the end of a row. Eyes burning angrily into hers. Glowering at her, in a way she has never seen before. Her heart stops. She is frightened. He is trying to kill her with his eyes. To suffocate her. To drown her. She stops walking for a second. The guard has to stop walking too. Stopping to gain the strength to pull her eyes away from him. In the distance of her mind, she sees Theo. Theo's gentle eyes push Sebastian's eyes away. Amber eyes melting her pain. Soothing her like honey.

16

Sitting in the car on the way back to prison, after the funeral, she is crying. Tears tumble silently down her face. She can't stop them. She wishes she had died at the same time as her sister. The day her sister died, her life also stopped. If only she had died instead. That would have been easier. This is no way to live. Body and brain numb. She cannot think. She cannot feel. She will never enjoy anything again.

The sight of her grieving mother sears across her mind, painful and corrosive. The sight of her sister's grieving friends. Of Sebastian's eyes. Sebastian's eyes telling her how much he hates her. That he never ever loved her. He always loved her sister.

If she lived in America, they would electrocute her. If she lived a hundred years ago they would hang her. In modern-day UK she needs to find a way to kill herself. She touches the discarded vicar's belt that is now — after she was uncuffed for a visit to the toilet — wrapped around her waist. Her stomach tightens. She is not quite sure what she can attach it to. But she will find a way. People frequently do, even in prison, in this day and age.

The guard she is cuffed to is watching her. His fingers reach for hers. He squeezes them. 'It will get easier,' he says. 'This will be the worst day. They will help you when you get back to prison.'

His words float in the air, ineffective, meaningless. Help. How can anyone help? Her desperation has gone too far.

Back to Eastwood Park. Back through reception. Back into the holding area, face wet with tears. Into a room where she is patted down gently by an overweight prison officer, who smiles at her indolently, at first. But his search becomes more thorough. His fingers probing and insistent. He finds the rope.

'What's this?' he asks, unravelling it from her waist.

She doesn't reply. She stands silently, still crying. He presses a buzzer to request backup. Within seconds two more prison officers enter the room.

'Watch her carefully. Watch her every move.'

He leaves the room, taking the rope. She sits down and continues to cry, while the two backup officers stand by her side, watching her like hawks. The overweight officer, whose thighs snake across one another as he walks, returns and steps towards her.

'I know this has been a very difficult day for you. We will do our very best to help you. We are taking you to a new cell in the special wing and sending a doctor to see you immediately.'

She is crying and crying, head in her hands.

The cell in the special wing has no sheets, just a blue mattress and a duvet too thick to roll into a ligature. No hooks. No sharp edges. Totally open plan to the bathroom with a large window in the door so that her every movement can be viewed at all times. Suicide watch big time. No privacy.

She has changed out of her own clothes and is wearing paper pyjamas; they have even removed her underwear. She lies on the bed beneath the duvet and continues to whimper. Time has evaporated. Become irrelevant. Somewhere as she floats in its vacuum, the doctor arrives.

The doctor has ginger hair and watery blue eyes. His skin is pale. Almost translucent. Like delicate fine bone china. He is young and slim and riddled with concern. He kneels at her side by the bed.

'I'm Doctor O'Byrne. I'm here to try and help you. Can you sit up and talk to me?'

She doesn't move. The crying stops for a second and then starts again.

'Please,' he begs. 'Please stop crying. Please talk to me. Otherwise, after the trauma you've been through today, I may have to sedate you.'

A movement beneath the duvet. Her head appears. She is inhaling deeply in an attempt to stop crying, her face blotched red after so many tears.

'How are you feeling?' Dr O'Byrne asks, leaning towards her.

'I can't live without my sister. I wish I was dead,' she says, tears still streaming down her face.

'Is that why you hid the cord? Because you wanted to use it to kill yourself?'

She wipes her face with her hand. 'Yes.'

'Were you thinking about your mother? How much she would miss you?'

'I've killed her, as well as my sister. My mother would be better off without me.'

'No. No. She loves you. She needs you. She will be here to see you as soon as possible.' There is a pause. 'I'm starting you on antidepressants, and I am recommending you see a counsellor urgently.'

He fills the plastic cup from her hand basin with water. 'Here, take these.'

THE PAST

17

Zara

We are sitting in the Roebuck pub by the fire, watching the flames twist and dance. I'm sipping a G&T; Sebastian is cradling a pint.

'Mother's visit went well, but I missed you, Sebastian,' I say.

'I missed you too.'

His eyes shine intensely into mine. I lose myself in them.

After a while, I ask, 'Did you miss me? Or just my body?' I'm trying to make my voice sound curious and light, deliberately adding an idleness to it.

'I missed you. All of you.' He reaches across the small mahogany table between us and takes my hand. 'Of course.'

I let him squeeze my hand and then I pull it away from his. 'But where did you go?'

He stirs uncomfortably. 'Home.'

'To see your parents?'

'No. They're away. On a cruise.'

'To see your friends?'

'They're all away.'

Silence settles between us. We return to watching the fire. We sip our drinks. Sebastian's face is strong and sullen. After a while he says, 'Zara, the truth is sometimes I just need a little time on my own.'

His words panic me. Is he about to finish with me?

'We all do,' I manage to say, flashing him what I hope looks like an understanding smile.

'Not like me.' His face is stormy now. 'Sometimes if I'm not alone, really alone for a while, I feel as if . . . as if . .' His voice stammers and stops. 'As if my world will end,' he continues. 'As if the sky will fall on me and crush me to death, if I don't escape somewhere for a while, totally alone.'

He reaches for his pint from the table in front of him and takes a large gulp. I watch his Adam's apple rise and fall as he swallows.

'As long as you wanted to come back,' I say.

His eyes soften. 'Zara, I will always come back.'

We return to the flat, go straight to bed and make love. Urgent, passionate love. Our bodies sing together with pleasure. When it is over we lie in bed replete, side by side, fingers touching. Sebastian whispers, 'This is it. Tonight. Let's cut.'

My stomach tightens. I roll on top of him and kiss him.

'OK, my love.'

I slip out of bed trembling with anticipation. A hint of fear. I fumble in my dressing table drawer to find the new pack of razor blades, hidden beneath my tights. Then I go back to the bed, take his hand in mine, lead him to the bathroom, and switch on the light. After the soft moonlight of the bedroom, curtains left wide open, the bathroom halogens feel cold and harsh. They push into our eyes and make us blink.

We stand in the middle of the bathroom, naked. My eyes adjust. He stands before me, long-limbed with dark downy hair on his legs and forearms, chest rippling with muscle. I love the snake tattoo that curls around his stomach, mouth open, forked tongue stopping at the stem of his penis. It really turns me on. He leans towards me. I melt into him. We kiss. Gently at first, then greedily. I pull away from him.

'Give me your arm.'

He trusts me. He gives me his arm. I lead him to the sink. I turn his inner wrist upwards and press it on the side of the sink. He turns his head and kisses me again, lips hard against mine. A bite not a kiss.

'You cut me,' he whispers.

'Hold it tight,' I instruct, voice trembling. With a shaking hand, I take a fresh blade and move it towards his wrist. I am vibrating with anticipation, not panic. I know how to do this. How to cut without causing damage. The therapist has taught me. I am an expert. Ever since my first accident I have learnt so much. No one knows more about cutting than me. I know how to really cut. Just how deep. Just how much.

I bite my lip. I move the blade towards his wrist. I touch it against his skin. I feel the skin separate. He inhales deeply. The inhalation of his breath, the way his lips part slightly, turns me on. I see the blood line. The seepage. Sweet seepage. Sweet, sweet seepage. Sweet release.

'Do you feel it?' I ask.

He closes his eyes. 'I feel it,' he whispers.

I stand on tiptoes and whisper in his ear, 'And now you must do it to me.'

We stop his blood. We wipe his wound with antiseptic, and dress it.

He is nervous. I sense hesitation as he cuts me. But it feels good. So good. The pain. The pain that takes pain away. The moment of euphoria. Euphoria that no one but a cutter under-stands. The euphoria that cannot be explained.

He helps me stop my blood, eyes holding mine as he band-ages my wound. We hold hands and snuggle back in bed, limbs entwined. We kiss for a while, snogging like teenagers for the first time at a party. Before snogging became foreplay. Suddenly Sebastian breaks off.

'I don't trust your sister,' he announces.

His words shoot into me like bullets. My body springs away from him a little. 'Why ever not?'

'She's twisted.'

'Twisted? You're joking. She's a rampant goody two-shoes, not like us.'

He is lying on his back now, dark hair tousled, distinct against the white pillow. I see in the moonlight that he is shaking his head.

'No, she's the one who's twisted,' he repeats.

I am knocked back by his attitude. Miranda, you always treat him so kindly, so thoughtfully. He spends so much time in your flat. Or at least he was doing until Mother visited, and now that she's left he's come straight back.

'She's very caring,' I say indignantly. 'Sometimes she comes over as a bit bossy. But her heart's in the right place. If she's too bossy sometimes it's only because she cares. I know she seems a little self-righteous at times . . . but . . .'

'Self-righteous. That's it,' he almost snarls. 'You've put your finger on it. It's the self-righteousness that I don't trust.'

It's the self-righteousness that I don't trust.

His words reverberate in my head. I shudder inside. For a split second I know what he means, here and then gone. I push his words away. I love my sister. Always will. Always have.

18

Sebastian

Jude, I don't like to admit it but the cutting turned me on. I am disgusted with myself. How could hurting the woman I love make me feel hot? You can't imagine that, can you? Maybe it's because it made me feel part of her. But it's not going to happen again. I am going to help her to stop. You must know I can't bear to hurt someone else I love. Not again.

I walk across the bedroom and reach for my diazepam. I sit, head in hands, waiting for it to calm me. I close my eyes and see you all once again on the driveway, waiting for me to get the car out of the garage.

The turn of Mother's head. Father smiling, putting his fingers to his mouth and stroking his moustache. You stand there looking at me, afternoon sun shining from behind your head like a halo. That is how I think of you sometimes. Like an angel shining down at me from heaven, surrounded by the flowers that lined the driveway: lupins, dahlias, delphiniums. I couldn't even bear to keep the flowers that grew there. I removed them. The driveway is surrounded by shrubs and bushes now. No colour at all.

19

Miranda

Ten o'clock on Monday morning. Sitting at my desk. Anastasia Sudbury, our accountancy partner, is walking towards me, flanked by Sebastian, who is carrying a cardboard box. What can she want? Except for our assessments, she doesn't usually communicate with staff as junior as Sebastian and me. She normally looks through associates as if they are air.

They arrive at my desk, Sebastian grinning like a fox.

'Good morning, Miranda,' Anastasia says.

That's something. I didn't think she could remember my Christian name.

'Tax and Acquisitions are merging together for a new case, and Sebastian is coming to work with you for a while,' she says, gesticulating towards him with her right hand.

He nods and his grin widens. Over-whitened teeth so perfect he should be in a toothpaste advert. She points at the empty desk space next to me. Sebastian sinks into his new chair and starts to unpack his box.

'Notes on the acquisition you're dealing with,' Anastasia says, thumping a thick manila folder onto the middle of my desk. 'Seb's dealing with the acquisition cost. You're sorting out tax liability.'

'What about my current tasks?' I ask.

'Obviously they'll have to be kept in the air too,' she snaps.

I sigh inside. I'm already so busy. But what Anastasia wants, Anastasia gets. I know from experience it's best not to argue with her. Although, for my sins, I've tried to no avail on a number of occasions. However difficult it is, I must cope with this.

'OK. Fine. I'll get on to it, right away,' I reply.

'Please do. I need the first indicative briefing in three days' time.'

Three days. Doubtless I could do with three months. She saunters away through the junior office, back towards her lair, ignoring everyone as usual. Everyone pretending to ignore her. Silence reverberates across the thin layer of pretence. As soon as she has gone, happy background chatter begins again. I turn to Sebastian. He is still unpacking his files and papers.

'Welcome,' I say and try to smile. But I am worried about how much work Anastasia has just asked me to do; and about having to sit next to him. So the smile doesn't manage to spread around my face. 'When did you know about this?' I ask.

'I've known for a while, but Ana asked me not to say.'

'Ana? Are you on familiar terms with her then?'

'Is anyone?' he replies.

I laugh. 'Well, talk to you later. I really need to get my head around this.'

I open the file in front of me. The largest tax and acquisitions merger in the history of Harrison Goddard. Hours and hours of work. I close my eyes and try to stop thinking about all the other things I need to do. But I can't. Tax accounts for Edmonson's International, Berlin Bank, J. J. Cohen solicitors, Abe Pharmacy, AJT Consultancy, march across my mind. I need to keep calm and get on with it.

At first I can't believe what's happening. I feel a hand stroking my inner thigh. Thinking I must be imagining it, I grab it instinctively and push it away. Then I feel it again. I open my eyes. Sebastian. His hand *is* on my inner thigh. He is leaning towards me, grinning.

I gasp for breath. 'What the hell do you think you're doing?'

He doesn't reply.

'Sexually harassing me?'

'No.'

'What are you up to then? Making a pass at me?'

'Giving you an opportunity to feel a real man's hand on your body.'

I try to think of something clever and witty to say, to demean him. But my reactions are too slow. Instead, I jump up and rush to the toilets, locking myself in the first cubicle, putting the lid down and using the toilet as a seat. I sit, head in hands, trembling. I have never been sexually harassed before.

I'm not sure what to do about it.

Well I am sure.

I need to complain, immediately.

But Sebastian is my sister's boyfriend. And she is so vulnerable. I can't believe this has happened. I need time to think. Why did he do that? What's the matter with him? I can't tell Zara. If I do she won't believe me. If she does believe me, the knowledge of what he's done will destroy her.

I sit on the toilet seat for half an hour before finally leaving the sanctuary of the ladies' lavatories. I know, however difficult it is, I must try to get Anastasia Sudbury to move Sebastian to another task. Breathing deeply to keep calm, I manage to wheedle my way past her PA, into her office.

'Please can I work with the other new associate rather than Sebastian? He's my sister's boyfriend. Our relationship is too close,' I beg.

Slowly, slowly I watch her eyes harden to granite.

'You're wasting my time.' There is a pause. 'I don't appreciate pointless interruptions like this.' She pushes her hair back from her eyes. 'Sebastian has far more experience in the relevant areas than the other associates. That's why I chose him.' A shrug of her slender shoulders. 'It's a simple choice. You work with Sebastian or you leave. Decide what you want and please leave my office.'

20

Zara

I am laced in his arms as he drifts towards sleep. The sweet fingers of sleep are touching me, pulling me towards oblivion. I feel as if I am floating. Floating. Flying. Weightless. All-powerful. Eternal.

But something has happened. Shouting. Someone is shouting. Someone is kicking. Someone is screaming. I wake up. It is Sebastian, still fast asleep. Eyes tightly closed, fighting the bed covers, kicking and twisting them around his legs. Thumping and kicking. He thumps me in the chest and shrieks. I shriek back at him, grab his shoulders, and shake him to wake him up. He opens his eyes and groans. He clings to me tightly like a frightened toddler.

'I had a nightmare,' he whispers.

He is shivering. I stroke his back. I stroke his hair. His breathing slows.

'Calm down, calm down,' I mutter. 'What happened?'

'I dreamt I was in a car.' His voice tremors. 'I was driving.' He pauses. 'Everything was woolly. Unfocused. The other driver didn't see us.'

'Us?' I pause. 'Who else was in the car?'

He pulls away from me, sitting upright in bed now. 'Nobody . . . I can't remember.' His body is no longer shaking. He is breathing steadily now. 'I must have had too much to drink last night. I have graphic dreams when I drink too much.'

21

Miranda

Sebastian seems to spend nearly all his time with us. In my flat. It's all happened so quickly. From the minute you saw one another, you just had to be together. He doesn't seem to want to spend much time in his family home. He doesn't get on too well with his parents these days apparently. He is even giving me some money for rent now. Zara, you insisted. I didn't feel happy as it makes the arrangement too formal. Too difficult to break away from.

I still have to work with him too. Fortunately he hasn't sexually harassed me again, thank goodness. So perhaps it was an aberration. A one-off. I would so love to believe that. But can a leopard change its spots? I think I'm right not telling you, Zara, when you love him so much. But sometimes, just sometimes, I think not knowing his true nature in the end may cause you harm.

As soon as I think that, my mind twists, remembering the fear I felt both times when you almost took your own life. It comes back to me with such clarity. Walking through the hospital not knowing whether you were alive. Then I remind myself you must never be told about Sebastian's behaviour. Deep inside I know that is right.

So for the first time in our lives, since you met Sebastian, we are experiencing a slight distance between us. We, who were always so tight. Despite all our differences. Despite the way you fluffed your A levels and didn't go to uni. Despite my success, my degree, my job. Despite your popularity when I am so quiet. What has caused this? Is it my fault? Is it because you've never loved anyone else as much as me, until now? Until now, whenever I've needed you, I've always had you to myself.

THE PRESENT

22

Her mother is here. In a private visiting room. They are using the legal visit area, because the prison governor is so concerned about her vulnerability and is affording her special treatment, special privileges. Today the prison officers have trusted her to dress in her own clothes. Today she is wearing jeans and a T-shirt. She is hardly eating and so her jeans are hanging off her. Thinner than thin. Paler than pale.

Her mother looks like a ghost of her previous self as well. As soon as her mother sees her she takes her into her arms. She holds her tightly against her body as she did when she was a baby. She strokes her hair. She strokes her back. She kisses her. Her daughter's body relaxes a little, melts into hers.

'I love you,' Mother says. 'You told me what happened. You know I understand you had no choice. You need to come to terms with what happened. You need to forgive yourself.'

'I will never be able to forgive myself.'

Her daughter pulls away from her to sit at the plastic table in the visiting room, continuing her whimpering and crying, head in hands. Her crying is uncontrollable. Panic simmers inside her mother's heart.

'Stop it. Please stop it,' her mother says. 'I've lost one of you. I can't, I won't, lose you both.'

She moves across to the table and bends down next to her daughter, clinging to her body as much as she is able.

'Please hold it together,' she begs. 'I love you so much.'

23

Every day feels the same. Solid. Blurred and grey. They are giving her so many tablets, antidepressants, anxiolytics, sleeping tablets. First thing in the morning. Last thing at night. In happier times, she would have made a joke about it, said she rattled with all the pills she takes. But she is so diminished, jokes are a distant memory.

It is a relief at night to fall into the numbness of a drug-induced sleep. Sleep that isn't sleep. Sleep that doesn't refresh her. When she wakes in the morning she feels as if she is pulling herself out of a coma. Her head pounds and feels heavy, so heavy. As if made of solid metal, not bone and tissue and flesh. Her neck aches. It hurts to hold her head up and light pierces, like a painful laser, into her eyes. When she moves, her limbs feel as if they are pushing through solid brick.

The prison officers don't trust her. She doesn't always trust herself when she is left alone. The clothes she is given are still made of paper in case she uses them to hang herself. But they don't really need to worry – she doesn't have the energy to commit suicide; it would take too much momentum.

Sometimes her mind clears for a while and she steps back in time.

Walking hand in hand with her sister down Fisherman's Path in Tidebury. The silence of the sandy walkway pressing towards her. No footfall here. Her sister's palm hot against hers. The sweet smell of the pine trees. The wind from the sea whispering across her cheek. For a few seconds, she forgets. For a few seconds, she feels her sister with her as if she's still alive. But then she remembers and heaviness engulfs her.

Sometimes her mind reaches back still further. She is a child again, sitting with her sister on her mother's knee. Her mother smells of vanilla and lavender. Her mother is wearing her favourite mohair sweater: the one that feels so comforting when she rests her head on her breast.

It doesn't last long. Her mother and her sister fade. Searing loneliness invades again. Locked up in solitude from 5:45 p.m. until breakfast. The pain of loneliness is sharp. But sometimes, just sometimes, the pain pushes the grey away.

THE PAST

24
Zara

I return from my late-night photographic workshop to find you lying on the sofa, flat on your back, a half-cooked stir-fry on top of the oven. The flat is eerily quiet.

'What's happened? Where's Sebastian?'

You open your eyes and sit up. Your eyes are red and swollen. 'We had an argument. He stormed off.'

'An argument? What about?'

You look away from me. Your chin wobbles. You swallow hard to stop yourself from crying. 'I don't want to talk about it. Please ask him.'

'But you are my sister. I want to know what's upset you.'

You reach for my hand and squeeze it. 'I really think it's best if you ask him.'

I give up. I know of old when you are in a mood like this I won't be able to get you to talk.

I text Sebastian. He is waiting for me on Harbourside. I step back out into the sharp October night, drizzle on the wind. Out of your beautiful flat with its brand-new kitchen, brown leather sofas, and 50-inch TV. Miranda, I know Sebastian and I have invaded your home. Your life. I know that by upsetting you we are skating on thin ice. But I need to live with you. I can't afford to live anywhere else, and I need to be with Sebastian too. He's saving up for a deposit to buy a flat for us. When he does we will both move out. Please, Miranda, keep your patience with us; soon we will both be gone.

I find Sebastian pacing up and down outside a noisy bar, smoking a cigarette. He must be upset. He hardly ever smokes. As soon as he sees me he throws it to the ground and stubs it out.

'Come on, let's go inside, have a drink.'

The pub smells of chips and stale beer. The stench punches into my nostrils, making me feel nauseous. But drizzle has turned to heavy rain, so we decide to stay put rather than get drenched trying to find anywhere else. I head for a table in the corner. Sebastian goes to the bar. He buys a glass of wine for me, and a pint of beer for himself. As he is putting my drink in front of me, I ask him what he and Miranda argued about, shouting above the house music, which is pumping out at high volume.

'I don't know where to start.' He pauses as he sits down. He takes a sip of his drink. 'Your sister is tetchy. Touchy and diffi-cult.'

'That's usually how I've been described. Are you sure you've got it the right way round?' I pause for a sip of wine.

'I was only trying to help with the cooking. She got very ratty and asked me to get out,' Sebastian says.

'Is that all? How ridiculous. I'm worried about her. She's not acting herself. Maybe her job is stressing her out.'

I think back to how well you have always coped. The look on your face when you opened the envelope containing your A level results. Ecstatic, jubilant. Knowing you were off to Bristol to study maths. I knew you'd end up with a hot-shot career. You were always a bit of a know-it-all. Always winning an argument. Do you remember the heated discussion we had a few years ago, as to whether China was a communist country or not? I thought it was, but you knew better, didn't you, Miranda? You always know better. Your clever argument that it wasn't really communist as they recognised the concept of private property. You always know best. That's why you got the top first in your degree. Why you slipped so easily into a job at Harrison Goddard. Why you have a mortgage on a flat, even though Mother coughed up the money for the deposit. Tell me the truth, Miranda, is your demanding life finally catching up with you?

'Do you think she's starting to suffer from stress, like me?' I ask.

'She certainly works very hard,' Sebastian says as he sips his pint. 'I see her every day at work. She barely has time to smile. She hardly ever lifts her eyes from her desk.' He smiles at me with his eyes. 'Maybe she just needs to learn to chill.'

Maybe. Maybe that's it. She just needs to learn to chill. After all that's always been the problem with me. I need to help her. I need to hold this together.

'Sebastian. I love you very much. And I love my sister. Do you think we could just both go to see her and you could apologise?' I pause. 'Please. Just to keep the peace?'

25

Miranda

'I'm sorry,' Sebastian says, 'for getting in your way while you were cooking.'

My stomach tightens. My teeth clamp together. Getting in the way while I was cooking. But I manage to smile sweetly and pretend to forgive him for the time being, for your sake, Zara. But I can assure you, in the long run, there is no way I will let this man destroy you. And I won't let him destroy me.

26

Sebastian

What a fuss about nothing, Jude. The lightest of touches on Miranda's breast, when she was fretting over the stir-fry. Why are women so sanctimonious about their breasts? It's only body tissue. Miranda will never forgive me. I see that. In the flash of her eyes. The turn of her head. Miranda. A woman with a mouth almost permanently pointing downwards. A woman who gravitates towards darkness. A woman Zara needs to step away from. I need my beautiful Zara. I need her to myself.

27

Miranda

Relationships at our age are an emotional battle. Winners and losers. So much to play for. Sebastian must lose, and you must win, Zara. No other outcome is acceptable for your mental health.

Saturday morning. Sebastian is out jogging. You are washing your hair in the shower. I pad towards the kitchen to make coffee. I hear running water and humming. You always hum when you are happy. Pulsing water relaxes you. You've always loved moving water. You've always loved the sea. All those walks, along Fisherman's Path to the beach, almost every Saturday. From when we were small with Mother. For years when I came back at weekends.

I push my memories away.

Coffee in hand, I flop onto the sofa and start to drink, Saturday stretching relentlessly in front of me. Nowadays I never seem to know what to do with myself when I'm not at work. I think of you and Sebastian clinging together as you do on my sofa, like ivy, and panic rises inside me. Zara, can't you see him for what he is?

Your purse is on the arm of the easy chair. You must have

left it there last night and forgotten about it. Your small leather change purse. I put my coffee down and lean across to pick it up. Three cards, a few receipts, some loose change, and a twenty-pound note, rammed in. I remove the twenty-pound note, zip up the purse and slowly, slowly, tiptoe past the bathroom. The shower has stopped but I can still hear humming. Tiptoeing into my guest bedroom where you both live.

The room is dishevelled. The duvet needs straightening. Piles of clothes nestle either side of the bed, random and scattered as if they've been pulled off in a hurry. The chest of drawers is coated in bottles of perfume and make-up. Not like my room, which is antiseptically tidy. I place the twenty-pound note in the pocket of Sebastian's favourite weekend jacket.

Just as I step back past the bathroom, you appear, head and body towel-wrapped. Face flushed from your piping hot shower.

'Good morning.'

'Morning,' I reply.

There is nothing good about Saturday morning any more. Not now we both have to put up with Sebastian.

28
Zara

'What was going on between you and Miranda this morning?' Sebastian asks. 'You were shouting as I returned from my jog.'

I sit on our bed nursing a mug of coffee, watching him peel off his Lycra.

'I was a bit worked up because I'd lost twenty quid.' I pause. 'I found it in your jacket pocket.'

He stiffens. 'I didn't take it.'

'I never said you did.'

He leans towards me, mouth in a line. 'I guess your sister implied it.'

'She did. But I know it was her.' I take a sip of coffee. 'I had just checked my purse for cash, after you went jogging, before I got in the shower. Just wondering whether I needed to go to the cash point. That was when it went. You were out jogging. She and I were in the flat.' I let out a breath. 'Why would she take money from me, and plant it on you?'

'It's obvious, isn't it? She's trying to come between us.'

I shake my head. 'But why, Sebastian, why would she want to do that?'

He raises his eyes to the ceiling, shrugs his shoulders, and smiles. 'She's jealous. She's never really been properly close to a man.'

'But why would that make her resent me having you?'

I close my eyes to think as Sebastian reaches for his dressing gown and trundles off to the shower. Sebastian is right, you have never really been close to a man even though you went out with Adam for two years, and Jonathan for nearly five. You didn't seem sad when you split up with either of them. As if you hadn't really connected, as if you were just stepping along together in the same time zone, for a while.

Adam was your university boyfriend. Joint activities: going to the library, occasional coffee breaks. Were logarithms and simultaneous equations your dirty talk? Adam had looks that melted into a crowd easily. The only thing I remember about him was the lack of expression on his face. He finished with you, just after your finals. You came back to Tidebury shortly afterwards, emotionally disconnected, as if the relationship hadn't ever happened. Perhaps that's why he finished with you. Because your relationship never took off.

Jonathan, your most recent boyfriend. You were an item for five years, breaking up three years ago. He was an accountant, like you. He lived in Bath. I can't remember how you met him. You saw him every other weekend. You never varied the pattern. Whatever the weather. Whatever was going on in your lives. After you finished with him, I asked you whether you would miss him.

'No. That's why I ended it,' you replied.

So why did you spend five years of your life with a man who made no difference?

I have moved on so often. But now I have Sebastian. Can't you see, Sebastian is lightning, electricity, the eye of the hurricane?

Why do you react against him so much?

29

Zara

I come home in my own private panic to find you back before me, already sitting at the kitchen table, sorting out the mail. Most of it seems to be being thrown straight into the bin beside you. Colourful adverts for curry houses and takeaway pizza. Free magazines. Free newspapers. You look across at me and smile. I do not smile back.

'What's the matter?' you ask.

'I've messed up the timing on my coursework.'

You abandon the mail and walk towards me, eyes full of concern. 'What do you mean, Zara? By how much?' you ask. There is a pause. 'Will they give you an extension?'

You have always been overly concerned about my lack of education. From the look on your face anyone would think I'd just told you I had terminal cancer.

'I thought the deadline was next week, but it's tomorrow.' I shrug. Your shoulders widen. 'So I've just got to stay up all night to finish it.' I pause. 'After supper could you two get out of my hair? Bugger off to the pub.' You stiffen, reminding me that this is your flat. 'Sorry to be so cheeky,' I continue. 'It's just I really need to spread out and use the kitchen table. And any noise from the TV will distract me.'

Sebastian appears. Standing outside my bedroom. He must have overheard. You look at him, a frown whispering across your forehead.

'That's fine,' he says. But you still have not replied. You are watching him, eyes bursting. With dislike? With lust? But you are Miranda Cunningham. Miranda Cunningham never ever lusts.

30

Miranda

After supper Sebastian and I visit the pub as requested. We sit watching a game show on the large TV in the corner. After a few drinks, we set off home. It is a cold night. The water in the harbour has turned into a mass of dappled neon because of the reflections from the streetlights and restaurant fronts. We walk along the quayside in silence watching the water, molten in the reflected light, its surface rippling in the evening breeze. Feeling a little squiffy after too much Chardonnay, I stop and stand looking at it. Sebastian stands next to me.

'Pretty, isn't it?' he says.

I nod. And then, after being quiet and respectful all evening, he pulls me towards him and attempts to kiss me. My body stiffens with distaste. I push him away.

'What are you doing? Leave me alone. Stop it.'

'I don't want to stop.'

'But,' I stammer, 'what's going on? What's the matter with you? Are you just playing with my sister?'

'Zara and I were not meant to be together forever.'

'Does she know that?'

'If she doesn't she should.'

He smiles. 'Do you fancy me, Miranda?'

'No. You know I don't. And even if I did, it's not relevant.'

'Nothing could be more relevant.'

He pulls me towards him and tries to kiss me again, but I fight against him, harder this time, pinching him, thumping him. He stands back calmly and raises his eyebrows.

'So you love Zara more than you love me.'

'You know I don't love you, Sebastian.'

He laughs. A hollow laugh, like a pantomime baddie. I march angrily back to my flat with my nemesis following me.

31
Zara

After a rather turgid, conversation-less supper, you have both
gone out for a drink, to get out of my hair, leaving me alone
to finish my puppet theatre. My coursework. I nearly had a
complete meltdown when my tutor asked to see me to discuss
it because he hadn't seen its plan. And it's due in tomorrow. I
don't know how it happened but I'd got the date mixed up by
a month. I will lose ten per cent automatically because I haven't
handed in a plan.

Ten per cent. Fuck.

So sitting in my tutor's office, walls plastered with his speciality – photographs of moving water – my body and my brain
started to go into exam-style panic. But I managed to pull
myself back from the brink. I went to the toilets and cut. That
energised me. Then I went and sat in the park. Art and
photography are very different from when I fluffed academic
exams, so long ago now. I am in tune with photography. I have
creativity in my heart. I knew if I took some amphetamine and
stayed up all night I would be all right.

Amphetamine. I knew I had some that Sebastian had given
me, stashed in my knickers drawer in the flat. So I came home,

with the framework of my theatre and its contents, and hid it in the bedroom. I didn't want you to see it, Miranda – not yet. You try to be interested in my photography, but I know from the way your voice slows a little when you talk to me about it that you have to make a concerted effort. I swallowed a few tablets before supper.

Now you have both gone out, I feel even more positive. Full of creative energy. I take an extra amphetamine for good luck, open a bottle of white wine from Tesco, pump up the music in the flat, and get cracking. I cover the kitchen table with newspaper. I fetch my cardboard box theatre from the bedroom, and my three papier-mâché puppets: two girls, one man. They lie limply on the bed. I pull on their sticks and strings to breathe life into them, then I fetch my folder of photographs of us. The theatre's wall and stage will be plastered with them. The puppets' faces, hair, and clothes will be made of ripped parts of our photographs.

The point of it is: we are all puppets controlled by the circumstances of our lives. Clever isn't it? But you won't get it, Miranda. Your mind is mathematical, logical. One plus one always makes two. No amount of creativity or optimism could turn it into three.

I dance around the table, drinking and buzzing, sticking photographs to cardboard and papier-mâché, having a blast. Really, really, enjoying myself. Really making progress. Dance trance music pumping out.

Until, finally, after an hour or so, I am interrupted by you two coming back.

'Hey for heaven's sake, turn the music down. What will the neighbours say?' you ask.

'OK. OK. Cool it, Miranda.'

I turn it down, but I get some glue on the remote.

'Are you pissed?' you ask.

'I'm creating,' I tell you. 'I'm in flow.'

Your eyes narrow in disapproval.

Sebastian looks flushed. He walks towards me and kisses me, lips lingering on mine playfully, trying to tempt me to abandon my work.

'I'll wait for you in bed,' he whispers.

'Don't wait for me. Go to sleep. I'll be up all night. I'm determined to finish this. To hand it in on time.'

'Clever, clever, clever,' he says, eyes twinkling at me as he disappears into the bedroom. 'I'll just dream of you then.'

Miranda, you look so worried. Is it because you've guessed I've taken something? Is it because I'm pissed? Let me tell you, Miranda Cunningham, drink and drugs will not detract from my amazing puppet theatre. They will only help.

32

Sebastian

Jude, the sister started to kiss me back. Just for a split second. She wanted to, you know. A stupid frivolous bitch, always pretending she isn't interested in me. She is interested. I know she is.

33

Miranda

'Still feeling guilty about kissing me, are you?' he asks as he catches up with me on the way to work.

'I didn't kiss you,' I hiss.

He puts his head back and laughs. 'But you started to, didn't you? You wanted to.'

He turns and stands in front of me, putting his hands on my shoulders. He leans towards me. His breath mingles with mine.

'I didn't want to.'

'Do you think your sister will believe you?' Brown eyes darken to black.

'My sister doesn't need to know what happened.'

A slow forced smile. 'Deceitful little minx, aren't you? Don't you care about lying to your sister?'

THE PRESENT

34

She is sitting in front of the psychotherapist, who has visited the prison for her appointment. He is a middle-aged man with a bald head. He has brown eyes infused with kindness and a wide, friendly mouth that always looks as if it is on the brink of a smile.

'Are you feeling any better?' he asks.

'A little. But starting from a low point that's not good.'

He leans back and waits for her to continue.

'I feel punctured. Exhausted. As if I can hardly hold my head up.'

'And what about the crying?' he asks.

'It has almost stopped.'

'Good.' He pauses. 'But when it comes, what triggers it?'

She shrugs. 'Anything. Nothing. I've no idea.'

'Keep a notebook. Maybe that will help. Then when you come to see me next we can discuss it.'

She closes her eyes. She remembers. The last time she cried was as soon as she felt air on her cheeks walking around the quad during association. Being outside. A sudden reminder of how her life used to be.

A few hours later she is sitting opposite Theo Gregson in the legal visit area. Theo is dressed down today, wearing jeans and a rugby shirt. His abundant hair is freshly washed and the room smells faintly of his herbal aftershave. Of oregano. Of sage.

'Mr Mimms is busy,' Theo explains. 'He's the duty solicitor today – the only one on, so he's up to his eyeballs.' He pauses. 'So I decided to come alone. I just wanted to know how you're feeling?'

How can she answer him? She doesn't want him to know how bad she has been. She doesn't reply; she just sits looking into his amber eyes.

'What have you heard?' she asks after a while.

He shrugs his shoulders. 'Nothing.' There is a pause. 'I just thought this would be a bad time for you after the funeral. I wanted you to know I've been thinking about you.'

She can't tell him that since the drugs started to work and she stopped crying all the time she's been thinking about him too. How old is he? Is he still single like her? Could a man as attractive as him still be free?

She pulls her eyes from his and looks at the floor. 'Thank you.'

'Does it help at all, knowing other people are thinking about you?'

She lifts her face and looks back into his eyes. 'Yes.' She smiles. 'Of course it does.'

'Good. Well I'll continue then.' He leans back and crosses his legs. 'Have you heard from Sebastian recently?' he asks.

Her stomach tightens. 'No.'

If only she could explain to Sebastian what happened. Why hasn't he visited? Where has he gone? Is he having one of his claustrophobic periods when he fears the sky will move towards him and crush him? One of those times when he can't communicate with anyone and needs to be alone? What does he think happened? What does he think she has done?

'I need to check up a few things about him,' Theo Gregson says.

Her heart quickens. 'What do you want to know?'

'About his family life. His background.'

Golden amber eyes are holding hers.

'Well, he comes from Bristol. You know that. I gave you his address. My sister and I both visited his house. His parents are doctors of some sort.' I shrug a little. 'But we never met them.' Her voice is cracking. 'As it turned out, we knew him for less than a year.'

Almost a year of knowing Sebastian. The longest year of her life.

'As it turns out, you don't seem to know very much about him.'

'Is that a question or a statement?'

'A question. I saw him at your sister's funeral,' Theo continues. 'He was staring at you a lot, wasn't he?'

'Yes. His look frightened me. It was so intense.'

'I noticed.'

Silence rises in the air between them. Theo crosses his legs and leans back in his chair. 'Has he tried to contact you at all since you've been on remand?'

'No.'

'Don't you think that's strange?'

'Yes. Of course I do. He must be so freaked out by what's happened.' She pauses. 'I've written to him again.'

'Have you?'

'He still hasn't replied,' she tells him. She shrugs. 'Maybe he didn't get my letters.'

For a second his eyes cloud with worry. He is frowning. Theo usually looks so positive. She watches his frown soften.

He curls his lips into a smile. He leans down and opens his briefcase. His barrister's black leather box with handles. He pulls out a bag from Waterstones.

'I brought you a few more books and a box of chocs. Lightweight chick-lit. Thought it might cheer you up.'

Choked by his kindness, she says, 'Thanks.'

THE PAST

35
Sebastian

Preparing to lie to her sister. I really caught her out. She makes me shudder. Not worthy of Zara, who is so virtuous and kind, like you always were, Jude. Zara and I are sitting watching TV. My mind isn't here, but in another place embedded deep in my memory. Do you remember our final skiing holiday, Jude? The special day when we escaped from the rest of our party? When we went off-piste for the first time, just the two of us?

I followed you down the mountain. You were easy to see in your lime green ski-suit. I skied behind you because I wanted to protect you. Help you up if you were to fall. The snow so fresh it glistened with moisture. Fluffy to touch, like duck feathers. But you didn't fall, did you? You were such a good skier, so elegant. Gliding down the mountain as if your feet were wings.

Sometimes, I still close my eyes and hear the silence of those mountains. Feel sharp air cut across my skin. Smell wood smoke and pine trees.

At the end of the day, as we wound our way home we had to ski back on piste. After the fresh snow, the piste felt icy. Flat and weird. We stopped at the last bar, on the last corner of the lowest piste. Some elderly Austrians having a party, dancing in their ski boots. We sat and watched them. You always liked people-watching, like me. We asked for two large beers and they brought us giant glasses, a litre each. You were red-faced and exhilarated, wide-eyed and happy.

You trusted me so completely. You didn't know then that six months to the day, I would kill you. We had so little time left then, and we were so happy. Looking back it was better not to know, don't you think?

THE PRESENT

36

She has not cried at all for several weeks. She feels flat, but purposeful. Little by little she's on the way. She doesn't believe in God, but someone is looking out for her. A prison officer came to her cell yesterday, a dark-haired woman with brown eyes – dark bags beneath them – and a gold stud in the side of her nose. Asian beautiful. Slim and elegant. She stood in the middle of her cell and smiled.

'I've come to tell you that you've been allocated a job in the library.'

'Thank you.'

'Report there tomorrow morning at free-flow.'

Free-flow. The time the prison community is allowed to move around. Five minutes in the morning to get to your job. Doors unlocked. Doors soon locked behind you again. A life of doors locked behind you. A life of listening to turning locks.

Free-flow and she is walking along the corridor. She finds herself walking along next to Jane – her favourite listener. Listeners: prisoners who have been trained by the Samaritans, to listen to other prisoners who need help. And she has been so distressed she has needed a listener almost every day. Jane has come to see her so often she's become a friend. She is a middle-aged mousy blonde, with a pale voice, pale skin, and pale eyebrows. Eyebrows so pale they are almost non-existent. There is nothing forceful about Jane. She must have been stitched up by someone else to end up in here.

At the moment Jane's gentle passivity is all she can cope with. Jane is kind. Kindness is what she needs. She reaches for her hand and they walk along the corridor together, fingers entwined. She last saw her a few days ago.

'How's everything going?' Jane had asked then.

'Not too bad,' she'd replied quietly.

'That's good then. That's an improvement.' A pause. 'Are you still beating yourself up?'

She had burst into tears.

'Have I said the wrong thing?' Jane asked.

'My sister and I used to use that expression sometimes,' she managed between sobs. 'I guess I will always beat myself up now.'

'It'll diminish.'

'How can you be so sure?' she asked.

Jane looked at her with sad eyes. Sadder than sad. 'I've been there, you know,' she said.

Jane so kind and gentle; she couldn't believe what she was hearing.

'Missing the person you *killed*?' she asked, her voice ringing with surprise.

'Missing someone I'll never see again.' Jane paused and sighed. 'In the end the longing will decrease.'

'No it won't. I killed my twin sister. She is part of me.' A silence.

Today, as they walk along the corridor together, Jane asks, 'Where are you going?'

'I've got a job in the library.'

'Congratulations, Professor.'

'Hardly a professor.'

'You've been to uni.'

'So has everyone these days.'

'Not in here, they haven't. You have to be a professor to get a job in the library.' Jane squeezes her hand. 'You're a professor to me anyway.'

THE PAST

37
Zara

I am sitting in bed watching Sebastian getting dressed; pulling up his jeans and fastening the press stud just above the tail of his snake tattoo.

'Next weekend I'm going to the Lake District with my parents,' he announces.

At the mention of his parents I stiffen. My Achilles heel. We are so together, but I still haven't met them yet.

'Where are you going?' I ask, trying not to sound waspish.

'Borrowdale.'

'Lucky you,' I reply, hoping for an invite.

But an invite doesn't come. He continues getting dressed, pulling a black V-neck top over his head.

'Walking I presume?'

This is beginning to sound like an interrogation. He nods his head and smiles. A short, uncertain smile. Nowhere near as flamboyant as usual.

'Any particular special occasion?'

His eyes darken. 'Mother's birthday.'

I can't hold it in any longer. 'Sebastian, why don't you want me to meet your parents?'

He comes and sits next to me on the bed. He takes my hand in his. 'I'm sorry, it's just not possible yet.'

'But why not? We've been going out for months now. What's the matter? Are you ashamed of me?'

He holds my gaze in his. 'It really isn't like that.'

'What is it like then? Tell me. It's serious. I feel excluded from a major part of your life.'

'I'll sort it out soon, I promise,' he says.

'I wish I could believe you,' I reply and break eye contact to look out of the window.

'If you loved me you'd believe me,' he says.

'I can't love someone who doesn't love me back.'

38

Miranda

Something is wrong with the lovebirds. Sebastian has left my flat looking thunderous. You haven't emerged yet. Are you about to split up?

Two hours later. Sebastian hasn't returned. You still haven't appeared. I am pottering about my flat, tidying up a bit. Drinking coffee. Flicking through the newspaper. Curiosity pricking. I make a cup of tea and knock on your bedroom door.

'Come in,' you say weakly.

I open the door and step inside. I inhale a tangle of over-sweet perfume and stale sweat. Don't you ever open the window? I step across a river of discarded clothing and progress towards your bed. I cannot see you, Zara. All I can see is a lump under the covers.

'I've brought you a cup of tea,' I say brightly, too brightly I suspect for you this morning.

The lump under the cover moves. Your head appears, hair more tousled than ever, eyes red. I sit on the edge of the bed beside you, and hand you the tea.

'Thanks,' you say and sniff.

'What are you doing today?' I ask.

You shrug. 'Not sure. I'm annoyed with Sebastian.'

'What's he done?' I ask.

'He's going away next weekend with his parents and he hasn't invited me. It makes me feel uneasy about him. As if I am not important enough to him.'

This is it. This is my opportunity.

'I don't blame you for being annoyed. It's high time you met them.'

My tone was perfect. Casual. Impartial. Ideal for making sure you listen.

'They're not doctors you know,' I continue.

39
Zara

Your words pierce into me.

'What do you mean?' I splutter, almost spilling my tea.

'His parents. I got a friend to look them up in the medical directory. They're not listed.'

Your face looks so jubilant. What is the matter with you, Miranda? Why are you so keen to catch Sebastian out? What has he ever done to harm you?

'Maybe they have different professional names,' I say.

Your grey eyes are tighter than usual today, like a beady hamster's eyes; small and round. I do not know how to respond to you. For despite my angry words this morning I don't want to believe that Sebastian has been lying. As soon as he left the room in a temper, I knew I would do my best to pull us away from this argument. I never want us to be apart. He would only lie to me for good reason. And even if he has been lying, I will forgive him, for I love him. But then I pinch myself. You would only lie to me for good reason too. I feel stretched and torn. Tired.

'Have you got a set of keys to his house?' you ask.

'No. But I know where he keeps a spare set. Why?'

You lean towards me. 'Next weekend, when his whole family are away, let's go in and search around, see what we can find out.'

I look at you, open-mouthed. What is the matter, Miranda? You seem so highly strung right now. So out of control.

'That's trespassing, isn't it?' I ask.

'Not really. You know where the key is.' Your grey eyes shine to silver. 'If anyone finds out, just tell them you lost your credit card, and had to check whether you left it there. It's really quite simple.'

'It might be simple for you, Miranda, but it's not simple for me. He's my boyfriend. He trusts me.'

'Trusts you?'

You raise your eyebrows in a condescending way, which annoys me. 'Yes,' I snap.

'So you think trust is important?'

'Of course,' I reply with a sigh.

'Then we need to go through with this. You need to know more about him, to be able to trust him back.'

110

40

Zara

The following Saturday, despite my reticence, I find myself walking along with you towards Sebastian's parents' house. When we arrive, I lift the large stone hidden beneath the *choisya* bush by the front gate to retrieve the spare keys. As we walk to the front door I feel them jangling in my pocket, making me feel guilty.

We pad up the driveway, past the immaculately ironed front lawn. Past the rest of the carefully designed shrub border. I ring the bell. Footsteps in the hallway. Someone is opening the door. I can't bear this. I wish I was invisible. I am so tense. I close my eyes and open them again. Sebastian is standing in front of us. He looks unkempt. He hasn't shaved. His hair needs washing. He has dark circles beneath his eyes from lack of sleep.

'Oh my God, Zara, Miranda, what are you both doing here?' he asks.

'We could ask you the same thing,' I reply.

'I'll leave you two to talk,' you say.

I hear your footsteps crunch across the stones of the driveway as you step away. Miranda, I am so glad you are going. I want to sort this out in my own way. Sebastian and I stand looking

111

at each other. I am not sure which of us is more surprised. He isn't smiling, but he doesn't look angry. My stomach is churning. My heart is racing.

'Come in. Let's talk about this,' he says softly.

Perhaps his parents are here. Perhaps I will meet them now. But as soon as I step inside I feel only silence, and I know they are not here.

'Why didn't you go to the Lake District? Where are your family?'

'Come into the sitting room, and I'll explain.'

We sit on opposing leather sofas, still looking at one another with surprised eyes. I am aching for everything to be all right. He looks so lovable, so familiar. So much part of my life.

'Something cropped up with my mother's work, at short notice,' he says.

'Really?' I try to stop my voice sounding waspish. But I'm not sure I manage. 'I'm confused. I've just found out your parents aren't listed in the medical year book.'

His eyes flatten. 'They're not medics.'

'You said they were.'

He pushes some hair that has flopped across his forehead away from his eyes. 'You must have assumed they were medics.' He pauses. 'I said they were doctors.'

I try to focus my mind back to our first meal out together. I was sure he said his dad was an obs and gynae consultant and that his mother was in community medicine. Maybe I didn't hear him properly.

'You've got it mixed up,' he continues. 'I never said they were medics. They are doctors, PhD doctors. Into scientific research.'

I so want to believe him, it hurts.

'What's their speciality, so I can look them up? I mean, they're your parents, Sebastian. I love you. I want to know about them.'

'You won't find them on the internet. They work at Porton Down. Their work is confidential. I'm sorry, Zara, if I misled you. It's because their work is sensitive.'

'But, but,' I splutter, 'why didn't you let me know that you weren't going?'

His face crumples. 'I'm sorry.' There is a pause. 'I told you before about the blackness. Sometimes I just need time alone.'

He gets up from the sofa and moves towards me. 'Now you *are* here, can I persuade you to stay the night?'

As he takes me in his arms and kisses me, I melt inside.

41

Miranda

As I walk back to my desk after our cross-departmental meeting, I see Sebastian slipping across the office towards the coffee machine, treating me to a snake-like grin. After the debacle of his aborted trip to the Lake District, I thought Zara would see sense and begin to mistrust him – but unfortunately she seems to be more embroiled in him than ever.

She wanted to know if I minded him continuing to live with us if he paid a bit more rent. I didn't really know how to say no, so I acquiesced. Pretending to ignore him, as I always want to spend less time with him, not more, I turn my computer on. Twenty emails that need dealing with have come in over the last hour. I groan inside. One day. One day it would be nice not to be so busy. I start trawling through them. Then a new one pings.

! Important. Anastasia Sudbury.

She wants to see me in her room immediately. However much I have to do, I can't refuse.

I arrive as requested, and I am kept waiting fifteen minutes. Not too bad for Anastasia Important Sudbury. When her PA finally invites me to enter her office I find her sitting behind her desk, whippet thin, wearing a painted-on grey dress. Despite her unsuitable attire her face is so stern she looks as if she is about to attend a funeral.

'Sit down,' she commands.

I obey, dropping into the low-level chair in front of her desk. She looks down at me over the top of half-rim specs.

'Have you any idea why I want to see you?' she asks.

I shake my head, slowly.

'I have evidence you wrote an unpleasant email, and tried to pass it off as Sebastian's.'

'That isn't true,' I reply.

'Maybe you didn't quite hear me. I have evidence. I know you're an accountant not a lawyer, but even so you must know what that means.' She leans forwards with granite eyes. 'The IT department has traced the supposed attachment from Sebastian back to your computer. Have you anything to say for yourself?'

'Can I see it?'

'Fine.'

She taps on her laptop keys; and then turns the screen towards me. An email from Sebastian bad-mouthing one of our major clients. This is madness. How dare she accuse me of this?

'I didn't write it. I didn't send it,' I splutter.

'The IT department have traced it. It definitely came from your IP address.'

I can't believe this is happening. I pinch myself to try and check whether it is a dream. It hurts. This is happening. This is real.

'You've got to believe me; I've been set up. I had nothing to do with this.'

'I am willing,' Anastasia says very grandly, flourishing her right arm in the air, 'to overlook this just the once.' She pauses. 'The email chain has been deleted. Sebastian dealt with it as soon as he saw it. We told the clients we had been hacked, and

115

that we have now upgraded our security.' She leans back in her chair expansively. 'You are a good worker. We don't want to lose you just because you may be having a domestic wrangling with your sister's boyfriend. Just make sure nothing like this ever happens again.'

42

Zara

It's my turn to 'cook' tonight. I have bought three M&S ready meals for £10, and a small bag of frozen peas. I have put them in the carefully pre-heated oven, so now all I have to do is shove the peas in the microwave four minutes before we eat. Sebastian has laid the table. Chores done. Time for a drink.

'What's your poison?' Sebastian asks.

'Vodka, I think.'

'Vodka shots? Vodka and tonic, vodka and orange? Vodka and ice?'

'Let's not dilute it. Let's go for shots.'

We snuggle up together on Miranda's brown leather sofa and start to drink. One shot down, I can already feel the warmth slipping down my throat.

'I got a distinction for my puppet project,' I tell him.

He grins from ear to ear, looking so genuinely pleased for me. He pours two more shots. We down them in one.

'I told you when you were making it how clever you were. Clever. Clever. Clever. Do you remember?'

Another shot.

'Course I remember.' I pause. 'Miranda will be pleased. I can't wait to tell her.'

'Frosty face Cunningham. She's never pleased about anything.'

'Frosty face? What's she done to deserve a name like that?' I lean towards him to see the expression on his face.

'Your sister's a difficult bitch,' he says matter-of-factly.

His face is serious. His eyes don't even have their usual twinkle. My stomach churns. Somewhere, buried deep in the narrowest crevices of my mind, do I sometimes agree with him? I push the feeling away.

'You're always complaining about her, and she's so kind to you, letting you more or less live in her flat. What has she done to rile you?' I ask.

'I don't trust her.'

I move away from him slightly. 'You don't trust her? The person I've trusted all my life?'

His face is still deadly serious. Serious and intense. I look into his eyes. Dark resinous eyes.

'Your attitude makes me feel uncomfortable,' I tell him.

'And I feel uncomfortable with hers,' he replies.

He fills our shot glasses again. The vodka is relaxing me. Diluting his words.

'What's happened?' I ask calmly.

'Nothing we need to bore you with. Something at work.'

'You always seem to get on well enough when we're all together in the flat.'

'It's what goes on behind your back,' he says with a cavalier grin.

Suddenly I feel cold inside. He pulls me towards him and kisses me. I taste the vodka on his breath. The coldness in my heart freezes, and my heart stops for a second. What are you doing, Miranda? Are you coming on to him behind my back?

Coming on to him at work? I bite my lip. No. Miranda Cunningham. You are as straight as a die. You would never do that.

43

Miranda

I am so angry with Sebastian. He must have set me up. He could easily have got into my computer at home, or at work. I have tightened up my password security. Now my computer is like Fort Knox.

'Good morning,' he smoulders as he walks towards our desk. Slow and deliberate.

What does he think he is? Sex on a stick? He sits down. As usual I edge my chair as far away from him as possible. He grins at me. A slow leering grin. He shakes his head.

'Anastasia is pretty disgusted by what you did. You've got to be more professional about working with me.' he says, sliding closer towards me again, overdosing me with an aroma of mint. He must have just cleaned his teeth.

'What *I* did?' I glare at him and stare him out.

For once I win. He pulls his eyes away first.

But I am over-aware of him as he sits at the screen of his laptop, frowning and staring, occasionally typing an amendment.

The phone on his desk rings. He picks up. 'Hello Anastasia,' he says, voice throaty and deep. 'Of course. I'll come to your office immediately.' He stands up, raises his eyebrows and announces, 'Anastasia wants to see me. Do you think she's going to promote me?'

'If she is the company has more money than sense.'

'Thanks Miranda, for the help and encouragement. I appreciate it so much.'

As he saunters across the office, grinning at his own sophisticated wit, my dislike for him rises like a volcano inside me. I look across to his part of the desk and see he's left his computer on.

Two can play your game, Sebastian, I say to myself through gritted teeth.

I reach for his computer to see what he's been doing, click on the document he's working on and alter the numbers a bit.

44

Zara

Miranda looks more serious than ever at the moment – a sour look on her face. Mouth turned down. Sebastian is quirky and awkward whenever she is around. I am sitting on the toilet in our bathroom with the lid closed, having a break from them both, contemplating their relationship. Contemplating the way Miranda avoids touching Sebastian or looking him in the eye. The way he pushes normal conversation away and relies on sarcasm when she is in the room. Why is he using sarcasm to protect himself? What is he protecting himself from? What can I do to bring them together? Is the distance between them my fault?

I take my blade out from inside my iPhone cover and put a ligature around my wrist, ready to cut. I hold the blade in my trembling hand and sit awhile, looking at the line of scars on my left arm. I breathe in deeply and out again, to prepare myself. I cross my legs. I press my left arm hard against my slightly raised leg. I bend forwards to steady my arm. My right hand moves down ready to cut. But something stops me. I can't quite manage it. My body isn't ready for the pain. Not yet.

I close my eyes and think about Sebastian's face at the point of climax. Then I open my eyes and cut. I cut the second scar down from my wrist. Blood seeps out. Slowly at first. Then a line. A river. Oh the sweet, sweet euphoria of blood.

45

Miranda

Sitting at my desk at work, smiling inside. When should I draw attention to Sebastian's mistake? A frisson of excitement rises in my stomach.

The phone on my desk rings. I pick up. Anastasia.

'Miranda, I need you in my office immediately.'

Perhaps she has discovered it already and needs someone to put it right. I feel triumphant. I've got him this time. I sense his eyes following me as I leave my desk.

As soon as I arrive outside her office, her usually overprotective PA ushers me in.

Anastasia. Cold-eyed and straight-lipped, as usual. Wearing a black pantaloon suit with a large gold chain around her neck. Strawberry blonde hair tied in an elegant chignon, at the back of her neck. We sit opposite one another, one on each side of her desk, eyeballs locked.

'What I am going to say to you, Miranda, is extremely serious.'

My insides tighten. My heart pulses.

'I'm giving you your first written warning of dismissal.'

Her words punch into me, winding me. She hands me a manila envelope with my name typed on the front.

'But why?' I ask struggling to breathe properly.

'You infiltrated Sebastian's computer.'

'No I didn't.'

'Oh yes you did.'

There is a pause.

'Do you want a pantomime conversation?' she asks.

I do not reply.

'Please accept what I said,' she continues. 'Sebastian filmed it on his iPhone. He was on his way to see me. He had forgotten part of the paperwork we needed to go through so he walked back towards his desk, to collect it. When he was halfway back across the office, he noticed you were typing on his computer. So he got his iPhone out and filmed it. He came straight to me with this. And now we've checked the figures and they are all obviously wrong. The tax liability data for a very big client. This is a serious breach. I've downloaded the film of your actions onto my computer. Let me show you.'

She turns her computer screen around, and sure enough, it shows me leaning across my desk, reaching for Sebastian's computer and changing the data. Sebastian must have left his computer open on purpose, hoping I would do something stupid like that. I am mortified. How could I have let Sebastian goad me into doing something as stupid as this?

'We have already had a previous incident, which we have overlooked. Two more warnings and you're out.' Panic simmers throughout my body. 'I am sure you were made aware of the terms and conditions when you joined the company,' Anastasia continues.

I try to contain the panic and think rationally. There is only one solution. I need to explain.

'The first incident wasn't me,' I splutter, voice weak and breathless. 'It must have been Sebastian.' Anastasia's cold eyes harden. 'I shouldn't have tried to get my own back; it was very wrong,' I continue. 'But I love my job. Please give me another chance and let this go.' She is disregarding what I say, looking beyond me. Not concentrating. I must try harder. I lean towards her.

'Sebastian and I have been having a few problems.'

A flicker of interest. Her eyes lighten. She leans forward across her desk. Over the pile of reports in front of her.

'What sort of problems?' she asks.

If I tell her about the sexual harassment, surely that would make her understand how serious this is? How vulnerable I am.

But then I think about you, Zara. So much more vulnerable than me. And Anastasia's question remains unanswered. I cannot bring myself to tell her.

She leans back in her chair. 'I can't give you another chance. It's company policy. There's nothing I can do,' she says, closing the file on the desk in front of her.

I leave Anastasia's office feeling bereft. The world I have built for myself crashing around my feet.

46

Zara

Miranda has been in bed all weekend. I've been into her room a few times to check up on her and find out how she is feeling. All she says is that she's tired, that she wants to catch up on her sleep.

It is so unlike Miranda to be tired. She usually has so much energy. In the last ten years, as far as I know, she hasn't had a day off work. Over the weekend while she has been incapacitated, Sebastian and I have been all over town. Saturday night supper at Luigi's. Sunday lunch at Arnolfini; afterwards wandering about holding hands, admiring the artwork. But all our activities haven't assuaged my worry. So on Sunday evening, getting ready for bed, I know Sebastian and I need to discuss this.

'What's the matter with her? This isn't like her. Do you think she's really ill? Do you think she's all right?' I ask as I struggle to pull off my skin-tight jeans.

His face solidifies. 'I was waiting for her to tell you herself,' he says. 'She's low. She's in big trouble at work.'

His words cut into me like electricity. Miranda Cunningham. Big trouble at work. Miranda has always taken her career so seriously.

My jeans are finally on the floor. I sit on the edge of the bed in my top and knickers, looking across at him, wide-eyed.

'But she loves her job. What's happened?' I stutter.

He comes to sit next to me on the bed. 'I'm sorry to tell you she was caught deliberately changing data on my computer.'

I stare at him. 'But why?'

'In an attempt to make me look incompetent.'

'Why would she want to do that?'

He puts his arm around my shoulders. 'I keep trying to tell you, Zara, she's jealous of our relationship. She's trying to prise us apart. We mustn't allow her to.' He pauses. 'We need to fight back.'

He takes my hand and squeezes it triumphantly.

'My relationship with my sister has never been a fight,' I tell him, feeling empty inside.

47
Miranda

The supposed joy of Christmas is incubating around me, irritating me with its false joviality. Piped carols floating towards me from charity collectors and bars. Electric lights glinting at me from the naked arms of the birch trees on Harbourside, the neon-dappled water at night prettier than ever. Cold air pecking at my face as I rush to work.

Zara, I still haven't told you what happened at work. I can't. I'm too ashamed. So ashamed that the first weekend after it happened I had to take to my bed. What I did was so stupid and childish. You look at me from time to time, askance, and I know that Sebastian has told you. Let's keep it like that. You know. We don't need to discuss it. I'm burying it. Burying it so deep no one will ever find it, and it will never happen again. In time the warning will fade from my record, and I can have a fresh start.

Zara, you have managed to nag me into having a Christmas party, of all things. At first I resisted. I am not at all in the mood for Christmas. But you were so insistent that in the end I relented. You think having a party will cheer me up. Maybe I should try and let it. Sebastian has brewed his mulled wine recipe, filling our flat with the scent of orange, clove and cinnamon. Far too sweet for me.

'The secret is taking your time over this and reducing it properly,' he says with a wink.

Nuclear smiles and an extravagant dimple aren't enough. How naff. He has to add a wink.

Zara, you and I go to IKEA to buy a plastic tree and some cheap decorations. However hard we try to balance the tree it keeps falling over. Even Christmas seems difficult these days. You and Sebastian sort out our party playlist. Far too Seventies. Slade and Wizard. Slade is Sebastian's favourite Christmas song. Surely he is too young for stuff like that? His invisible parents must have poor taste.

And now we are sitting together on the sofa, drinking mulled wine in plastic cups just before the party starts.

'Mmm, not as bad as it smells,' I say.

'Told you so,' Sebastian replies, putting his arms around both of us, making me wince.

He rummages in his jeans pocket and pulls out a handful of coloured pills. I stiffen. E. What is Sebastian doing now? E, the preserve of irresponsible teenagers, when he is over thirty. He holds his hand out and offers the selection to you. I watch you studying the pills carefully, then choosing a pale blue one and swallowing it, washing it down with a slug of mulled wine. He takes one too. And then you both turn your eyes and fix them on me. He stretches his pill-filled palm towards me. I shake my head. I have never taken E. I have always managed my life without party drugs.

'Come on, Miranda; it's the friendship drug – try it. Give friendship a chance,' Sebastian pushes.

'It'll help you relax,' Zara says. 'You know, Miranda, you really need to relax.'

'Is that how it works? By making people feel relaxed?'

'Yes. Why do you think it's so popular?'

I don't know what is happening to me but because I have been feeling so low lately, I am considering it. My heart is racing. My stomach almost constantly tied in knots. Perhaps I would feel better if I could relax. Slowly, I reach my fingers towards his outstretched palm. I choose a pink one, lifting it cautiously to my mouth and swilling it down with mulled wine. It slips down easily enough. I sit on the sofa with you both and wait. Nothing happens. I feel just the same. The same knotted feeling in my stomach as Sebastian exhales onto my cheek. The door-bell rings. I jump up and go to answer the door.

The first guests. Three girls from your photography course, Zara; I don't recognise them. All dressed in black with garish red lipstick, as if they were auditioning for the *Rocky Horror Show*; black and red and fishnets. One of them, the curviest, has pornographic breasts and a ring piercing in the middle of her nose – at the front, like a bull.

'Come in,' I say as you appear behind me.

They push past me as if I am invisible and engulf you in their arms.

Soon my compact flat is teeming, pumping with Seventies music. Sebastian is dancing in the middle of the living room, waving his arms around in the air, bending, waving, thumping, surrounded by an entourage of people copying him. I stand in the corner, sipping mulled wine and watching. Watching, as I usually do, not wanting to join in.

But then the world moves towards me. The music grows inside me and I become part of it. I am in the middle of our sitting room, shoes off, gyrating behind Sebastian, shadowing his every move. He turns towards me, his grin high-wattage. Jumping to the music. Faster and faster. Through the sound barrier. We are the music. The pulse. The beat. The sound. We dance all night. Sometimes you are there, Zara, gyrating with us. Sometimes you are with your coven of red-lipped girls, rotating around each other: a red and black kaleidoscope in the distance.

And then Sebastian takes my hand and leads me off the dance floor. He runs me a glass of water from the tap in the kitchen.

'Drink this,' he commands.

Where are you, Zara? Still dancing with your coven of girls?

I sip the water; it tastes like nectar, so refreshing. I am feeling very peculiar now. Light-headed. Sebastian's face looks blurred.

'If I finish with Zara,' Sebastian says. Even though I feel strange, his words stab into me. What is he talking about? Finish with Zara?

'If I finish with Zara, will you go out with me?' he continues.

I stumble backwards slightly. 'No! Of course not. Why would I want to?'

'But,' he stammers, 'I'd be free.'

The room is moving beneath my feet. I'm continuing to sway to the music; it's slowing my mind down, making it difficult to think. Difficult. But not impossible. Through the pulse of the room and the music, I ask myself, who does he think he is? Where is he coming from? I know he has deliberately tripped me up at work. What is he doing now?

'Do you think it matters whether you are free or not? Except that I don't want you to hurt my sister?' I reply. Then I pause and sigh. 'I don't want to go out with you. You're not my type. And even if you were my type, she'd never forgive me.'

'So you love her more than you love me?'

Knots curdle inside me. 'I never said I loved you, Sebastian. I'm only putting up with you for the sake of my sister. Don't make up lies about me.'

I walk away from him, slowly, trying to hold my body and mind together. I find you, Zara, and dance with you for the rest of the night.

48
Zara

Thumping, gyrating, pounding at the Christmas party to the beat of the music. Dancing with Sebastian. Dancing with my friends from my photography course. Miranda, you call them my coven because they are all wearing black. Dancing with you, Miranda. Ecstasy suits you. You are the pulse of the party. The party gyrates around you. Earlier Sebastian was dancing with you too. Arms in the air happy. I'm so pleased you are getting on. At last. I've wanted you two to connect for so long. When Sebastian dances with me he pulls me towards him. He tells me how much he loves me. Life, he says. Our love is for life. How beautiful is that? Life. Love. Life. A beautiful life.

49

Miranda

We're sitting in a sandwich bar on Park Street.

'To what do I owe the pleasure of your condescending to come for lunch with me?' Sebastian asks the Monday after the party, eyes sparkling too brightly into mine.

I breathe deeply to calm myself. 'Because I want to ask you why you're still with my sister, when you were talking about the end of your relationship on Saturday.'

He leans back in his chair and folds his arms. He raises his eyebrows, staring at me contemplatively. 'You won't be with me. Staying with her is the only way for me to be close to you.' He reaches across the Formica table and tries to take my hand in his, but quickly, instinctively, I pull mine away.

'I don't believe you.' I pause, hands behind my back now. 'And how fair would an attitude like that be on her?'

He grins, a slow contrived grin. Too slow to be real. 'It's your choice, Miranda. It's not my fault.'

Anger and claustrophobia contort inside me.

'You're impossible, Sebastian,' I retort.

'That's what you like about me.' His voice is calm and measured.

My jaw and teeth are clenched as I try to suppress my emotion. Despite my desperate attempt, 'That's what I hate about you,' whistles out. My voice sounds venomous.

'There's a fine line between love and hate,' he replies, grin widening.

'Don't speak to me like that. Our relationship's not a cliché.'

'So you think we have a relationship?'

His tongue slithers provocatively over the word *relationship*.

'No.' I shake my head in frustration with the way he torments me. 'I don't think that. I never will. I never have.' I pause for a second and my anger builds into a torrent. 'Piss off, Sebastian. You need to leave me alone. Stop harassing me.'

His grin is no longer a grin but a snarl. 'Such eloquent language.'

I inhale deeply. 'I really mean it – from now on, you must leave me alone.'

'I've told you, I can't keep away from you. I can't leave you alone.'

His eyes are like black holes pulling me in. Making me feel frightened.

'If you hurt my sister, I'll kill you.' I pause. 'You need to treat her with respect. Fairly. If you don't want to be with her, then let her know.'

He lifts his eyebrows again and leans back a little. 'Should I tell the police you've threatened me?'

I lean towards him. 'Just try causing any trouble and you'll find out what happens.'

His snarl is softening to a grin. 'It's touching how much you love her.'

'It's crazy how much she loves you. The poor girl needs help.'

50
Zara

I am looking around the flat trying to find where I've left my watch when I tell you my news, as nonchalantly as possible.

'Miranda, I'm not coming home for Christmas. I'm going to stay with Sebastian.'

Our first Christmas apart. I have thought long and hard about this. Riddled with guilt for not going home to be with you and Mother, but Sebastian and I feel we need some time to be together – alone. You look up from sorting through your accountancy books. Open-mouthed. Shocked. As if you can't believe it.

'Mother will be so disappointed not to see you. Can't you invite him to ours?' you say softly.

The journals that were in your hands have fallen to the floor, but you do not seem to have noticed. I pick them up and place them on the coffee table. You are staring at me as if I am a criminal.

'Stop looking at me like that,' I beg.

You continue staring. Mouth still a little wide.

'We just want a bit of time together on our own whilst his parents are away. That's why we're going to his house.' I pause to take a deep breath and shrug my shoulders. 'It isn't that weird for a young couple to want time together alone.'

'Isn't it a bit weird that his parents are away again? Come on Zara, how much do you really know about him?' There is a pause. 'You need to know him before you can trust him.'

I raise my eyes to the sky. Not that again.

THE PRESENT

51

Theo Gregson is visiting her. He is wearing toffee-coloured chinos that tone with his eyes. Today she has had warning of his visit, so she has managed to spruce herself up a bit. Freshly washed hair. Subtle make-up. Her favourite Kid Rock T-shirt.

'How's it going?' he asks.

'Good,' she says and manages to smile. 'Almost enjoying my job in the library.'

'Almost?'

'Well, as much as I can enjoy anything these days.'

He leans back in his chair and folds his arms. 'Well, you won't enjoy this then.'

'Do you mean your visit?'

'Yes.'

'Why?'

'I'm concerned you've not told me the full story about what happened between you and Sebastian.'

Their eyes are locked. She sits motionless. She doesn't reply.

'You need to,' Theo continues. 'Otherwise we won't be able to get you the verdict you want.'

'What makes you think knowing everything will help?'

'When you're charged the best way forward is to tell the truth.'

'I can't,' she whispers. 'I won't.'

He leans across the table and takes her hand in his. 'Please,' Theo says. 'Whatever happened, let me help.'

'No one can help.'

THE PAST

52
Miranda

Christmas. Just the two of us. Mother, and me. Without you, Zara, our house in Tidebury is so quiet. No laughter in the hallway. No trance music pounding from your bedroom. No one to drink with in the local pub on Christmas Eve. No one to giggle and stagger towards midnight mass with, tinsel decorating our necks.

I am drinking too many cups of ginger tea, and not enough alcohol. Watching too many slapstick sitcoms. Listening to too much analysis of the news and the weather. Having too much dull conversation with Mother, without you to liven us up. At the moment it is a house with the fun sucked out of it.

Christmas Day. Despite your absence, Zara, we stick to the usual routine – opening our presents first thing in the morning before we are dressed. You left a scarf for me to open. Too infatuated with Sebastian, you didn't remember. I never wear scarves. You didn't remember we always said we would wait until we were old to wear them, when we had crinkly necks.

We eat at one p.m. in our compact dining room, piling our plates high with turkey, sausages, bacon, potatoes and sprouts. All the usual. Eating so much we can hardly move and then having to go to bed for an afternoon snooze. Then high tea. More food.

'You don't trust this Sebastian, do you?' Mother says as she offers me a mince pie.

'What makes you think that?'

'Every time I mention him you change the subject.'

'You're misreading me, Mother. Of course I trust him. He's Zara's boyfriend and she loves him. What's not to trust?'

I can't tell Mother the truth. When she worries, she tortures herself.

53
Zara

I miss you, Miranda. Despite your negative attitude towards the love of my life, Christmas apart from you doesn't seem right. It's the first time we've been separated at this time of year.

I miss watching your grey eyes turning lighter as we swap presents. Sebastian and I have agreed not to bother. I miss watching your regal profile that reminds me of a princess, your nose crinkling a little as you reach for another mince pie. I miss laughing with you in church. When Mother is taking the Queen's speech too seriously. When carol singers, who can't sing, caterwaul at the doorway.

It's midday on Christmas Day and Sebastian and I have already had too much champagne. My body feels thin and unsteady, not solid enough to balance properly. I have to strain to think. We are playing a dance compilation album through the Sonos system which is pounding around the house, and we are dancing a sort of funky waltz, bodies pressed together, singing along at high volume. Rocking through the hallway, gyrating around the living room, smooching into the kitchen. When we arrive by the sink, Sebastian suddenly stops and unwraps himself from me.

'I need to FaceTime my parents.' He waves the remote and snaps off the Sonos.

He reaches for his iPad from the counter in front of him, opens the cover, props it up with the screen facing away from me, and positions himself to speak. He spends ages arranging his body carefully on a stool in front of it, to give his parents the best view of himself possible, and then he presses to ring.

The watery ring of FaceTime tinkles into the room. It rings and rings as Sebastian continues to sit in a suitable position, angling his face and running his fingers through his hair. His parents don't answer. My stomach tightens. I'm not sure I want them to. I'm not sure I want to talk to them for the first time like this, rather inebriated and usurping their home. Thinking about it, do they even know I'm here? The trilling continues. Sebastian cuts it off. He tries again. Then with a deep sigh he switches it off.

'God damn it, I'll have to go into the garden where I can get 4G, and ring them on my mobile. The internet reception is too bad in here.' There is a pause. 'You stay inside to keep warm.'

He grabs his coat and saunters out into the garden through the back door. I stand at the sink and watch him through the kitchen window, pulling his phone out of his pocket and pressing speed dial. Walking down the garden with his back to me. He's got through. He's speaking to them. Pacing up and down, chatting to them. He must be so close to his parents; he has so much to say. Laughing, smiling, nodding his head animatedly. They chat for ages. When the conversation is finally over he ambles back into the house, takes his coat off, and enfolds me in his arms.

'Are they having a nice time?' I ask.

'Wonderful. Wonderful.'

His voice is overly jolly. Compensating too hard. Because he is missing them? Because they are so often away?

'What are they up to?'

'Relaxing on the beach.'

'I thought they were at the elephant sanctuary first.'

'That's next week,' he says as he leans down to kiss me.

'I must have got it the wrong way round.'

'They send their love to you.'

A fist tightens around my heart. He's told them about me? They know I'm here? That I'm his girlfriend? The love of his life?

'Maybe I'll speak to them next time they call?' I ask, looking into his eyes.

'Maybe.' His eyes darken. 'Maybe.' His voice has slipped into a whisper.

The fist around my heart releases and my heart beats faster. Or maybe this sending their love is a lie?

'Christmas together alone, what could be more perfect,' he says.

He holds me against him, presses my head against his chest as if I am precious. He runs his hands through my hair. I look up into his eyes. They crinkle into a smile, telling me that everything will be all right.

We drink another bottle of champagne, take two Es each and snort a line of coke. Then it's time to put the Christmas pizza into the oven. The Christmas pizza. A special from the local artisan bakery. We went to buy it yesterday. Thick-crusted. A tomato, basil and mozzarella layer, topped with turkey, stuffing and meatballs. A little tarragon too, the baker said. Twenty minutes in the oven and bingo. No need for all the fuss that Mother makes over Christmas lunch.

Pizza and champagne at the kitchen table. The pizza is a little greasy, swimming in tomato-coloured oil, but the dryness of the champagne takes the edge off the food. Sebastian's eyes take the edge off everything. We roll a spliff and smoke it. By the time we turn on the Queen's speech, I can hardly hear or see her. She mentions some of Britain's achievements in the last year, and we both start to laugh. Rolling around on the floor laughing. Laughing so much. Then Sebastian rolls on top of me, presses my hands above my head, and kisses me hard. A kiss so hard it feels like a bite. I close my mouth. I turn my head away.

'Stop it,' I say. 'I feel sick after that pizza.'

He doesn't hear me. He is pulling my knickers down.

'Stop it Seb. I don't feel well.'

He doesn't reply. He just continues to pull my knickers down. I try to push him away, but he is so much stronger than me that my attempts to hold him off are useless. He opens my legs with his knee and thrusts into me, as if he is in a trance. Thrusting into me as if he doesn't know or care who I am. Thrusting into me as if he can't stop.

I have never seen him like this. I am so uncomfortable. He is hurting me. I feel as if I am about to vomit. He climaxes quickly. Relieved it is over, I push him off. I rush to the bathroom and vomit. The bathroom tiles are circling towards me. I put my hand out to touch them. They slip backwards. Then they begin to spin around me. The world turns black.

I wake up the next morning wrapped in Egyptian cotton sheets. For a second I do not know where I am. Then I remember. Christmas at Sebastian's home. Greasy pizza. Sebastian thrusting into me. Being sick in his spinning bathroom. I can't remember anything after that.

But he isn't here. Where is he? He isn't lying next to me. Even as I sit up wondering where he is, he enters the bedroom carrying breakfast on a tray. Coffee and croissants and a miniature red rose. He places the tray on the bedside table, leans across and kisses me. A kiss as soft as satin.

'I'm so sorry about yesterday,' he says. 'I'm going easy on the drugs from now on. I love you so much, Zara. I will never behave like that again.'

54

Sebastian

I overstepped the mark with Zara yesterday. I do love her, Jude. I love her so much. Time stops when she lies in my arms. Usually a beautiful calmness engulfs me. I will never be rough with her again. I had one hit too many. I only took the drugs to cope. On Christmas Eve I had the nightmare again.

Driving along the motorway in the fast lane, Kaiser Chiefs pumping out on the car stereo. The lorry. Coming towards us in slow motion. Half time. Quarter time. Almost stopping. Grinding, slowly, slowly, across the central reservation. Large wheels crunching, swallowing metal. I sat mesmerised by the truck. Transfixed. I couldn't speak. I couldn't move. Fingers frozen against the steering wheel, useless and immobile. The lorry hitting the car. The car skidding sideways. The taste of panic in my bile as I let go of the steering wheel.

How many times will I be plagued to relive what happened? It is torture, Jude. I woke up trembling, in a cold sweat on Christmas morning. I took an E as soon as I made it to the bathroom, and another just before lunch. On and off all day I kept snorting coke – to dim the pain, to help me keep going. By early afternoon I felt bullish and aggressive, invincible, unstoppable. Desperate for release, for closure. So pumped up and hyper, I couldn't even slow down to consider the woman I love.

THE PRESENT

55

Christmas Day. She feels so bad this morning that she pushes the emergency buzzer in her cell. A prison officer appears and summons her listener immediately.

Ten minutes later, the gentle Jane Noble is with her. She hasn't got out of bed. Her feet haven't touched the floor. Jane pulls a chair to the side of the bed and sits on it, carefully watching her charge. Her face is swollen with tears. Shiny hair tangled and matted.

'Bad day, huh?' Jane asks softly.

She reaches for Jane's hand, tears streaming down her face. 'Bad doesn't quite cut it. I'm not sure I can move through this.'

'Christmas is always bad. Christmas Day. Just a day to get through,' Jane says. 'You can and you will.'

And somehow she does. She moves through the day. She showers and dresses. Somehow she keeps going. Somehow she stays alive. She looks out of the cell window. A grey day. Solid grey drizzle. Weather that spits in your face.

You can and you will. You can and you will. She walks along the corridor with the other prisoners, towards the canteen for lunch. She collects her meal and sits down, the smell of overcooked turkey and grease making her feel sick. Sitting in the prison canteen, having lunch at 11:30 so that most of the staff can go home early after the prisoners are back, safely locked up in their cells again.

She pushes a piece of dry turkey around her plate. She isn't speaking to the women on either side of her. She isn't really aware of them. She isn't listening to the piped carols. Until she hears Slade: Sebastian's Christmas favourite. Her mind pushes back. Back to last year. Her stomach rotates as she remembers. Sebastian, Sebastian. Why won't you see me? You won't even speak to me now.

THE PAST

56
Miranda

New Year's Eve. You step off the train into my arms, Zara. I hold you against me. You smell of roses and violets. You feel thin and fragile. As if you would snap in two if I held you too tight.

'I missed you so much,' I said. 'It's like living in a cemetery when I'm here without you.'

'I missed you too.'

Sebastian hovers awkwardly behind you, attempting to shower me with his grin, but not quite managing as I avoid his glance. When you and I have become untangled, he walks towards me and puts his arms around me.

'Did you miss me too?' he whispers in my ear. I feel the heat of his breath on my skin.

I stiffen and unclamp my body from his grasp.

It is a mild day for the time of year. Zara and I link arms as we amble back towards Heathfield Close. Sebastian links arms with you. Glancing imperiously about him, staring into the windows of every home we pass. Leering at everything. Passers-by. Parked cars.

'The beauty of suburbia,' he says with a smirk.

'What's wrong with that?' I ask.

'Too parochial.' He pauses. 'Conservative with a small c.'

'And Clifton is edgy and exciting, is it? Plenty of drugs and gun culture?'

'Music culture at least. The Stones and the Beatles played Colston Hall.'

'Shut up, Sebastian. Everyone knows the Beatles are from Liverpool.'

'Stop bickering, you two. We're almost home,' Zara says as we turn the corner into Heathfield Close. Past the beech tree. Past gardens bordered by hedges and leafy shrubs.

Sebastian continues to observe our hometown, turning his head from side to side haughtily, as if it's all beneath him. He has only been here ten minutes and he is already annoying me.

Mother answers the door wearing her second-best apron – her denim Jamie Oliver one, hands covered in flour. As soon as her eyes alight on you her face explodes with joy. She wipes her hands on her apron, and envelops you in a bear hug. When Mother has released you, she holds her hand out stiffly to Sebastian.

'Nice to meet you,' she says.

'Come on Sebastian, I'll show you the spare room,' you say, with a toss of your increasingly razor-indented hair with its strange shaved sections, taking his hand and pulling him inside.

He follows you upstairs, climbing up enthusiastically, two steps at a time. I follow Mother into the kitchen, where she is halfway through cooking her signature dish, beef bourguignon, the woody scent beginning to waft around the house.

'Do you think he'll like it?' she asks.

'He'll probably think eating meat is class divisive.'

'Come on Miranda. Tell me the truth: do you like this guy or not?'

'I like him some of the time,' I lie. 'But not as much as Zara does.'

57

Zara

It's good to be with my small family again. A formal New Year's Eve dinner by candlelight in our compact dining room, just the four of us. Mother has pulled out all the stops. Silver place mats, silver goblets, silver cutlery. Smoked salmon, beef bourguignon, strawberries and cream. Champagne and Chablis. Rioja and Sauternes. Mozart's Horn Concertos – her favourite music, trumpeting cheerily in the background. But behind the music there is an eerie silence. No one chatting very much.

'How was Christmas without me?' I ask.

You and Mother exchange glances.

'Fine,' Mother says, eyes flat.

'One big house party from start to finish,' you add.

58

Miranda

Our candlelit New Year's dinner looks as if it should be intimate, but the conversation is stilted. Mother, who is often quite chatty, seems flummoxed and nervous in front of Sebastian.

'What are your parents doing this evening, Sebastian?' Mother asks after a while.

'They've gone away together,' he replies.

'Where?'

'To a secret destination.'

'How romantic.' There is a pause. 'Did your father surprise your mother?'

'Maybe. I wasn't there. I wouldn't know.'

That is the end of the conversation about Sebastian's parents for now until later, when we are finishing off strawberries and cream and you suddenly pipe up.

'Your parents go away so much, don't they, Sebastian?'

Sebastian doesn't reply. He shifts a little in his chair, as if he is uncomfortable.

'I mean we had their house to ourselves all Christmas,' you continue.

'It's a big house, isn't it? Did you feel lonely?' Mother asks, changing the conversation unnecessarily, just when I wanted to know what he had to say about his family.

You look across to Sebastian, holding his eyes in yours. 'I never feel lonely when I'm with Sebastian.'

Sycophantic, Zara. So sycophantic. Is that what you really think? Christmas, in a soulless house, with the dreadful Sebastian. Why have you let this happen to yourself?

'What about you, Sebastian?' Mother asks. There is a pause. 'Did you miss your parents?'

He clears his throat, shrugs his shoulders. 'Well, I'm used to it. They go away so much. Always have. Always will.'

Mother and I catch each other's gaze for a second. She has always been here for us. She finds it hard to understand parents who would do anything less. She raises her glass.

'Well, here's to your parents, wherever they are in the world right now.' Her voice sounds clipped.

We all raise a toast: 'To Seb's parents.'

Sebastian's weird parents. I am fed up of hearing about them. The conversation dwindles on towards midnight, until five to twelve when I open a bottle of champagne and pour us all a glass. One minute to midnight. Zara, you count down in seconds using your iPhone. And then we hold hands in a circle and stagger around the sitting room trying to remember the words to 'Auld Lang Syne'. As usual Mother gets tears in her eyes.

Singing ritual over, Mother and I reach for one another and hug. We give each other a quick peck on the cheek. Zara, you and Sebastian are welded together near the Christmas tree, snogging. I break away from Mother and stand, glass in hand, watching. Watching your lips, Zara, pressed greedily against his. Watching his right hand stroke your buttocks playfully. You break away and reach for your champagne glass. You walk to the TV, wave the remote, and Jools Holland comes on.

'I love this programme,' you say, settling in front of it.

'How can you watch this middle-aged crap?' Sebastian asks.

For once I agree with him. Most people must like his show though or it wouldn't get screened so relentlessly.

'Shut up Seb. Don't spoil the moment,' you say with laughter in your voice. 'I watch it every year.'

Don't I just know it? I sigh inside. I walk to the front door and step outside, wine glass in hand. The midnight air is cold and clear. The midnight moon is full and sharp. I look up at the stars and think of a beautiful story I once heard about a village in Africa where each child is named after a star. On the night their star shines the brightest, it is their turn to fetch the water the next day.

I hear a click as the front door opens. I turn around. Sebastian has followed me outside. He steps towards me and takes me in his arms, so quickly I do not manage to stop him; too much wine must have slowed my reactions. He is trying to kiss me again. Furious, I close my mouth and stiffen. Managing to untangle myself from his grasp and pull away, I step inside and slam the door.

The TV is still on. A jazz band belting out an old-fashioned song I don't recognise, Jools Holland standing in front of them tapping his foot. You and Mother are glued to the screen, finishing off your champagne.

'Happy New Year,' I say and disappear upstairs as quickly as possible.

I slip into bed, Sebastian's attempt to kiss me still burning on my lips. I lie awake trying to breathe deeply. Trying to relax. Sleep is stepping towards me. I am half awake, half asleep. The door bursts open and someone steps in. I jump out of bed and snap on the light. It is Sebastian. Running his eyes down my nakedness. My breasts. The carefully trimmed mound between my legs.

'Get out. Go away,' I hiss.

59

Sebastian

Do you think I'm frightening her, Jude? Do you think this will push her away? Once again, she almost kissed me back. She wants me really. She just doesn't know it yet.

THE PRESENT

60

'I've bought you a Christmas present, a bit late,' Theo Gregson says. 'I'm sorry, but I wasn't allowed to wrap it.'

He hands her a cashmere jumper. Dark purple cashmere. Soft as silk.

'Oh Theo, thank you. You shouldn't have.'

He grins his wholesome grin. 'I wanted to give you something to cheer you up a little. You've been going through so much.'

She holds it to her face to feel the texture and buries her head in it. When she looks up, he is watching her, eyes so tender it makes her heart ache.

'I just can't thank you enough,' she says.

She stands up and moves towards him. She so wants to hug him to thank him. To behave like a normal person, not a prisoner. He stands up too, and moves towards her. She stops herself just in time. They stand looking at one another, eyes locked.

'I'm not allowed to hug you, am I?' she asks.

His eyes dance with pleasure. 'Unfortunately not. The prison officers will be watching through the window.' He smiles. She smiles back. 'You don't need to hug me to thank me. Words are enough. I just wanted to give you a present to say keep your chin up.' There is a pause. 'The good news is you'll soon have your QC.'

Her smile evaporates. She feels empty. 'But I've got you.'

'It's a murder trial. Legal Aid have to provide a QC.'

They sit down again at opposite sides of the table in the visit room, as usual.

'Even if I don't want one?' she asks.

'Yes. They have to offer you the best representation possible and that is a QC.' His voice is stern now, measured.

'But Theo, I trust *you*.'

'You'll still have me. But you'll have a QC as well.' He pauses. 'I promise it's for the best.'

She is so upset. So depleted. The trust she has for Theo is burning and intense.

'Will you still be able to come and see me?' she asks, almost in tears.

'Yes. The QC's very busy on another case as well right now. So we've already agreed – I'll continue to make the legal visits.'

She lowers her shoulders and exhales with relief. 'That's good. Thanks.'

THE PAST

61
Zara

Back to university after the Christmas holidays. I am on a high. Scoring distinctions in all my coursework, on the most fantastic photography course. Our photography course is the top-rated one in the country, according to the *Good University Guide* I found on display in the library. So how fantastic am I?

But what I am more proud about than anything, is that I have given up cutting. It hasn't been easy. I have managed it with the help of my counsellor and Sebastian. The more days I get through without cutting, the easier it becomes.

Sometimes when I wake up in the morning I still want to cut. And on those days, that feeling doesn't go away. Even on my good days, sometimes for no reason, just as I am waiting for the bus to college, or walking to Tesco, I think about cutting. The release. What it used to feel like. I distract myself, with something else that makes me feel good. I close my eyes and think about Sebastian telling me that he loves me. Or I think about the last time we had sex. The feel of him inside me.

Last night before I went to bed (Sebastian had gone home for a few days), I wanted to cut myself so badly I cried. I stood looking at myself in the full-length mirror in our bedroom, wondering what Sebastian sees in me. What is there to love? Miranda, you are always telling me how good-looking I am. How you envy my looks. But you are so dark and sultry and sexy – how can you envy me my ordinary looks? I've always had far more men than you but that's only because I'm friendlier. Men like women who are friendly. They make them feel comfortable. Haven't you noticed the way men look at you these days? Even my darling Sebastian sometimes – although he very quickly averts his eyes.

So I stood looking at myself in the mirror, thinking about how chubby I am becoming. These days I am trying to eat as little as possible, just enough to have the energy to live. The lowest calorie ready meals I can find. Sometimes I even make do with a few tablespoons of your healthy rabbit food, Miranda. But still I have over-ample breasts and cellulite. A plethora of orange peel decorating my inner thighs. If I am already developing cellulite at thirty, what am I going to look like by the time I'm sixty? Someone who should only go out on Halloween?

I was standing looking at my cellulite in the harsh halogen light of the bathroom, pushing my inner thighs towards the mirror, pummelling them with my fingers. Wanting to take my blade and do something that would make me feel a lot better. To gouge a good lump out. The pain would be breathtaking. I would feel a sense of relief, knowing I had done something about my cellulite. My body deserves the punishment. I would be exhilarated by my audacity, by my bravery.

But I didn't do it. And I am so pleased with myself. I can't wait for Sebastian to come back so that I can tell him. It would have hurt me so much. It would have still hurt now. I would have gouged deeply. I would have gouged clumsily. It would have taken a long time to stem the bleeding and stung terribly when I rubbed it with antiseptic. The wound would probably have been so deep that it started weeping. I would have packed it with Savlon and kept my fingers crossed.

I think I would have needed to see a doctor. And when you're a cutter going to see the doctor is never good. They look at you with patronising condescension, and advise you to see a therapist. If you tell them to mind their own fucking business and that you're already seeing one, they'll probably send you for anger management, and write something damaging in your notes. So that's another reason I am so glad I didn't cut.

And now today, I've been having a good day. A shout from the top of the mountains, good day. Right from the moment I woke up. Meeting you in the kitchen, Miranda, laughing with you over a cup of early morning coffee. Walking to the bus bathed in January sunshine: young, happy and in love. My classes finished by lunchtime and so I am almost back at the flat. You're both still at work so I will have the flat to myself. I need to think about the next project for my degree. The final project, worth half the year's marks.

Last bit of the journey, footsteps echoing on concrete paving stones as I walk along the ornamentally landscaped pathway towards Harbourside, towards our flat. I turn the key and enter.

Today our shiny flat shouts at me like Tracey Emin's bed. Telling me about our life. The tangle of our love. Empty beer cans and unwashed wine glasses stained by wine dregs. Unwashed dishes in the sink. Overflowing laundry baskets. Our unmade bed. It is no longer a flat but a representation. It represents the rush, the flow, the passion of our love.

I have come back to the flat alone on purpose. I get very little time here alone. I want some peace to design my next photography project. I roll a spliff. I light it and lie on our bed to smoke it. I pull it in. Inhale. Inhale. Inhale. I close my eyes as I hold it in. I open them as I exhale.

My next photography project will be elemental. Powerful. It will encompass the power, the energy of the universe. The moon. The wind. The waves. The sky. Another hit. Holding in longer this time. I think back to our family holidays. You and I, Miranda, holding hands and running into the sea. Jumping over the crests of the waves and laughing. That's it. Miranda, you've helped me to find my project. The power of the sea.

62

Miranda

Anastasia's words from a few months ago reverberate in my mind.

'It's a simple choice. You work with Sebastian or you leave.'

They contort in my head. Work with Sebastian or leave. Before you leave, damage him. Before you damage him, leave. Work. Damage. Leave.

I cannot damage Sebastian at work, so I will damage him at home. Saturday morning. Home alone. Sebastian has gone for a jog along Harbourside. Zara has popped to Costa to get some fresh coffee. I step into their bedroom. What a disgrace. A carpet of laundry. Overflowing waste bin. A river of beer cans on the bedside table.

I wade through the mess, towards Sebastian's computer, and grab it from the top of the dresser. I sit on the bed and open it. Minimum time. Maximum damage. Downloading. Downloading.

Download complete.

63

Zara

Sitting in bed drinking my Costa latte. It tastes uplifting. Saturday morning. A lazy day of bliss ahead of me. Sebastian's laptop on the bed next to me. First things first. I fancy to catch up on the *Daily Mail* website: celebrity gossip, my favourite. I heard a bit about Tom Hiddleston and Taylor Swift, and I just want to check it out. Maybe, after I graduate, I should consider doing some celebrity photography on the side to earn a bit of money.

I pull Sebastian's laptop towards me and open it, tapping the keys to get in. But before I reach gossip and glamour, I am bombarded by naked thrusting bodies, pumping and panting. Orgasmic wailing. Pink nipples. Sweat and orifices. I cannot bear to watch. I switch it off. As soon as I have closed the screen Sebastian walks into the bedroom, red-faced after his jog.

'What's the matter?' he asks.

I open his computer and switch it on again. The pornography starts up. Three men on one woman. It looks like group rape. It makes me feel sick. Really sick. I retch in my mouth and swallow it back.

'Look at this,' I say turning the screen of his Mac towards him.

He watches, face ashen. Shaking his head. 'It wasn't me. I didn't download this.' His eyes are spitting with anger. 'It's disgusting. I don't watch this sort of stuff.'

'What sort of stuff do you watch?'

He holds his eyes in mine. 'I don't. It wasn't me.'

'Who was it then?'

Eyes darkening to black. 'Your stupid bitch of a sister again, I expect.'

64

Zara

Good days. Bad days. Good days. Bad days. Right now there are more good days than bad days. Speaking to my psychotherapist from home on Skype every day helps. Sebastian is helping me more than anyone. Sebastian has pulled me back from the brink.

Four o'clock in the morning, or about that time. I sense it from the way I feel inside. I have more energy now than at four in the afternoon. My circadian rhythm out of sync with the rest of the world. Sebastian is asleep next to me; I feel the steady tide of his breath and hear the insistent background hiss of rain spilling from the sky. As I lie here, listening to the rain, it happens – the thing I can't prevent. The desire to cut. A sickness inside me that pulsates. I lie and let it cascade through my body. If I stay calm it will go away.

But tonight it doesn't. I toss the covers away and pad to the bathroom to splash water on my face. Perhaps herbal tea will help. Mother loves herbal tea. Thinking about how disappointed Mother would be if she saw me restless like this, struggling not to cut, I step into the living room/kitchen and put the kettle on. In the silence of the night, the kettle sounds like a furnace.

When it has reached its crescendo, I pour boiling water onto my tea bag, releasing the gentle scent of lemon and ginger. You appear in the kitchen doorway looking concerned. You are wearing the yellow fluffy dressing gown that Mother bought you, and your lamb's wool slippers from the market.

'What's going on?' you ask.

'Sssh. Don't wake Sebastian,' I say, putting my fingers over my lips.

You step towards me.

'What is it, Zara? Why are you up in the middle of the night?'

'I'm giving up cutting. Sometimes it makes me restless.'

You stand staring at me.

'Do you fancy a cup of tea?' I ask. Perhaps like Mother, like me, herbal tea will calm you, distract you. You look uptight as well.

'Is tea the answer then?' you ask with an amused, almost condescending smile.

I love you, Miranda, but I don't like it when you are condescending. You have always been the clever one. You really do not need to add condescension to your repertoire. It doesn't suit you. Leave it out please.

Your smile relaxes and widens. Condescension evaporated.

I make the tea and we sit next to one another on the sofa, sipping it. The sofa is sagging in the middle, pushing us together. My thigh rests against your leg.

'It's such good news that you're giving up cutting. How have you found the strength?'

'Sebastian,' I tell you.

Your body stiffens. You look the other way.

THE PRESENT

65

'Legal visit,' the officer says as he walks towards her. 'Time to meet your QC.'

She sighs inside. She doesn't want a QC. She wants Theo. No QC, however experienced, could possibly look out for her better than Theo Gregson.

The prison officer walks with her along the convoluted corridors that lead back towards the visit rooms. White paint. Curved metal. No natural light. No windows. The prison officer is Sam, an elderly man with a grizzly beard, who looks close to retiring. But he has a voice much stronger than his body, and he is always ready with a kindly word and smile.

'Your trial must be coming up soon then?' he asks.

'A couple of months,' she says, biting her lip nervously.

'A couple of months and you'll be good to go.'

Her stomach jumps a little as he says that. Could that ever be possible? A life again, without doors locked behind her. A life under her own control.

Good to go.

Sam knocks on the door of the visit room and they enter. He nods his head at the waiting occupants and retreats, leaving her alone with her QC, and her rock star brief. Theo nods at her encouragingly. He is smartly dressed today. Ironed and suited, golden eyes blazing towards hers.

Her QC is sitting behind the plastic desk in the middle of the visit room, next to Theo. She is about forty, with sculptured cheekbones, and a balanced face. She looks a bit like the blonde from ABBA did in her heyday. What is it with her lawyers, that they remind her of musicians? Roger Daltrey. Agnetha Fältskog. Mr Mimms? Mr Mimms' overtired eyes do not remind her of anyone glamorous. Her mind goes blank.

'Sarah Little, QC,' Theo says enthusiastically.

Her QC stands up and leans across the desk to shake her hand.

'A pleasure to meet you,' Sarah Little announces.

'I wish I could say the same. I would be happier if we were meeting in different circumstances.'

'I can't blame you for feeling like that.' Sarah's voice is crisp. Her consonants clipped and decisive.

She smiles a long, slow smile, but it is solid and contained. It doesn't travel around her face. Sarah Little is wearing Margaret Thatcher blue that fits like a glove. White tights. Black court shoes. Nails and face perfectly manicured. What her mother would call Bandbox smart.

'I just wanted to meet you.' She pauses. 'I understand from Theo that you would have been very happy for him to act alone if that were permitted.' Another pause. Another contained smile. 'I don't blame you for having a high opinion of Theo; in my opinion, too, he is first class. But I will present in court, because that is what I am trained to do. He will continue to be your main liaison in the run-up to the trial, and please be reassured I will be relying very heavily on his work during my prep.' There is a pause. 'I think it will go swimmingly.'

'I hope so. I hope so.' Her voice echoes around the room, plaintive and desperate.

Sarah Little looks at her watch. Her iPhone buzzes. 'Sorry.' She smiles. 'I have to go.'

She leaves the room, her perfectly tailored powder-blue suit caressing her perfect body. Skinny legs. Pointed knees protruding. Graceful. Poised. Important. Sarah Little. Busy and important.

'See you in court,' Sarah says casually, as she leaves, as if they are soon to meet in a pub or a restaurant. As if meeting a QC in court is perfectly normal.

And Sarah Little is gone, leaving a little of herself behind in the room. Her solidity. Her confidence. Her perfume of gardenia.

A comfortable silence falls.

After a while, Theo says, 'Sarah Little is good. She knows what she's doing. And I am still here for you. I want you to know that.'

She feels the pulse of his breath. The warmth of his smile. And the elastic band that was tightening in her stomach begins to relax.

THE PAST

66
Zara

This wet Wednesday evening, it's my turn to cook. For once I actually *am* cooking. Only something simple from a BBC recipe: ham and cheese pasta bake. But even that, for someone like me who has never been interested in domesticity, has taken some reading and planning. It's in the oven right now, and the comforting smell of cheese and garlic is wafting around the flat. Maybe I should try to be a domestic goddess more often. And I've treated us to several bottles of Rioja – perfect with cheese and ham.

The key turns in the lock and, Miranda, you are home, hair and coat wet from the rain. Your look so low. So flat.

'What's the matter?' I ask.

You smile limply. 'Nothing.' There is a pause. 'Apart from the rain.' You take your coat off and hang it on the hooks by the door. You sigh. 'I'm just tired. I've been working hard. Struggling with a document I'm drafting.'

To me accountancy is so tedious, no wonder you seem stressed. I think about my sea project and my heart opens out.

'Where's Sebastian? Isn't he back yet?' you ask.

'I don't know.' I smile and shrug. 'I don't own him.'

'I thought you did.'

Your voice sounds sharp. Always sharp at the mention of Sebastian. I know I must keep calm. One day you will learn to handle me being in love.

Footsteps on the pavement. A key in the lock. And he is here, even wetter than you. The rain must have got worse. He grins wildly at me, moving towards me, taking me in his arms and kissing me. Rain from his coat and hair falling onto me and tickling my skin. He takes his coat off. It is so wet he hangs it in the bathroom, and then I watch him sit down at the table next to you, Miranda.

'Hi there, good evening,' he says, leaning across and kissing you on both cheeks.

I watch you wince as he touches you, as you avoid his gaze. He likes to pull people in. You push him away.

I carry the bake across to the table and place it down. It stands, steaming, in the middle of our small IKEA table. As I serve the food, Sebastian opens the wine and pours us a glass each.

'Cheers,' we say and clink glasses. But despite all my culinary efforts, the atmosphere between us is subdued tonight. It raises a little as we eat our food and drink our wine. At least my recipe is a success. I hope my news will liven things up.

'My sea project has been selected for a prize,' I announce as I top up our wine. 'A bit of funding to film it.'

Sebastian smiles. He seems so pleased for me. I look at you.

'Wow,' you say, eyes sparkling, pleased but not surprised. Letting me know you believe in me.

'I'm going to Weston-super-Mare this weekend to start work on it.'

'Sounds good. Can I come too?' Sebastian asks. 'I fancy a change of environment.'

I put my hand on his and shake my head slowly. 'Sorry my love. You're too distracting. It's just one weekend. You'll have to stay at home.'

67

Miranda

After your tasty pasta bake supper, Zara, Sebastian slips off to the pub for a quick pint, leaving us alone together to load the dishwasher. I take a deep breath.

'Do you think Sebastian would mind giving the key to my flat back while you're not here?' I ask as nonchalantly as possible. But my voice doesn't sound nonchalant. It is thin and strained. You stop rearranging the mugs on the top shelf, and turn around.

'Why? I'm only away for two days.'

I stand looking at you, feeling embarrassed, shifting my weight from my right to my left leg, nervously. Another deep breath.

'I don't really want him here while you are away.'

You react as if I have hit you. Or stung you. Your body stiffens. You stand in front of me wide-eyed.

'I thought he was our friend.'

You put your hand on my arm. You push your golden eyes towards mine. 'Miranda, I want him to feel part of our family.' Your eyes are filling with tears. 'Don't make him feel excluded. You've been upsetting us both with your spiky attitude towards him.' You wipe your eyes. 'I love him so much,' you continue. 'Don't antagonise him *again*, Miranda, please.'

68

Zara

The next weekend, Sebastian helps me onto the train, and lifts all my heavy camera cases onto the overhead shelf.

'Are you sure you'll be all right at the other end?' he fusses, looking down at me, his eyes infused with love.

'Yes, of course. Someone will help me get them down, I'm sure. Then I'm jumping straight into a taxi, remember.'

His eyes are still holding mine. 'I'll miss you, Zara.'

'It's just for the weekend. I'll miss you too, but making this film is a big opportunity.'

'I know. Good luck.'

He leans down and kisses me. His tongue rotates around mine. It arouses me. He turns and ambles away, filling the passage of the railway carriage with his broad shoulders and toned denim-clad backside.

As the train pulls away, leaving him on the platform with you, Miranda, I feel the passion of his kiss in my mind.

69

Miranda

Friday evening after work. We wave you off from Bristol Temple Meads railway station for your filming weekend, weighed down by a plethora of camera equipment. So much so that you struggle to get on the train. Sebastian helps you carry it on board and only just manages to get off in time, as the guard blows his whistle.

Once you're away, he walks towards me along the platform, airing his generous smile. My insides tighten as we watch the train depart.

'Freedom for the weekend. What shall we get up to?' he exclaims, putting his arm around my shoulders. I stiffen at his touch. I feel it like a burn.

We walk down the steps from the platform and meander towards the station exit. His arm is still around my shoulders.

'I'm working most of the weekend,' I tell him, removing it gently.

'Haven't you even got time for a quick drink at the pub tonight? I could do with a bit of company.' He pauses. 'Zara so wants us to be friends. Just one drink?'

Zara's tears haunt me, so against my better judgement I relent. 'OK. One quick drink.'

We go to the Roebuck. He has a pint. I have a G&T. It tastes sharper than usual – abrasive against my tongue. We share a large packet of cheese and onion crisps, ripping the bag wide open and placing them on the table between us.

The pub is Friday-night jovial. An atmosphere I usually miss due to my long hours at work. A Friday-night world of loud voices and laughter. People excited to see one another. People having fun. But sitting here with Sebastian I do not feel part of it. I do not know what to say to him. The way he keeps coming on to me behind your back really, really unnerves me. I can't work out what motivates him. For however much he tries to get off with me, whenever he is with you he seems totally engrossed.

'She's given up cutting,' he says as he sips his pint.

'I know.'

He raises his eyebrows. He seems surprised. 'She told you then?'

'Yes.'

A leering grin. 'Does she tell you everything?'

'I shouldn't think so. Nobody ever tells anyone everything.' I take a sip of my gin. It is so bitter I wince. 'I'm thrilled she's given up cutting,' I continue. 'I've been worrying about it for years.'

He pushes his eyes into mine. 'Have you ever cut yourself?' he asks.

'No.'

'Ever been tempted to try?'

'No. Twins don't always want the same things.'

'How do you know if you don't try?'

'We don't even want to *try* the same things.'

His eyes are like black holes, trying to pull me in and destroy me.

'Pity.'

177

My heart is pulsating. I finish my G&T and bang my glass onto the table in front of me. 'Thanks for the drink, Sebastian, but I need to go home now – I've got a few chores to do.'

I am standing up, putting on my coat, but I feel a little dizzy and sit down again.

'What's the matter?' he asks. 'Do you feel all right?'

I am looking at him and his face is swimming a little. I know I need to sit for longer before I walk home.

'Can I get you another drink?'

I shake my head. 'No.' I've had enough.

'A soft drink then?' He pauses. 'A tonic water, perhaps?'

I give in. 'OK, thanks.'

He leaves me and heads for the bar. I watch him amble across the room, his full head of wavy hair, his confident stride. I feel light-headed. But despite that, I am beginning to feel relaxed and happy. Perhaps, after all, it is fun to be part of the Friday-night crowd. Perhaps it is good to be out in town. I watch the groups of people standing in the bar chatting. They are beginning to look shiny and exciting. Sebastian returns with another pint of beer for himself and a tonic water for me. And another packet of cheese and onion crisps.

'Thanks.'

We demolish the crisps very quickly. An unhealthy treat. Afterwards I feel very thirsty and gulp the tonic water down gratefully. He suggests we go home. Now I do not want to leave the warmth of the pub, but I make myself stand up. I have a lot to do tomorrow. It is sensible to go.

He links arms with me as we walk back. I allow him to do that. Linking arms seems platonic enough. When we arrive at the flat, he unlocks the door and opens it. I step inside. He follows me. Feeling woozy, I walk towards my bedroom, planning to get inside and lock the door. Suddenly I want to sleep and sleep.

But I don't get that far. He pulls me into his arms and kisses me. His tongue is in my mouth. For once I don't seem to mind what he is doing. It feels nice. I kiss him back as we move towards my bed. He is undressing me. I am allowing him to. Then I lie, arms above my head, completely naked, watching him strip off. First he kicks off his shoes and rips his socks off. Then he peels off his skin-tight jeans, revealing muscular legs, and a large snake tattoo. T-shirt next. Then underpants. He is hairy. I am fascinated by his naked body. He is so dark and swarthy. So mysterious. He is fully erect as he stands looking at me.

'That's good. That's good,' he whispers. 'I'm ready for you. I want you to be ready for me.'

He is on top of me, kissing me, rotating his tongue across my skin. Down my neck, onto my breasts, biting, playing with my nipples.

He takes it slowly. He turns me over. He enters me from behind. He builds gradually, relishing every stroke, every thrust, gentle at first then more insistent. He guides my hand. He encourages me to squeeze his balls. His breathing is becoming faster and faster. His groin pumping in overdrive. He grunts in my ear and his body goes limp.

It's over.

I feel so tired and confused. Not sure whether I have dreamt this, or whether it has really happened. I snuggle against him, feeling as if my body is not my body but a puppet being controlled by someone else. When I wake up in the small hours, entangled in his arms, I look at his face child-like in sleep, and cannot believe what I have done. I am shaking. I feel sick.

I slip out of the bed and pad across the flat to the shower. I shower in scalding-hot water, to disinfect myself, to take his scent away. I want to bury what has happened so deep inside myself that it will vanish. So that nothing like this will ever happen again.

I wrap a towel around my naked body and creep back to the bedroom to get my stuff, hopefully without waking him up. I need to get away from here. To be alone. To cry. To think. But he is wide awake with the light on, lying naked on top of the cover, erect again.

'Not so frosty-faced today,' he says.

'Frosty face. Is that what you call me?'

He doesn't reply. His grin widens. I feel like crying as I stand in front of him. I feel ashamed. So ashamed.

'Sebastian. I made a terrible mistake. I really shouldn't have done that.'

'You seemed to enjoy it.'

'Whether I enjoyed it or not isn't relevant. It is enjoyment that may cause a lot of pain.'

'No pain. No gain.'

'Don't be flippant. Sebastian, I made a mistake. I'm sorry. I don't want to have a relationship with you.'

'How are you going to manage that when you're so attracted to me?'

'Don't worry, I'll manage.'

He puts his head back and laughs. 'Come here, sweet Miranda. Let's do it again.'

'No.'

He gets off the bed and walks towards me. He pulls my towel off and draws my body against his. I stiffen. I struggle against him, using my full force to push him away.

'No Sebastian. No.'

'You were greedy for it before. So greedy.'

I don't want him to remind me. I want to blank it from my mind. Never to think of it again. I try and stick my elbow in his ribs.

'No. Sebastian. No,' I tell him.

But he is much stronger than me. He overpowers me. He shoves me face down onto the bed, mouth pushed into the duvet so that I can hardly breathe. Clamping my arms so tightly behind my back that I can hardly move. My buttocks are curved awkwardly over the edge of the bed. I cannot stop him. I cannot protect myself. I suppose I am still wet from earlier and he enters me easily from behind. But this time it hurts. It really hurts. A burning pain in the walls of my vagina. A burning pain that I fear will never go away.

70

Zara

When the train arrives at Weston-super-Mare no one helps me with my cameras, but I manage. I lump them together over my right shoulder and hobble off the train. As soon as I step off the train I am embraced by the flavour of the sea. The smell. The sweet, sharp, salty tang of the sea. The cry of the gulls. So high-pitched. So haunting.

The taxi winds through the higgledy-piggledy streets behind the seafront. So far Weston-super-Mare looks to me as if Bath and Bristol have been shaken up together in a jar, and Weston has appeared as a mix-up of them both. I see a curved row of yellow sandstone town houses, very fine and balanced, very Georgian. I see line after line of Edwardian comfort, built in pale stone slabs with creamy sandstone window frames. Substantial and comfortable surrounded by the smell and taste of the sea.

I arrive at my hotel, dump my bags, grab one small cine camera, and head straight for the seafront. Having allowed myself to fall in love with the architecture of Weston too quickly, the brutal architecture of the seafront disappoints me. It's too Victorian. Ugly grandeur. Bold and unforgiving. Telling tales of another era, not accepting that life has moved on. Buildings with an artificiality about them. As if they are trying to pretend life was better then, when we now know that for many it was far worse. Fronted by the pier, a spiky contraption that spoils the sweep of the bay. It is so dark that as I walk away I can only see the outline of its monstrous bulk, shining between the street lamps. I step onto the beach, my back to the pier. Unencumbered by the sight of architectural ugliness, I move towards the sea. Black sea churning and heaving in the moonlight.

I sit on the sand at the water's edge and take my camera out. I watch the sea through the lens. Listening to the waves explode across the sand, so mesmerised I do not go back to the hotel. Waiting to watch dawn break across the horizon. Fingers of orange, peppered with red. The sun rises whole, like an egg yolk, dousing the world with pale early morning light. An ebony sea turns to lace-trimmed hyacinth. A cold icy blue.

I am cold. I am hungry, but still I do not move. The waves speak to me of continuation. Of eternity. Of love. Of freedom. Of my freedom from cutting.

71

Miranda

He grunts in my ear like a stuck pig as he climaxes. I vomit in my mouth and swallow it. He pulls out of me. The burning pain he was causing me increases. It is almost unbearable. I do not move, even though with my head stuffed into the duvet I can hardly breathe. I cannot bear to pull myself out of duvet and look at him. I hear him moving about my bedroom. I presume he is gathering his clothes. What can he be thinking? Is he pleased with himself? I hear the bedroom door open and close. Now he is gone, I feel able to move my head so that I can breathe more easily.

I lie there, anaesthetised by shock, for what seems like hours and hours. Until the heat in my body has gone and I am shivering as I think about what has happened between us. At what he has done. At what I have done. I lie there numb until a voice in the distance of my mind begins to call. A voice telling me to carry on. Not to let this man defeat me. Get away from him. Go to a hotel for the weekend. Get away from him. Stay safe.

So I pull myself to standing, feeling faint. The burning pain between my legs starts up again. I manage to find some clean clothes and get dressed. I cannot bear to wear the clothes I was wearing when we first ripped them off. I leave them on the floor where they fell. I shove a random selection of clothes and toiletries into my backpack, along with my computer, my phone and some books. Quietly, quietly, I creep out of the flat, without hearing him. Without seeing him.

It is early morning. Six a.m. No one is about. A cat skulks in the shadows near the bins. A solitary taxi sweeps past the end of the road. I step around the corner to the Ibis Hotel. I think of you, Zara, so excited about your project, so unaware of what has happened while you are gone. I cry inside. I love you, Zara. I am sorry. So sorry for what I have done.

When I get to the Ibis, I press a buzzer on the door and a pale young night porter lets me in.

'Do you have a room?' I ask. 'To check into now?'

'Funny time to be asking,' he comments.

I stand staring at him without smiling. He taps his fingers on his computer keyboard, consulting his screen.

'You're lucky, I've got one left. Wouldn't usually at the weekend. Had a last-minute cancellation.' He frowns as he continues to consult the computer screen. 'Checking in at this time, you'll still have to pay for two nights. Special offer: £120.'

One hundred and twenty pounds to avoid Sebastian for the rest of the weekend. Cheap at the price. I hand him my credit card and he swipes it.

'Room 107. Use the lift on the left to get to the first floor.'

I smile limply.

'Thanks.'

The young man is staring at me, as if he wonders what I'm doing checking into a hotel on my own in central Bristol at this time in the morning. Watching me to see whether I'm off my head on drugs, or whether I'm pissed. Too drunk to get home after an all-nighter at a club, he probably thinks. Let him think what he wants. I don't care, I tell myself. But I do care. I hate the way he is looking at me. I hate being judged. I know tears are beginning to well in my eyes. I swallow hard to try and push them back. The pain between my legs is rising. I wince. I turn away from him and walk slowly towards the lift. But his eyes are burning into me and I can't wait to be rid of his gaze.

The hotel bedroom is shiny and clean, benign and sterile. Its anonymity wraps itself around me and makes me feel a little better. A little better to be away from him, to know that I am safe. A little better to be away from where it happened. I step into the shower and scald myself with burning water for the second time today. Then I dry myself and slip into this impersonal bed. No scent. No smell. No memory. But it doesn't work. I cannot sleep. I cannot bury the memory.

'No. No,' I say.

'You know you mean yes. You know you want me.'

By morning I am not sure whether I have been awake or asleep. Awake or asleep a montage of what happened keeps running through my brain. The sound of his climax. The taste of my own vomit. The look on your face, Zara, as you reach for his hand. By morning I know I have to get hold of a morning-after pill.

72

Zara

A perfect weekend, totally alone. I was surprised how much I enjoyed it. How much my own company left me feeling at peace. Being alone gave me time to free my mind to concentrate on my project.

Although exhilarated, I was tired and cold on Saturday after staying up all night and filming the darkness and the kaleidoscope sunrise, so I was very glad to return to my hotel at just the right time for breakfast. I couldn't eat much, too energised by my creative experience. But brain and stomach loaded with hot coffee to warm me up, I snuggled into the most comfortable bed I have ever been in and fell asleep like a baby.

About four hours later I woke up totally refreshed and returned to the beach. The same routine. Ignoring the Victorian architecture, sitting at the water's edge, filming the sea. But I didn't stay up all Saturday night. Without any amphetamine pills – I'd left them at home – I couldn't do an all-nighter twice.

So, Saturday night I had a break from my artwork. A few chips on the seafront. A seafront I was now coming to like. Softening to the charms of its faded grandeur. It somehow didn't seem so brutal any more. Pacing along the pavement, head down to protect my face from the wind. Then red wine and TV in my room.

Sunday I became sea-engrossed again.

But now I am on the train home, longing to see Sebastian to tell him about my experience. Longing to see you, Miranda. The train is searing through the countryside, cutting a line between shades of green. And I am smiling inside, knowing that being a representative artist is what I want to do with the rest of my life.

'We are now approaching Bristol Temple Meads,' the guard announces.

I gather my lumpy belongings and wait at the end of the carriage. Brakes whine. The train slows and stops. The person in front of me opens the door. I stagger onto the platform. Sebastian is here. Walking towards me. Kissing me. Taking most of my cameras.

'How was it?' he asks.

'Fantastic.' I pause. 'I just can't tell you how fantastic. As soon as we get back to the flat I'll tell you both all about it.'

'Well it'll just be me.'

I raise my eyebrows hopefully. 'Has Miranda got a date?' I ask.

'She's in bed with flu. She's been away all weekend. I had a quick drink with her on Friday night then she cleared off – didn't tell me where she was going.'

'Has she met someone?'

'I don't know – not that she's admitting to. She came home when you were almost back and went straight to bed saying she felt as if she'd caught flu.'

'Poor thing. I'll check up on her as soon as we get back.'

'I wouldn't go near her if I were you. You don't want to catch it.' There is a pause. 'I've already taken her a Lemsip.'

'You've taken her a Lemsip and I'm not allowed near her. How does that work?'

'Come on, Zara. You know she's got an awkward streak.'

73

Miranda

Sitting in our living room, on the brown leather sofa, holding your hand. Laden with guilt about what has happened between Sebastian and me.

I can't understand it.

I've never found him attractive.

I felt so strange. So sleepy and distant. Out of it. And now I feel so ashamed. I can't bear to contemplate what happened the second time he penetrated me. A nightmare perpetually runs through my head. A nightmare I can't move away from.

You show me the first edit of your sea film. It plays through the TV from your computer. It is so good. If I was feeling normal it would be engrossing. But today it can't take me away from my worries. I look across at you, lost in your film of the sea at night. The intensity. The darkness. As you admire the golden beauty of the dawn that the film is drawing into, for a second I envy you. You look so enthused. But then my envy turns to pity, as my mind reverberates back to your boyfriend.

'You've not been yourself since I went away. What happened?' you ask.

I do not reply. I turn my head back to the screen. Another wave cascades towards me.

'Do you think you ought to go and see a doctor? Maybe you're just a bit run-down?' you continue.

'Come on. Let's not talk about it. Not now when I'm so enjoying your film.'

'You're not getting away with it that easily. Even if I have to arrange the appointment myself.'

You take my hand in yours and squeeze it. You lean across and kiss my cheek.

Sitting at my desk in the office, trying to get on with my work. Not concentrating. Sometimes I wonder why I ever decided to be an accountant in the first place. Many years ago when I was a maths student I was excited by its intellectual complexity, the challenge. But now the practicality of the job seems so far removed from the theoretical maths that I loved. It seems so boring. So flat. At the moment I can't sleep. I can't concentrate. The numbers in front of me are meaningless and dissociated.

My phone buzzes. You Zara. A text.

I'm outside. Come and see me right now.

OK, I text back, sighing as I leave my desk. My boss won't like me leaving the office in the middle of the day. But the way I feel right now about my job, about everything, what does it matter?

I step outside to find you waiting for me on the pavement outside my office block, wrapped in the new coat you chose with Sebastian. A blanket of a coat that makes you look like a hippy.

'Come on,' you say. 'Chop, chop. I've booked you an appointment.'

'An appointment?'

'With our GP.'

I groan.

'Yes. I told you I would. And you *are* going to see her.'

'When?'

'In ten minutes. Got a cancellation. And I'm coming with you, to make sure you get there in time.'

'OK, OK. I'll text my boss to tell her I've an urgent doctor's appointment. She has to let me go I suppose.'

I text. She replies.

Fine. Thanks for letting me know.

Polite for Ms Sudbury. I expect I will have to make up for it later. Perhaps she will have me redacting documents into the small hours. It's a cold day. Watery sunshine. The first scent of spring in the air, as you link arms with me, and accompany me on the five-minute walk to the medical centre.

We sit next to one another in the waiting room, which is full of people coughing and spluttering. People ignoring one another, staring at the wall in front of them. Fiddling with their iPhones. I join in the endless modern ritual, and fumble nervously with mine too.

No new emails. Nothing much on Facebook. The Twitter feed is moving as fast as ever, lots of silly comments from people whose names I don't recognise. BBC News: nothing much new happening there. Something unpleasant in Syria. But then there is always something ghastly happening in Syria. I watch shots of an explosion, and buildings that look like decimated concrete moving towards me as if from another world, completely dissociated from mine.

After what seems like forever, the doctor calls me.

I stand up. You stand up too.

'You're not coming with me.'

Your face crumples with concern. 'Are you sure you don't want me to?'

'Yes. Yes. Thanks, but I really want to go alone.'

You shrug your shoulders. You sit down. I walk along the corridor feeling as if I am walking through space. I can't believe I am finally here to see the doctor. Something I know I should have done sooner, but I just couldn't bring myself to. I suppose I didn't want to admit what had happened, not even to myself. I knock on the door of Dr Dale's consulting room.

'Come in,' a cheery voice floats out.

As I enter the consulting room with its grey walls and thin orange curtains, a woman swathed in pink cashmere that clashes with the colour of the curtains is looking up at me from her swivel chair, smiling condescendingly. Her smile makes me feel uncomfortable. It doesn't look natural. It extends too far around her face.

'What can I do to help?' she asks.

I do not reply. I sit down. My mood has swung full circle. I shouldn't have come in. What was I thinking of? What has happened is private. It only belongs to Sebastian and me. I am sitting on the edge of an abyss, about to fall in. She leans towards me, smile evaporated now.

'Are you all right?'

Still I don't reply. I try to but my lips don't move.

'Please,' she says. 'You can't shock me. I've heard everything.'

The silence is solid. Tangible. From somewhere behind it, I hear myself speak. 'What makes you think my problem's embarrassing?'

'You just seem a little hesitant.' She leans back in her chair a little and folds her arms. 'Try me. I don't bite. There is nothing in my job that I haven't seen or heard.'

'OK.' I take a deep breath. 'I've got a burning pain between my legs.'

She raises her eyebrows a notch. 'Since when?'

'A few days ago.'

She picks up a pen and pulls the notepad in front of her a little closer. 'Does it hurt when you pee?'

'No.'

'So when do you get it? Is it there all the time?'

'Just sometimes. I can't figure out why.'

She makes a few notes, then she looks up at me. 'Do you mind if I examine you?'

I say no, but I do mind. I mind very much. After what has happened I feel so very embarrassed about my private area. It feels distended, violated. Ugly. I feel heat burning in my cheeks and realise that I am blushing.

Her eyes soften as she watches me. She gets up from behind her desk, rips a fresh piece of giant kitchen roll from the holder on the wall, and places it carefully on her examination couch.

'You can leave most of your clothes on. Just take off your knickers and tights. And then sit up on the couch.'

I move towards the couch. She turns the area around it into a cubicle by drawing curtains around it and steps outside to allow me to sort myself out. With trembling hands I pull down my tights. And I am back. We are on my bed. He is undressing me. He is pulling my knickers down. I am crying. Tears run down my face.

When my knickers and tights are rolled up in a ball pushed inside my handbag, I pull myself up onto the couch and sit up as she asked.

'Ready,' I shout over the curtain.

Dr Dale reappears wearing thin plastic gloves, and her surprisingly un-reassuring smile. She has a speculum in her right hand and a little torch on her head. I look at her moving towards me and shudder inside.

'Open your legs,' she commands.

He overpowers me. He shoves me face down onto the bed,

pushing my mouth into the duvet so that I can hardly breathe. Clamping my arms so tightly behind my back that I can hardly move.

'You're greedy for it,' he says as he puts his head back and laughs.

I clamp my legs tightly shut, knees pressed together. Tears are streaming down my face. I know because I can feel their salt as they reach my mouth. She puts her hand on my knee.

'Please Miranda, I promise I won't hurt you.'

I concentrate. I close my eyes. Slowly, slowly, I move my knees apart.

'I'm going to take a swab, just to make sure there's no infection,' she says as she pushes something inside me. He enters me from behind. It hurts. It really hurts. A burning pain in the walls of my vagina. A burning pain that will never go away. She pushes something inside me and I cry out in pain. She pulls back. She pulls it out, puts the swab in a test tube and seals it.

'Sorry. Did I hurt you?' she asks.

The burning pain is escalating. My insides are on fire. 'It hurts. It hurts so much.'

'I'm sorry. Get dressed, and come and sit down. I'll run through what I think,' she says disappearing through the gap in the curtain again to leave me in peace.

Shivering and trembling, I pull on my knickers and tights. I move back to the patient's chair again and sit, watching and waiting. Watching her watching me. Wondering what she is thinking. Waiting for her to speak.

'Miranda,' she says. 'It all looks healthy down there. There doesn't look to be any tissue damage. Nothing to suggest anything is wrong. I've taken a swab, which I'll send to the lab, just to make sure. And we'll get a urine sample just to make sure there's no UTI. But as it doesn't hurt when you pee that

194

situation is unlikely.' She pauses. A long considering pause, head on one side. 'Please Miranda, tell me, are you having a sexual relationship with anyone at the moment?'

I shake my head and try to push back the tears that are prickling behind my eyes. She is watching me too carefully. It's making me feel nervous. The tears start to fall. I wipe them away with my handkerchief.

'Has anyone forced themselves on you?' she asks gently.

I know I should tell her. I should speak out to protect other women. But I cannot tell anyone about this – Zara must never find out.

'Of course not,' I say, still wiping away my tears as I stand up to leave.

74

Zara

Miranda, what is wrong with you? Why won't you tell me? Where have you gone? Only the shell of you is left. Are you anaemic? Diabetic? Depressed? Historically, you were the calm, confident one. Now our roles have been reversed. University life invigorates me. Being an accountant is destroying you. I am sitting in the waiting room at our surgery, waiting for you to come out of Dr Dale's consulting room, eager to hear what she has to say to you. I look at my watch. You've been nearly half an hour. What's taking so long?

I want you back, Miranda, the way you used to be. Sebastian keeps telling me to stop worrying. He thinks I'm trying to be a surrogate mother to you.

'It's not good for twins to be too reliant on one another,' he said this morning as he was getting out of bed.

'In what way?' I asked sleepily, still languishing beneath the covers.

'Over-reliance is damaging.'

He had a sharpness in his voice that made me wake up. I pulled the duvet away and sat up, blinking in the halogen light. He was wrapping himself in his stripy dressing gown.

'I don't know what you mean. I thought support of family and friends was essential for feelings of belonging and wellbeing. Miranda feels like family *and* friend to me. In fact, until I met you I'd say she was the centre of my life.'

He was staring at me, eyes sparkling. He raised his arms in the air and shrugged. 'Exactly. You've proved my point.' There was a pause. 'Combining family and friendship. Too much pressure. Too much intensity. You need to spend more time apart.'

He walked back towards the bed.

'Why are you saying this?' I asked.

He sat on the edge of the bed, pulled me towards him, and kissed me. As usual when he kisses me a pulse of electricity ran through me.

'Maybe it's because I want you to myself,' he whispered.

I push the memory of his touch away. The taste of him. The smell of him. As I watch you walking towards me across the waiting room, shoulders down, bereft. As you come closer, I can see you've been crying again. Now you are trying to suppress more tears. I know the tell-tale signs. Swollen eyelids. Red blotches all over your face. You are sniffing and searching in your handbag for a tissue. I walk towards you and put my arm around you.

'How'd it go?' I ask.

You don't reply. Worry escalates inside me.

75

Miranda

A week has gone by. A week with no change, no improvement in my symptoms. No return to my usual level of concentration. So far I don't think anyone has noticed. Except Sebastian who keeps staring at me at work. He must have noticed my endless trips to the lavatory to try to get away from him for a few minutes, to compose myself.

I have come back to see Dr Dale today, to get my test results. She is sitting hands clasped together on her knee. I am in her patient's chair watching her, waiting for her to speak. She is a smart dresser. Wearing cream upon cream. A creamy cardigan. A creamy blouse. Creamy pearls curdled around her neck. Leaning forward and staring at me intently. I wish she would tone herself down, put those eyes away.

'All your tests are clear,' she says in a chirrupy, singsong voice.

I do not reply. She leans back in her chair and folds her arms, not taking her razor eyes off me, not even for a second.

'All your tests are clear,' she repeats. 'The swab. The urine. The blood test. The internal examination.' There is a pause. She crosses her legs now too. Arms and legs crossed, making her look streamlined, as if she's into yoga. 'So you've no infection. No trauma. Nothing.' Her eyes are simpering with pleasure.

I do not respond.

'Aren't you pleased?' she asks.

I continue to sit silently, dwelling on my negative results. I still feel so rotten. What can this mean?

'But . . . but . . .' I finally splutter. 'It hurts me very much. I'm not imagining it. There's something wrong with me and we don't know what it is. Why should I be pleased?'

She smiles. Half a smile. As if she finds consulting me difficult.

'It means you don't have anything serious.'

'Are you sure? Does it?'

A frown ripples her face. She bites her lip. She swallows. 'There is one thing that concerns me.' She pauses. 'Sometimes rape victims have symptoms like this.'

'Like this?' My voice is plaintive. Desperate.

'Yes. Real physical pain left by the psychological trauma of the event. A sort of post-traumatic stress syndrome.'

'Like soldiers get?'

'Yes.'

Anger explodes inside me. How dare this woman speculate about my private life? She knows nothing about me. I do not want her to guess what happened. I will not come and see her again. I am trembling, every bit of me. My tissue, my guts, my sinews. My fingers, my toes, my lips.

She is scribbling down notes as I leave.

76

Miranda

Driving up the motorway, escaping from Bristol, back to Tidebury for the weekend. Maybe seeing Mother will help.

I hate Anastasia Sudbury.

Second written warning indeed.

One more written warning and I am out. How dare she. Patronising, sycophantic bitch. The memory of her voice, with its overemphasised vowels and artificial resonance as she 'mediated' between me and Sebastian makes me feel sick. Second written warning for not working efficiently with him. I clutch the steering wheel so tightly my fingers ache.

I turn the car radio up in an attempt to drown my thoughts in classical music. But my mind is pumping. Plaintive violins and resonant cellos don't help. I cannot stop thinking about Sebastian and what he did to me. I feel his hands all over me. I feel him entering me again. I hear his grunting climax. I feel a knife grating the walls of my vaginal passage. As I drive I breathe through the pain.

I stop at a service station and sit in the car, head in hands.

Back on the motorway, I know I need to pull myself together. It isn't safe, even in the slow lane, wedged between heavy lorries, driving when my mind is a kaleidoscope of hate, guilt and pain.

Classical music. Perhaps that will help. Four hours of listening to Classic FM later, at half past midnight I finally arrive home.

Mother opens the door. She hugs and kisses me. I step into the hallway. I see our patterned rug, the parquet flooring, the limited edition print that you chose when we were on holiday in the Lake District, so many years ago. Being home intensifies my thoughts of you, Zara. So many shared memories. I hoped coming home would make me feel better, but I feel worse as I stand in the hallway surrounded by echoes of happiness that has passed.

'Would you like a tea, a coffee?' Mother asks.

I don't reply.

'Something stronger perhaps? I'll open a bottle of wine, and pour us both a glass.'

I follow Mother into the kitchen and watch her taking a bottle of Beaujolais Villages from the wine rack and start to open it.

'What's happening?' she asks with her back to me. 'Why are you here?'

'You make it sound as if I never visit.'

She turns towards me, eyes soft. 'I miss you both, you know that.'

And I step towards her and hold her in my arms. I pull her against me; my small, resilient mother who has done so much for us, brought us up on her own.

'I need to talk to you,' I mutter.

She opens the wine and pours us both a glass. We settle in the sitting room. The room is a time warp. Mother hasn't changed it since we were ten. A dresser with our school photographs on. A vase containing silk flowers that we bought her one Mother's Day. I take a large gulp of wine.

'I'm thinking of leaving Bristol,' I announce.

Mother's mouth opens, like a guppy. 'But I thought you loved it there?' she splutters, almost spilling her wine.

'I need a break. A fresh start. I'm an accountant with almost ten years' experience now. I could work anywhere in the world.'

'But what about Zara?'

'She's not my responsibility. She's really happy in Bristol. She loves her course. She loves her boyfriend.' I pause. 'She doesn't need me.'

'I need you. I need you to stay in Bristol to keep an eye on her,' Mother says, her voice thin and plaintive.

My stomach tightens. It hurts me to breathe. 'It's crippling me living there with her and Sebastian.'

'Because?' she asks.

'She's better now. They just ignore me.' I pause. 'And I've told you. I need a fresh start.'

Mother leans towards me. 'But you've always been there for your sister. What's happened?'

'Nothing has happened.'

'I don't believe you.' Her eyes are wide with concern. 'It's late. You've had a long journey. Let's sleep on it and talk in the morning.'

I nod, drain my wine, and kiss my mother. 'Good night.'

The familiarity of my bedroom folds around me and makes me feel worse. I want time to go backwards. I want never to have gone to Bristol. Never to have met Sebastian. I wish I was dead. I take my clothes off and look at my body, the body he has desecrated. I weep myself to sleep.

I wake up in the morning suffused with a feeling of dread. Knowing something awful has happened, but not sure what. Then I remember. The written warning. The sex. The rape. As soon as I remember the rape, the scraping pain begins again. I shower for far too long, soaping my body, pushing soap up

202

inside myself to clean him away. That makes it hurt more. Feeling heavy inside, I get dressed and walk downstairs.

Mother is in her kitchen domain as usual – laying the table for breakfast.

Pouring out orange juice she says, 'I didn't sleep all night, thinking about what you said.' She pauses and looks up at me. 'You can't leave Bristol. If you do, you'll have to pay me back the deposit I gave you for the flat.' Another pause. Head on one side. 'I really want you to stay and be there for your sister.'

77

Sebastian

The nightmare is back. Making me scream, making me sweat. The stench of blood, sickly and sweet. Rolling and tumbling in it. It clings to my skin. Sirens wail. The emergency services are here, circling like birds of prey. The fire brigade. Cutting me out. The police giving me the Breathalyser. I am lifted into an ambulance. On the way to hospital. I don't know where I am. I don't know which hospital. My mouth isn't working. I can't ask questions. I don't know where they are taking you. I wanted to say goodbye. Slipping in and out of consciousness. I will never say goodbye.

I wake up in a private room attached to machines, my arm and leg in plaster. I can see out of the window to a small courtyard, with a bed of fleshy bushes. It is raining. The first thing I do is look for you, Jude, for Mother, Father, for my family. What has happened? Why aren't you here to look after me?

And then I remember. This nightmare is my life.

78

Zara

You return from visiting Mother looking thunderous. Stomping around the flat tidying up. Banging the plates I had left in the sink into the dishwasher. Eyes dark. Frown mountainous.

'Sebastian is out tonight. Any chance of a girly trip to a wine bar?' I push through your mood and dare to ask.

'Is he visiting his invisible parents?' you snap.

'Yes.'

You relax your mouth a little.

'OK then, I accept,' you reply.

79

Miranda

We go to a quirky wine bar near the Crown Courts. Your worry about me tunnels towards me and makes me feel worse. Surely you must realise it is hard enough coping with my own problems, without feeling guilty about yours?

But everything seems a little better, a little brighter, over a glass of wine in an artificial environment. Alcohol and artificiality pushing the world away. The flicker of candlelit shadows. Knees pushed together against an old wine cask masquerading as a table. An underground cavern of stone walls. For a while I feel all right. My real world steps away. The wine bar is full of young professionals straight from work. Youthful responsibility fills the air.

'How's your job going?' you ask.

'I don't want to talk about work,' I hear myself bark.

You reach across the wine barrel and take my hand in yours. I don't want you to touch me, but I don't pull my hand away. Your hand feels hot in mine. You lean towards me. Your golden eyes fragment a little; your irises become misty.

'What's going wrong, Miranda?' you ask.

I don't reply. I sit looking at you in your dangly earrings

and your gypsy dress from New Look. Your golden brown hair the colour of syrup. Your soft toffee skin. So like Mother. You two are like peas in a pod. I am the odd one out.

I take a large sip of my red wine. It feels heavy on my tongue. I put my glass back on the wine barrel table. 'I've hit a bad patch.'

'A bad patch? What did you say to Mother? She phoned me – she's worried.'

'I told her I want to leave Bristol.'

Laser eyes widen. 'Leave Bristol? Nothing momentous then! You told her but you hadn't told me?' You shake your head. Your voice is high-pitched. Indignant. You are almost in tears.

'It sort of all came over me while you were away.'

'What did?'

'Everything.' You frown. You look confused. 'It reached a crescendo,' I continue to explain.

You bite your lower lip. 'Where do you want to go?' you ask.

'Anywhere. Hong Kong. The Cayman Islands.' I pause. 'Anywhere but here.'

80

Zara

Even though I am not religious, I pray somewhere deep inside that you do not mean this. You can't mean this. You can't move away.

'No. No. Please don't go. Don't ever leave me,' I beg.

I lean across the wine cask and take your hand in mine. I tighten my fingers over yours. A friendly squeeze. You don't respond. Your hand remains flaccid in mine.

'But you've got Sebastian. You don't need me,' you reply, your voice flat. Robotic. Telling me with your voice, and your eyes, that you don't feel any better about my relationship with Sebastian.

I move past the way your attitude hurts me. 'I want you both,' I tell you.

'I'm not sure that's possible,' you reply.

'I don't just want you both, I need you both,' I continue.

You don't reply. You stare into the air beyond me, as if I am invisible.

'Miranda, I can't bear it if you go,' I plead. 'I've always needed you and you've always been there for me.' I pause and watch you take a sip of wine, your lips pressing a little too hard against the glass. You are still gazing into mid-air, as if I wasn't here.

'And I've been waiting for the right moment to tell you,' I persevere, 'I think it's important for you to understand just how good Sebastian is for me as well. With his help, I've not cut myself for two whole months.'

You look straight at me now. Eyes focused.

'I need you both so much,' I beg with a final plaintive flourish.

81

Miranda

You've not cut yourself for two months. I need to talk to Sebastian as soon as possible. Yet again I am reminded that you mustn't guess what's happened between us. That I must continue to laugh at his jokes. To accept his 'platonic' kisses. Whatever I think of him, he has helped you to stop cutting, in a way that Mother and I could not.

'Sebastian, I thought maybe we could walk to work together,' I say the next morning, as I make myself toast and coffee.

As we step together through the door of my flat, he offers me his arm. I shake my head.

'Walking to work together doesn't mean we need to touch one another.'

'Walking to work together doesn't mean you need to be prickly.'

Again it takes me all my effort not to retort. I smile weakly. It is raining. Discordant rain, hissing as it hits the pavement, thumping from blocked gutters. The road is a lake. Sebastian produces a knowing smile and a large shiny black umbrella. He opens it and pulls me beneath it, shading me from the bullets of rain. I am closer to him than I want to be, but if I move I will be drenched.

'Sebastian,' I say, 'she must never know about what happened that weekend.'

He holds my eyes in his. 'OK, OK. Calm down. She'll never know. I promise.'

82

Sebastian

I knew you were dead before I even saw your mangled body. The second you went I sensed it. I killed you, Jude. And Mother and Father. Bodies twisted and tangled. Shreds of metal. The meaty stench of blood. So much blood. The haunting pulse of the sirens that will never go away.

Jude. I love you. I miss you. I never believed in the after-life until you were gone. Now I know all your love, all your energy, must be somewhere. It was too powerful to be destroyed. Whether you have angel's wings and sit on fluffy clouds, or are a string of molecules light years away, swimming in DNA soup, I know you are still here, looking down on me, watching my every move.

Did you see how that young policeman treated me when I was in hospital still attached to machines? He was so young he looked as if he should still be at school. So smooth-faced I don't think he even needed to shave. As soon as he entered my room I resented him. He walked towards me with an expressionless face. No humanity. No empathy.

I was feeling particularly bad that day. Every day was bad. Still is. But some days are worse than others. That morning my back and my joints were burning with more pain than usual because the nurse was late with the drugs trolley. My head had a firecracker exploding inside it. Even my jawbone and my teeth were painful.

He stood by my bed. He didn't even greet me.

'I am arresting you on suspicion of driving under the influence of alcohol . . .'

He carried on with the rest of that stupid speech.

'You bastard,' I shouted, interrupting him.

I clenched my fists. I wanted to get out of bed and thump him. To beat him up. To get him on the ground and kick him in the head. I wanted to see him lose as much blood as you did. Still attached to machines, I couldn't move. So I pooled saliva in my mouth and spat at him. My spittle landed on his face. He wiped it from his cheek with his hand and stepped back. He repeated his spiel now, for assaulting a police officer. What a moron. What a plonker.

He continued, 'You failed the Breathalyser test at the scene, and later drugs were found in your blood. We look forward to seeing you in court.'

The lorry annihilated my family and he arrested me for drunk driving? What was the matter with him? Anger cut through my depression for an hour or two. But later that day my anger diminished, and I reached a new level of depression. A level of depression that could not be contained.

83

Zara

'You're still very worried about Miranda, aren't you?' Sebastian says, his voice soft with concern, as we lie next to one another, first thing in the morning, in bed.

'Is it that obvious?' I ask, wondering why he asks this right now, when we've just woken up.

'Yes.'

I roll on top of him and kiss him, gently. His body is soft and warm. He kisses me back intently. If I encourage him much more we will end up making love. I pull my lips away from his. I want to chat. I do not want to make love.

'We need to move out. We're stressing her,' I tell him. I have been awake half the night worrying about this.

'Is that what you think?' he asks.

'Yes.'

I feel his body stiffen beneath me. 'We can't afford to. Not yet.'

I run my fingers through his strong wavy hair. 'What about living with your parents?'

His eyes flatline. 'That's a mad suggestion. You'd retract that if you'd met them.'

'Well, we need to do something to get away from here.'

214

84

Sebastian

A glimmer of hope, Jude. The twins are beginning to think separately. Miranda has mentioned moving abroad. Zara has suggested moving out of Miranda's flat. Progress at last. Progress indeed. Not long to go now.

85

Miranda

Sitting at my desk trying to concentrate. Sebastian sitting next to me. A smoky aura hangs over him. It's obvious he has the occasional cigarette behind our backs. In these days of health consciousness the scent of cigarettes seems edgy. Rebellious. But then everything about Sebastian is like that.

He leans towards me, eyes glinting dangerously. 'I know what you like. Remember, Miranda.'

My hand itches to slap his face. But we are in full view of half the Tax department, so I manage to restrain myself.

'Why don't we go for a coffee?' I hiss.

He gives me a buttery smile. 'OK.'

He stands up and I follow him out of the office. Even the way he walks is showy. He rolls his thighs across one another, confidently. Flamboyantly. Today, the café is swimming with even more accountants than usual, as Harrison Goddard are hosting a conference. I fetch two Americanos from the machine whilst Sebastian nabs a table. Too many people. People invading us with elbows and bags as they pass. Someone jolts the table and coffee floods onto my lap. I pat it off with a napkin.

'Not very private in here, is it?' Sebastian says.

'Private enough for us,' I reply.

'Come on, Miranda, you only ever buy me coffee for a reason. What is it?' Black eyes shine like a stag beetle's back.

'To remind you about your promise.'

Black eyes darken. 'There's nothing contractual about a promise; if you were a lawyer you would know that.' A smile with a snarl in it.

I put my hand on his arm. 'Please Sebastian. Please don't tell Zara about what happened between us.'

'You sound as if you're begging.'

'I am.'

'I like it when you beg.'

86

Sebastian

When I had come out of hospital, I had to go to court. You were watching that too, weren't you Jude? A little part of you floating in the spectators' gallery. How did it make you feel? Outraged by my treatment? My barrister, an uptight little woman with large breasts and an educated accent, didn't do a very good job, did she? I was found guilty. Of causing death by dangerous driving, after alcohol and cannabis consumption.

It makes me so angry. Anger incubates inside me. What about the lorry driver who lost control on the other carriageway, ploughing into our car, and pushing it beneath a coach? He was a cherub, was he? An innocent?

Did you see me, Jude, the day I received my sentence? Trembling so much, wishing I'd taken even more drugs. I'd already had a shedload of cocaine and amphetamine in the morning to help me get out of bed. Just before I left my flat to go to court I took some blues. My body was in such distress; I should have maxed on the blues.

The judge gave me two years. The cocksucker. At least it was a suspended sentence. And my licence was suspended too. Not that I wanted to drive anyway. The judge also handed me two hundred hours of community service. Community service. Thanks. Picking up litter will really help me to cope with bereavement.

Thanks a fucking bunch.

87

Miranda

Sebastian. In my bedroom, walking towards me. His face dark and blurred.

'I like it when you beg,' he tells me.

The bread knife is under my pillow. My fingers clench around its wooden handle. He is leaning over me. I feel his breath against my face. I pull out the knife, swing it round and push it into his stomach, just beneath the breastbone. Angling it up as high as I can. Higher and higher I push. I feel his body stiffen, and I know what I have done. I roll away from beneath him. I am sweating. I am trembling. I slip out of bed, snap on the light, and reach for my phone to dial 999.

And then the fug in my mind becomes finer. What has happened? I turn around. The bed is empty. No Sebastian. I have had a dream so real I woke without realising it was a dream. Still trembling, I reach for my dressing gown and pad to the bathroom, clean my teeth, and step into the shower.

I like it when you beg. I like it when you beg.

And I feel him penetrating me again. I want to maim him. To hurt him. Enough so he couldn't come to work for a while.

Some respite for me. If I just had some respite I could cope with him better.

I soap myself in the shower. The water is soft, the bubbles generous. I rub and rub, and bubbles and foam come up. A waterfall of bubbles rising and sinking. A myriad of rainbow-hued colours reflected beneath electric light. For the first time in a while I almost feel happy. Or at least content. Self-indulgent. Thoughts of maiming Sebastian are helping me.

Sebastian showers straight after me. If I make it as soapy as possible there is an outside chance the bastard might slip. I tighten my grip on the block of soap and rub it and rub it until it starts to disintegrate. I spread the gunky, gluey mess across the shower tray with my fingers. Across the middle of the bathroom floor. I accidentally leave my slippers just inside the door. Trip, bastard, trip. Break an arm. Break an elbow. Break a leg. Come on Sebastian, break a leg.

88

Zara

Soft in love, lying in my lover's arms, thinking about the day ahead. This morning I have an early start for my still-life photography course. It sounds like a bit of a bore. I prefer topics with movement. Clouds. Wind. Sea. I sigh inside. I wish I could just stay here all day. I force myself to pull away from Sebastian, twist my feet out of bed, and plant them firmly on the floor. He whistles appreciatively at my naked body as I walk across the room and lift my dressing gown off the back of the door.

'I'll shower first today,' I tell him as I cover myself up and step towards the bathroom.

I am daydreaming. Thinking about Sebastian. The heat and pulse of him. First I trip over Miranda's slippers, but I manage to catch my balance. Just. Leaning heavily on my right leg in front of the sink. My right leg slips. I land with a thud onto my left shoulder and yelp in pain. The shock of hurting myself so much when I least expected to makes me burst into tears.

I hear Miranda and Sebastian calling to me through the locked bathroom door. Carefully, I pull myself up to standing. I hobble awkwardly to the bathroom door, gradually realising that I am all right. I open the bathroom door and fall into Sebastian's arms.

'What happened?' he asks.

'It's slippy in here. There's soap everywhere! You mad cow, Miranda, you didn't clean up properly.'

89

Miranda

On the way to work, trying to keep ahead of Sebastian whose footsteps are echoing mine. Breathless along Park Street. But his legs are longer so he soon catches up.

'What caused the debacle this morning?' he asks, his breath mingling with mine.

I step sideways, away from him, and continue walking. 'I was late, so I didn't clean up after myself as well as I should have.'

'You don't say.' He pauses. 'You made a hell of a mess.'

He moves closer to me, grabs my wrist with his hand, and squeezes so tightly it hurts. The pain makes me cry out. I stop walking and stand looking into his eyes. His eyes are as dark as the night. I feel as if I can hardly breathe.

'Don't forget again or we might think you did it on purpose,' he hisses.

'Don't bully me,' I reply.

90
Zara

After my clumsy episode in the bathroom this morning, fortunately I made it to my photography class on time. I didn't want to be late – this is part of my course assessment and I'm heading for a first. Who would have thought, little old un-academic me, heading for a first.

I'm a bit bruised. No real damage. So here I am looking at a bowl containing an apple, an orange, a pear and a pineapple. I've arranged it perfectly. Still life. Far more interesting than I expected. My camera is clicking repeatedly. Shadows and light. Dust and softness. Intensity and vibrancy. The shadows and light of life.

91

Sebastian

Jude, did you see it all? Did you see me rushing to the probation offices? Standing by the minibus with the other 'criminals' – not that I thought of myself like that. I ignored them and looked at the ground until the supervisor arrived. The supervisor, Bert, was an emaciated man, with crevices on his face rather than wrinkles. A recovering heroin addict I expect. Bert doubled up as the driver, and drove us around three corners to the park.

We spilt out of the minibus – men, mostly middle-aged. Hair in short supply. Beer bellies abundant. I was the youngest by far, except for a pimply youth with a nose stud. Bert issued us with our equipment for the day. First, our bright orange high-vis jackets with COMMUNITY PAYBACK written in giant letters on the back. Specifically designed to make us feel ashamed of what we have done. A public shaming. How barbaric. Out of fashion in sophisticated cultures, ever since the Middle Ages. And I used to think Great Britain was great. Next we were given our litter grabbers and bin-bags. Whoop de whoop. Fun on a summer's day.

All day collecting litter, melting in the heat. I was still recovering from the accident, so I found it very painful. We had our lunch break at a local café. That was when I overheard one of the men talking. It was better to turn up a few minutes late for the minibus, apparently, because if there's no space on the bus you are exempted from a day's service; people frequently get left behind. I never arrived early again. And that's how I managed to skip half my hours. Clever, don't you think? But then I always was a clever guy.

92

Miranda

The one time I leave work before Sebastian, Anastasia steps out of her office and bumps into me as I am going. Today she is wearing a leather dress. It looks stiff and uncomfortable. As soon as she sees me she makes a point of glancing at her watch. I don't smile at her. I don't speak to her. I just continue rushing down the corridor to try and make it look as if I am going somewhere important.

In fact, I am escaping early because I am determined to make a special casserole for supper. An apologetic supper to compensate for the mess I left in the bathroom this morning. I stop at the supermarket around the corner from work to buy the ingredients. Chicken. Bay leaves. Tarragon. Shallots. White Burgundy. I have every intention of making this meal gourmet.

Back in the flat I turn the Sonos up loud and treat myself to a dose of Harper. Her music is uplifting. I relax into it. I must cook the chicken very carefully. Listeria has been increasingly found in supermarket chicken lately. The government have been issuing guidelines advising people to be very thorough. To be on the safe side I have taken Delia's advice. Mother always says you can't go wrong with Delia.

I peel the shallots, and fry them in butter, with garlic. Onions and garlic. They smell delicious. I cut up the chicken and add it to the pan, keeping the raw juice in a jug. When the chicken has browned, I add a bit more butter and the flour, the herbs, then I slowly, slowly add the wine. Forty-five minutes later the gravy is thick. It has reduced perfectly. The sweet smell of tarragon butter chicken permeates the flat. The lovebirds arrive home, hand in hand.

'Supper is ready when you are,' I announce.

You sit opposite one another, eyes locked, at the table I laid earlier. Sebastian, as is his habit, occasionally tears his eyes away from you to glance at me through the mirror above the table. When I am sure he isn't watching I pour the raw chicken juice into his portion of the casserole and stir. I bring the food, already plated, to the table and hand it out.

Much to my dismay, just as you are about to start to eat, you swap portions. His portion is too small and yours too big, apparently. I try to stop you but I can't. The right words just don't materialise. I just don't know how to explain.

93

Zara

I wake in bed, burning up like a furnace. Sweat pooling in all my crevices. I toss my side of the duvet away. My stomach feels as if I have swallowed a packet of nails. Nausea rises and I know I am about to be sick.

I leap out of bed and make a dash for the bathroom, arriving just in time to get most of my projectile vomit down the toilet. But some of it slimes across the bathroom floor, smelling of stale cheese. Its stench rises in my nostrils and makes me retch again. I strain every muscle in my stomach and neck. I retch so hard it seems as if my body wants to expel my innards. Somehow they manage to stay in place. I retch and retch until only coloured liquid comes out. No longer hot, I am shivering now. The retching softens and stops. But I feel so cold; my teeth are chattering, and my body won't stop shaking.

I creep back to bed, and bury myself in my duvet. Within seconds I know I am about to vomit again, and that however cold I am, I can't risk being away from the bathroom. I spend the rest of the night lying on a towel in the bathroom, bath sheet on top of me. Hot. Cold. Hot. Cold. Retch. Vomit. The longest, most uncomfortable night. Somewhere on the edge of my mind, I keep telling myself that in twelve hours I will start to improve.

But by morning I feel worse. The coloured liquid has turned back to vomit. Full-scale vomit. How can that have happened? All I have ingested is a few gulps of tap water. Every time I am sick, brown liquid spurts from my butt, like muddy water from a spout. I am so weak it is a major achievement to keep clearing the bathroom up. A knock on the bathroom door.

'It's Sebastian. Zara, let me in. Please.'

Legs like jelly, I pull myself to standing, open the door, and fall into his arms, not caring what I look or smell like. He comforts me by holding my head against his chest and stroking my hair.

'Let's hope it's just a twenty-four-hour bug and you'll feel better by tonight,' he says.

His words do not cheer me. Twenty-four hours feels like an eternity of hell right now.

He takes me back to the bedroom, fluffs up my pillows and the duvet. I sink back into bed gratefully. He puts the washing-up bowl next to my bed in case I am sick again, and a jug of water and a glass on the bedside table. If he gets bored of accountancy perhaps he should become a nurse.

'I'm off to work. I'll ring you at lunchtime.'

He kisses me on the forehead and leaves. At first I feel a little cheered by his attention. But not long after he has gone, I feel cold. So cold. Losing feeling in my fingers and toes. Sinking into the bed as if I will never be able to get out. Pain paddling across my stomach like a razor. A knock on the door. This time it is you, Miranda, entering gingerly.

'Zara, what's happened?'

'I must have a twenty-four-hour stomach bug, I've been vomiting so hard.'

Your face crumples. 'I think we should go to see Dr Dale, as soon as possible,' you say, voice stiff with concern.

'For a stomach bug?'

You push your grey eyes into mine. 'What if it's something more serious like Listeria? What if it's because I didn't cook the chicken enough?'

'How could it be? We all had the chicken. Only I was ill.'

Grey eyes darken. 'Maybe you're a bit run-down or something.'

'Why would that be?' I ask.

'Stress?'

'You're more stressed than me right now.'

Too much talking. Nausea is rising. I head back to the bathroom at double speed.

94

Miranda

I ring in sick. I need to stay at home to look after you. I skip a shower, hurriedly pull on my clothes, and sit in the sitting room area listening for your every trip to the bathroom. The feral sound from your throat as you retch. Every time you are ill my stomach hurts and I feel sick in sympathy.

From time to time I pop into your bedroom to check on you, and ask whether I can get you anything. But every time I do, you frown and wave me away. At around three p.m. you emerge into the sitting room, face as white as your dressing gown. You look like a panda with black bags under your eyes. Your hands are trembling.

'I don't feel quite as bad as I did,' you announce, sinking into the sofa opposite me like a rag doll.

'I still think we should take you to the doctor; because you ate that chicken.'

'But . . . But . . . Only I was ill.'

'Maybe it just hit you first.' I pause. 'You are my precious sister. I'm not taking any risks.' I stand up and pull my mobile out of my pocket. 'I'm ringing the surgery right now.'

I sponge your face and help you into an old tracksuit. I rub your back as you lean across the toilet bowl and vomit again. I squeeze toothpaste onto your now overused toothbrush, and you clean your teeth.

The drive to the surgery is difficult. You hold your hand over your mouth as the car bumps over potholes and speed bumps. After I have parked the car, we move through the entrance into reception, arm in arm. At reception you vomit again and catch it in your hand. Together we go to the toilet and I help wash you.

A receptionist fetches a chair and asks you to sit in the corridor, away from other patients in case you are contagious. She hands you a cardboard sick bowl. I stand next to you, guilt increasing. I can only just bear to look at you. I could have coped with doing this to him, but seeing you like this is difficult.

Dr Dale calls you into her consulting room. Her usually high-pitched voice sounds like a Dalek's over the tannoy.

'Can I come in too?' I ask.

You nod your head as you begin to pad wearily along the corridor. I hover behind you, bearing your bowl. We arrive at Dr Dale's room and knock.

'Come in,' she says in her singsong voice.

We open the door and enter her consulting room. We stand in front of her, side by side. Dr Dale. Pastel blue coordinates today. A blue ruffled shirt. Fluffy blue cardigan. Dangly earrings made of blue glass.

'Miranda. Zara. To what do I owe the pleasure of both of you?'

You collapse into the patient's chair. I step forwards to stand at your side and take a deep breath.

'I think I have given Zara Listeria poisoning by feeding her undercooked chicken,' I announce dolefully.

You sit shivering, holding the paper bowl close to your mouth. You cannot even bear to open your eyes.

'Only Zara?' Dr Dale asks, looking across at me, concerned.

'Only Zara,' I reply. 'I dealt with the portions separately.'

Dr Dale leans across to you and puts her hand on your arm. 'How have you been feeling, Zara? What's the problem?'

You explain very graphically. I feel ill just listening. Riddled with an ever-increasing weight of guilt.

'Is there any chance you could be pregnant, Zara?' Dr Dale asks softly.

You shake your head. 'No, I don't think so.'

'Fine. That's good. I'm giving you a seven-day course of tried and trusted antibiotics, just to make sure you have no infection in your gut.' She pauses. 'Don't start taking them until you've stopped vomiting.'

Dr Dale taps on the keys of her computer, prints off the prescription, and hands it to you.

'If anyone else is unwell please come straight back.'

You stand up slowly, wincing in pain as you move. I put my arm around you and guide you out of the consulting room.

Outside in the car park your iPhone pings. You pull it out of your pocket to read a text. A soft smile radiates across your face. 'Sebastian's a real brick. He's taking next week off work to look after me.' A deep sigh. 'I think I love him more than ever. If that's possible.'

My stomach tightens. Even though I've hurt the wrong person, I'm getting a week without having to put up with him at work. I look across at your love-infected face. Progress? Or is it? For someone who has been so ill, and looks as thin as a prepubescent ballet dancer, when you talked about Sebastian your voice was surprisingly loud. When will you understand? When will you use your common sense? As soon as possible, this man needs to go.

95

Sebastian

I sold our London flat, the home we so cherished. It was quirky, wasn't it, Jude? Overlooking Regent's Canal. You would jog along the canal to work. The flat was so stylish, with its glass coffee tables, and copious mirrors. Sometimes, when I least expect it, whatever I am doing, in my mind's eye I am back there with you. Laughing together. Remembering the way your eyes crinkled in the corners when you laughed. The resonance of your voice. The gentle turn of your head. The peace I always felt when I was with you.

The funerals. I survived the funerals in a fug of alcohol and drugs: cocaine, methamphetamine, whisky, wine, Valium, skunk. Skunk so strong I hallucinated. Jumbling what I took, depending how low or high I felt, and which way I needed to go. I achieved my objective. I don't remember the ceremonies. Not even the burials. But the impact of the crash never goes away. Nightmare after nightmare overwhelms me.

I couldn't bear to give your belongings to a charity shop. Charity shops reek of death. Its sickly scent clings to my nostrils as soon as I enter. You had too much life in your every sinew to end up diluted there. So I bundled your possessions into old suitcases, and stored them in the loft of the Bristol house. One day, I will be brave enough to look at them. One day. Maybe twenty years from now. Surely by then the pain of losing you will have diminished? But my love for you will never go away.

THE PRESENT

96

Another legal visit from her rock star brief. Just lately he has been coming to see her every other week. Her major visitor. Mother has cut back a bit, because it's such a long journey. Maybe that's for the best. Seeing her mother quadruples her guilt, and she drags her guilt around very heavily. A dead weight that never lightens, that never leaves her. Except sometimes, when she is with her rock star brief. Sometimes, then, just for a few seconds, it lifts.

Theo Gregson is sitting opposite her today, pad and pen in his hands. She notices his slender fingers and short fingernails. Once again she imagines him on stage – handing his guitar to a stagehand and moving towards the piano, about to break up the rock music with a power ballad.

'How's your week been?' he asks, interrupting her daydream. He asks this with concern, as if she is a friend, not a client. As if he really cares.

'Not too bad,' she replies. 'And yours?'

'The same.' They laugh. 'Well, I don't suppose they can have been that similar,' he admits.

'Not unless you locked yourself in your house all week, unplugged the internet, and ate the most tasteless ready meals on the planet.'

'No.' His grin continues. 'That didn't happen.'

'What did happen?' she asks.

He leans back in his chair. 'Not a lot. I've been in chambers trying to research your case. I've a couple of questions I need to ask.'

She sighs inside. 'About Sebastian again?' she asks, trying to keep her voice light.

'How did you guess?' he replies, laughing. 'Well I'll get straight to it then. Have you heard from him yet?'

His eyes are darker than usual – more serious now.

'No. And I don't want to,' she tells him.

He scribbles in his pad, writing down her answer. 'Is that because you've moved on from what happened between you?' he asks.

'It's because I've accepted he doesn't want to see me.' She pauses. 'I will never accept what happened between us.'

She almost bursts into tears. He leans forwards and takes her hand in his. She feels his warmth.

'When are you going to tell me about it?' he begs. She doesn't reply. 'Telling me would be cathartic. It would bring you comfort.'

Slowly, slowly she shakes her head. 'Burying it deep is the only comfort I have.' She swallows hard to push back the tears.

His amber eyes hold hers.

'Truth is freedom. You've got to let it out.'

He sits staring at her, a frown rippling across his brow. Then his expression lightens a little. 'I'm still trying to find out a bit more about Sebastian's background.'

'Have you made any progress?' she asks.

'Not yet. He's an elusive man. No internet trail. I sometimes wonder whether his identity is fake.' He pauses. 'Run through what he said about himself again.'

She sighs heavily and shrugs her shoulders. 'Again?'

'Yes. Again please.'

'He's from Bristol. He went to Cambridge University. His parents are both doctors. PhD doctors we thought. Neither my sister nor I ever met his family. He didn't want us to, and he didn't seem to want to meet ours.' She hears her words running together on automatic. She pauses. And then she continues, 'Just occasionally, for a split second, you remind me of him.'

As soon as she says that she is not sure where it came from. Is it because Theo is good-looking? Or because, for a barrister, he seems rather maverick? Not what most people would expect. Too young. Too fun-loving. Too handsome.

'Is that a compliment?' he asks, eyes twinkling into hers.

'I'm not sure I should answer that,' she replies.

Eyebrows up. Mouth playing with a smile. 'Why not? Would it give your game away?' he asks.

'What game?'

'The game you play about the depth of your feelings for him.'

'Theo, I can assure you I am not playing a game.'

THE PAST

97
Zara

You need to chill, Miranda, so I have asked Sebastian to go out for the evening, leaving us with some of his best Colombian Gold. You took a bit of persuading. You only smoke weed occasionally. But in the end you succumbed to my will.

Mood music. Lying on the rug on the floor, on our stomachs, facing each other. Miranda, looking into your dark grey eyes, savouring the moment. I have rolled the spliff. You haven't mentioned leaving Bristol again, so I am hoping you've changed your mind. That it was just a passing comment and you have already forgotten about it. We all think about escaping to a new life sometimes.

I take the spliff first. Inhaling deeply, so deeply, holding it in. Slowly, slowly, pushing it out. You look so pretty, so floaty. Your turn. I pass you the spliff. I watch you like a mirror image. I watch your eyes. So shiny, so liquid, so doleful.

We do not talk. We finish the joint. You stub it out in the ashtray between us. Now the edges of the room are soft and melty. The scent of the cannabis is heady. It wraps itself around me and makes me think of the colour purple. It comes to me clear as a bell. Cannabis is purple. A scent of purple smoke, as purple as heather on the mountainside. As purple as a bishop's robe, or a queen's regal gown.

'Have you met anyone recently you fancy to hook up with, Miranda?' I ask with a giggle. 'You've not been with anyone for a while.'

Even through the softening haze of cannabis, I see you look at me as if my words have burnt you.

'I'm happy enough on my own at the moment.'

The walls of our sitting room are moving in and out. It makes me feel a bit dizzy, but dizzy in a good way, a feeling I like. I am swaying. I am smiling. Giggling inside. The giggles feel like a bubbling stream running through the core of me.

'I like being on my own,' you repeat, not giggling and smiling. You are frowning. Your nostrils look wide.

'But it's fun having a man,' I reply. Giggles cascade out of my mouth. I can't stop them.

'Fun I can do without.' Your mouth is in a straight line.

'Why do you want to do without fun?' I ask with a shrug of my shoulders.

'Do you think you and Sebastian are having fun?' you ask, something wrong with your voice. It is cracked. Heavier than usual.

'Yes. I do think we're having fun. What's wrong with that?' I pause. 'Are you jealous of me, Miranda? Jealous of what I have?'

You don't reply. You put your head back and laugh. A deep-rooted, throaty laugh. A scorning laugh that doesn't sound real. Your coldness steps on my heart. Paralyses me with fear. Suddenly I wonder seriously – could you really be jealous of Sebastian and me? Is that what you want, Miranda? Is that what is wrong with you? I see the way you look at him some-times, as if he confuses you. Is that just an act? Maybe he doesn't confuse you. Maybe you love him. Maybe you are waiting in

242

the wings to take away Sebastian. To destroy me. To take everything I have.

Then you turn your head towards me and your eyes are soft and full of love. I take your hand in mine and I know that the cannabis is making me paranoid. It often does that.

98

Miranda

I wake up a few nights after our cannabis session with severe chest pain. I know I am having a panic attack. I can't control it. I can't stop myself. Someone is strangling my heart with their fist. Stabbing my left arm. Thrusting pins into my jawbone. I am struggling to breathe. A cry for help, a pitiful cry from the edges of my mind, but no sound comes out. The pain is increasing. I'm dying. Please, please, someone help. I'm shouting. I'm screaming, but still no sound comes out.

Something rips through the silence. A groan. A feral sound. And my bedroom light is snapped on. I blink. You are here, Zara, wearing a tracksuit; eyes wild, hair dishevelled. The pain in my chest increases. You rush to my bedside. Even through my pain I see that you look frantic.

'What is it, Miranda?' you ask.

'I'm having a panic attack. Or a heart attack. Not sure which,' I manage. 'I feel really bad. Call an ambulance, now.'

'Sebastian, quickly, quickly,' I hear you shout.

You sit on my bed and hold my hand. I feel your fingers trembling in mine. You lean across and kiss my cheek. I can smell the remnants of yesterday's perfume on you, mingled with sweat and fish. The faint fishy smell makes me feel sick. I hear his grunting climax. I feel a knife grating on the walls of my vaginal passage. The burning pain rises like a volcano inside me. I breathe through the pain. Sebastian is here, standing behind you. The pain in my chest tightens.

'The ambulance is on its way,' he says.

He is standing over my bed watching me. His black eyes are suffocating me. I turn my head into my pillow so that I don't have to look at him. I hear a siren. The paramedics are here. Surrounding me. Moving my head away from my pillow. Force-feeding me oxygen. A burly man with short brown hair is cuffing my arm and taking my blood pressure. A man with dark hair and dark eyes is attaching electrodes to my chest.

'We're taking your ECG,' he explains. 'How's the pain now?' he asks.

'Bad. Still very bad.'

The portable screen by my bed explodes into darting lines. He watches it intently. I close my eyes and breathe deeply, trying to cope with the pain. I open my eyes. He is standing over me, and you are standing next to him, face twisted with worry. Sebastian hovers behind you, hands on your waist. I see his spiky fingers, clasping onto your jeans. Spiky fingers that clasped onto me. I am sweating profusely. Sweat dripping off me like a tap.

'Terrible. The pain is getting worse.'

'We're going to take you to hospital to get you checked out,' the paramedic says.

The burly man and a woman I hadn't noticed before are wheeling a trolley into my bedroom. Gently, gently they lift me from my bed onto it, wrap me in a red blanket, and strap me in. I feel you next to me as we move into the ambulance. The journey is short and uncomfortable. Bumpy. The pain in my chest is still here and I struggle to breathe as the siren echoes around the ambulance, its every resonance reminding me there is something seriously wrong with me. Reminding me that I'm dying. I still feel you here, Zara, holding my hand. Somewhere along the route I am given oxygen again.

Into the hospital. Straight into a curtained cubicle. Curtains pulled around me by a jaded nurse with dry skin and bags beneath her eyes. Circled by doctors. An ECG again. Needles. Blood test. Oxygen. A cuff on my arm. A drip.

A young woman is walking towards me, soft red curls simpering around a heart-shaped face. She is a doctor. No uniform. Stethoscope around her neck. She stands by my bed.

'Miranda,' she says, 'the good news is that so far all the test results are clear. We know it isn't a heart attack. We think it is a panic attack as you feared.' She leans towards me. Her pale brown eyes are misty with concern. 'We're keeping you in overnight for observation.'

You are sitting in an armchair in the corner of the cubicle. Your eyes catch mine. You stand up and walk towards the doctor. 'Panic attack? That's not in character.'

The soft red-haired doctor turns to look at you inquisitively. As if she's only just noticed you're there. 'Isn't it?' she asks.

'No,' you reply. 'That's my territory.'

'Are you sisters?'

'Non-identical twins.'

'Do you think it's possible that you're both predisposed to it?' the young doctor suggests gently.

Zara and I exchange glances.

The doctor turns from you back to me. 'Is there anything worrying you more than usual?' she asks, picking up the clipboard with the notes about me from the end of the bed, and flicking through them.

I don't reply.

She is looking at me caringly, head on one side. 'This panic attack has made you very ill. We'll look after you tonight. Tomorrow we'll discuss how we're going to help.'

99

Zara

Back from the hospital, walking to the pub with Sebastian. It is a mild moonlit night. The violet sky almost translucent. I feel subdued, heavy. Sebastian senses my mood. We don't talk. All I can hear is our feet pounding along the pavement, my heart thumping against my eardrums, and the occasional cry of a seagull.

As soon as we arrive at the pub, Sebastian heads for the bar and I go to find a table. Our usual table is occupied by a group of elderly men cradling their pints, already glued to the football we have come here to watch. With no other choice I grab an uncomfortable spot too close to the noise from the bar. I sit down and my mind turns back to you, Miranda. Reliving my fear that you were having a cardiac arrest. The sight of your dank hair, damp with cold sweat, plastered to your forehead, to your cheek.

Sebastian sidles back from the bar, drinks in hand.

'Old sods taken our table have they?' he says. 'Shouldn't be allowed.' He places our drinks on the table. A pint for him and what looks like a pint of white wine for me. He sits down and starts to sip the top off his drink, eyes holding mine.

'So tell me more about your sis. What do you think the prognosis will be?'

'They'll confirm tomorrow, but they think she's had a panic attack and she needs help. Therapy.'

He puts his pint on the table, eyes riddled with concern. 'What sort of therapy?' he asks.

'CBT, I expect.'

He frowns, sips his beer, and cranes his neck to watch the football. He becomes engrossed in the game. I continue to worry. After a while Liverpool score. The Liverpool crowd sing their anthem to us through the television. 'You'll Never Walk Alone' hums out.

Sebastian moves his chair away from the table closer to the television. I follow him. One-nil. Chelsea up the defence. Liverpool don't seem to be able to get close again. Suddenly from nowhere Willian kicks across field and, at last, Morata gets an opportunity. He slides the ball past the defenders from a wide angle and hits the back of the net. The pub turns electric. Everyone stands up and cheers. Sebastian is swaying and singing the Chelsea anthem.

I join in. And by the time I have almost finished my pint of wine, and my world is becoming softer and easier, Chelsea have scored another goal and won the game. I wasn't watching properly. I'm not sure who scored the second time. Sebastian lifts me in the air and kisses me.

After the jubilant post-match interviews, the publican switches off the TV. The elderly men leave. We get our usual table back. Now we are sitting by the fire, finishing off our drinks and watching the flames. I am still thinking about you, Miranda. Now the football is over I can talk to Sebastian properly.

'I just don't understand what's triggered her problems,' I say. 'She was always so calm, so collected. So much stronger than me.'

His eyes harden and he slowly shrugs his shoulders. 'Maybe she was never as calm as you thought. She's certainly finding the tax case she is working on very difficult, spending far too much time without taking a break.' Another shrug. 'Maybe university was her academic zenith. Maybe she's not as bright as you think.'

'Of course she's as bright as I think. Harrison Goddard haven't given her a lobectomy,' I snap.

'OK, OK, sorry.' He raises his hands as if to say truce. 'What about another drink?'

'Yes please.'

I watch him walk to the bar. Broad shoulders. Painted-on jeans. My heart lurches as it always does when I see him from a distance. I watch him talking to the barmaid. She is smiling. She has her head back laughing. She leans towards him. He whispers something in her ear. Now she giggles like a school-girl. He has such an effect on women. Women always like him. A stone coagulates inside me.

Except Miranda.

I see Miranda, stiffening when he touches her. Why can't she relax with him? I look across at him, charming the barmaid, at his characterful angular face. Is the weird idea I had a few days ago that Miranda is in love with him true? The sudden fear pulsates towards me again. Is she torn in half by jealousy? Overcome by his charm, by his looks? Miranda, in love with Sebastian? If it was the case surely there would be more obvious signs? It's just a passing thought. A passing fear. I push it away.

Sebastian returns with our drinks. 'It's almost Easter,' he announces as he places them on the table. 'Are you going to come home with me? My parents are away.'

'Away again?' I pause. 'I didn't even know they had come back. Where have they gone this time?'

What has he done to deserve parents like this who seem

250

so uninterested in him? He doesn't reply. His dark eyes hold mine.

'Keep me company. Leave Miranda here.'

'I'm so worried about her. How can I leave her alone right now?'

He frowns in concern. 'She told me a few days ago that she wanted the flat to herself for the holidays.' He pauses. 'And she'll be over whatever she's going through by then. Having some time to herself will do her good.'

'Do you really think so?'

He puts his hand on my knee. 'Come on. What do you say?' His eyes are goading me.

'Give me time to think.'

100

Sebastian

A crack in the armour again. I am getting there at last. Miranda is definitely beginning to see how difficult her sister is. Their relationship isn't as perfect as they think. Not like ours. There never was a relationship as golden as ours. A pair of birds with gilded soaring wings. Birds I thought would fly together forever. Fly and fly, and never, ever fall.

101

Miranda

Lying in the hospital, drifting towards sleep.

Sleep. Is this sleep? Dreaming I am in bed with Sebastian. He is lying next to me holding my hand. He rolls on top of me, smelling faintly of tobacco, of testosterone-fuelled sweat. He is inside me. I scream as I climax. I scream as I reach for my knife. My climax encourages his. Men like it, don't they, when you enjoy it? It makes them feel in control, powerful.

The knife pulsates in my fingers. The knife pulsates into his stomach. I thrust it up. I push. He grunts like a stuck pig in my ear as he climaxes. He climaxes at the moment of his death. I push him out of me, away from me, and calmly, slowly, cover his already stiffening body with a sheet.

Naked, I pad to the shower to wash his scent away, to soap myself. I rub the soap hard across my body and it froths up like bubble bath. Surrounded by bubbles and froth. It is a long time since I felt so relaxed. Sebastian is dead and I can sing about it. Heart and mind singing about his demise. But no. He is here. He has come back to life. Naked. Erect. Walking towards the shower. Walking towards me to take me again.

'I thought you were dead,' I say.

'You will never win, Miranda, you will never kill me. Like a cat, I have nine lives.'

He sounds and walks like an automaton. His movements are slow and stiff. Alive, but not alive. Pallor translucent. He opens the shower door and steps inside. He smells of rotting meat. I back away from him. But he is strong, so much stronger than me. He puts his fingers around my throat and tightens them. I can't think. I can't breathe. I knee him in the groin as hard as I can. He loosens his grip on my throat for a second and I thrust him away with as much force as I can muster.

He slips on the floor of the shower, which is covered in a sticky, glue-like substance. He slips, and bangs his head so hard on the glass shower door that he slumps in the shower tray, unconscious. Blood is spurting from his head. It soaks across the shower tray. It seeps across my feet. It is sticky. He has stopped breathing. Dead once again.

I put my head back and laugh.

I wake up in the hospital bed still smelling his blood. I am no longer laughing. I am shaking. This is serious. I need help.

102

Miranda

You have gone to Sebastian's house for an extended Easter break, and thankfully I am having some time away from you both. Away from the pitying looks you have been giving me since I came out of hospital. Away from the ever-increasing temptation to hurt your lover. I know I need help, and I am getting it. The doctors at the hospital have referred me on.

The psychotherapist I have been assigned to works from her own home. I arrive outside a balanced Georgian town house in the prettiest part of Clifton and walk up the drive, past a shiny grey Mercedes, to ring an old-fashioned pull bell that surprises me by still working. The door is answered promptly by a young woman wearing copious mascara, a short skirt and flat shiny pumps.

'Come in,' she says. 'Are you Miranda Cunningham?'

'Yes.'

I step into the hallway. It is beautiful. Oak planking. Indian rugs. Original paintings. Tasteful and old-fashioned.

'Do follow me to the waiting room.'

The waiting room is the family sitting room. Soft golden walls, sofas of gold-tinged cream. Photographs everywhere.

Bose sound system. Large TV. A display cabinet full of treasures and ornaments. Greeting cards on the mantelpiece, a mixture of congratulations and thanks. One day in a better life I would love a house like this. Full of mementoes and memories. I think about the emptiness of Sebastian's house and a chill runs through me. Sebastian. At least I don't have to see him for a while.

After a few minutes a middle-aged woman steps into the room. 'Hi, I'm Jill Watson-Smith. Welcome. Pleased to meet you.'

She pushes her hand towards me in greeting. I stand up and take it. She shakes my hand vigorously and flashes a high-wattage smile at me. Her large blue eyes radiate intensity.

'Follow me. Please, come into my consulting room.'

Her consulting room is a tiny panelled space off the side of the family sitting room. It contains two easy chairs and a coffee table. It has a very small window, the view from which is blocked by a contortion of ivy. The panelled walls display a strange mix of paintings and photographs. Wedding photographs. Degree photographs. Small framed prints.

We sit in the easy chairs looking at each other. Large blue eyes appraising mine.

'Shall we start by talking about your sister?' she asks.

She leans back in her chair, relaxed, waiting for me to speak. I do not know what to say, where to begin. The silence between us is becoming claustrophobic. I must say something. I need to start somewhere.

'I do not resent my sister.' My voice sounds strained and waspish.

'Why did you say that?' she asks.

'Because that's what I think you think.'

Jill's face is gentle and relaxed. Her eyes and mouth soft and ready to smile. 'I don't think anything. I'm here to help.'

'I don't understand.' I pause. 'If you don't think anything, how can you help?'

'It does help. If *you* talk about the things that are worrying you, I can guide your thoughts.'

I do not reply at first. I sit hands together on my lap, contemplating this. I do not want to open up, but I know I need to. I am not managing very well on my own. After a while I look up at Jill. She holds my eyes in hers.

'It's her boyfriend I resent.'

Jill scribbles something on the notepad in front of her. 'Why?' she asks.

'It's complicated.'

Her eyes melt with kindness. 'Try to explain.'

Just thinking about the situation makes my stomach feel as if it is tied up in knots. That is what our life has become. A knot. A tangle. The more I try and hold things together to help you, Zara, the more the knot tightens. The more the knot tightens the more I know I need to explain. But I can't find the words today.

103

Zara

Easter. At Sebastian's house again. Trying not to worry about you. But it's not quite working out. I keep seeing you lying on the bed, struggling to breathe, and then I feel awful that you are in your flat, alone. I telephone every day, and you assure me that you're OK. Are you, Miranda? Are you really OK? Your voice sounds thin and strained.

The house seems emptier than ever, as if some more things have been removed. I sometimes wonder if his parents are ghosts. He no longer mentions the possibility of me meeting them. Is he ashamed of them? Or of me? They travel at every major holiday, for a long time it seems. I wonder what they must be like, these strange people who hardly ever seem to live in this house. This house with no photographs. But then again, not everybody is as mad on photographs as me.

The garden is still perfectly maintained. A sea of daffodils trumpet beneath the weeping willow in the middle of the lawn.

As soon as we arrive, Sebastian raids his parents' wine cellar.

'Let's start with some white,' he announces, using a bottle opener that looks like a gynaecological instrument and pouring us both a glass.

We sit together on the sofa in the drawing room.

'What film would you like to watch?' Sebastian asks, grabbing the remote and putting his arm around me.

'I don't,' I say, pulling away from him a little. 'I just want to chat. I want to know about your life. Your parents.' I pause. 'It bothers me that I've still not met them. They never seem to be here.'

Sebastian puts the remote down on the coffee table in front of us and stirs uncomfortably next to me. His face develops a strange look I have never seen before. A shadow of the Sebastian I know.

'I should have told you the truth earlier. We've had an argument. I'm trying to patch it up. They don't mind me staying here from time to time when they are away but we're not comfortable spending much time together.'

I can't believe this. It is so very sad.

'But,' I splutter, 'you chatted to them so long on the phone at Christmas. You looked so happy as you spoke to them.'

Sebastian's eyes are flat. Solid. 'We can be polite at a distance. But at close range it's difficult.'

'It must have been an awful argument for you to spend so little time together.'

'It was.'

I look down at his hands. They are trembling. I reach out to him and hold them in mine. My mind contorts as I try to imagine what could have happened to cause such a rift. Just thinking about it makes me want to cry.

'I can't face talking about it yet,' he manages, voice breaking with pain.

I massage his hands with mine, to comfort him.

'You may not want to talk about it right now, but I'm here for you when you do.'

'Thanks Zara.' There is a pause. 'I love you so much.'

He kisses me. I melt into him.

'I love you too.'

'I promise you, by next Christmas I will have solved this. Healed the rift, and we can all have Christmas together.'

'I hope so, Sebastian. So much.'

For the rest of the week, Sebastian and I live in his house, drinking wine, ordering takeaway, and watching late-night films on his enormous TV. No cutting this visit. That's over for good. And not *too* many drugs. Sleeping wrapped together in Sebastian's black Egyptian cotton bed sheets. But, for the rest of the week I do not feel comfortable being here. All I do is worry about you, Miranda, and try to stop my mind bursting with curiosity about why Sebastian and his parents argued. You were right, Miranda. We need to get to the bottom of this. It needs sorting out.

On the last morning of our visit when we're packing to go, I am checking the bedroom drawers in case I've left anything. Tucked at the back of one drawer I find something wrapped carefully in scented tissue paper. I put it to my nose. I inhale rose and lavender. It feels hard and rectangular, like a photograph in a frame. A photograph. At last a photograph. Hands trembling, I unwrap the tissue. It is a photograph. In a mother-of-pearl frame.

A dark-haired woman is sitting in a bath chair, with two small babies cradled on her knee. Her hair is dark and wavy like Sebastian's. My heart misses a beat. Does this mean Sebastian is a twin? He said he was interested in twins when I first met him. Is there some sort of heart-wrenching tale of separation at birth? Forced adoption?

Sebastian walks into the room. I look up and brace myself to ask.

'What is this, Sebastian? Are you a twin like me?'

104

Sebastian

A twin like me. She's finally guessed the truth, my beautiful brother. Jude, my beautiful twin, so much more beautiful than me.

105

Zara

'What is this, Sebastian? Are you a twin like me?'

He walks towards me, takes the photograph, and looks at it.

'It's my aunt. My mother's sister. The twins are my cousins.'

Lips in a line. Eyes like stone. Sad and convincing. And yet. And yet. Why hasn't he told me about his twin cousins? When I am a twin? When I would have been so interested?

'But . . . but . . .' I splutter, 'you never mentioned you had twins in the family.'

'As you already know, there are a lot of things I don't mention about my family.'

His voice is twisted and sharp. I step towards him and put my hand on his arm.

'But when are you going to tell me?' I ask gently.

He shakes his head. His eyes are moist with tears. 'I can't. Not yet.'

'You will have to soon.'

'I know.'

A tear rolls down his cheek. I brush it away and my insides crumble. What has happened to distress him this much, a strong vibrant man with his whole life in front of him? He clamps against me, and I hold him so tight. I want to protect him. But how can I protect him if I don't know what has happened to him?

'Your aunt looks very much like you,' I whisper.

He pulls away from me. 'Why wouldn't she look like me?' he replies. 'She's my mother's sister. She looks like my mother. That figures, doesn't it?'

'I suppose so.'

I sit down on the bed. I feel exhausted. Depleted. 'Why is that the only photograph in the house?' I ask.

'I'm not sure it is. I haven't gone through all the drawers like you.' His tears have dried. His voice and his eyes are acidic now.

I stiffen inside. This is unfair. 'It wasn't like that, Sebastian. I was just checking I hadn't left anything behind. I'd forgotten where I'd put things.'

'Come on Zara, we've only been here a week.'

His voice is contorted. With hate? I have never seen him like this.

'I'm sorry. I didn't mean to pry,' I say, trying to placate him.

'My father must have kept the photo. My mother isn't one for photographs.'

'Why keep one of your aunt?' I ask. 'Is your father in love with your aunt?'

I lift my head. He traps my eyes in his. 'Of course not. Stop making up stories.'

His words twist in my head.

'If people don't tell you the facts, that's what happens. Stories appear in your mind,' I reply.

'Well keep them short and succinct. You're not writing a novel.'

I try to push down my anger. I take a deep breath. 'We need to move past this. You need to tell me about your parents.'

I watch his face close down.

106

Miranda

Sitting in Jill Watson–Smith's study, looking into her large blue eyes. They are radiating intensity. The knots in my stomach feel metallic. I am bending forwards in pain. I close my eyes and turn my mind in on itself. Somewhere deep inside I find the strength to relax.

'What do you think you can do about your situation?' she asks, softly.

The knots in my stomach begin to unravel. 'I think I need to stop feeling so responsible for Zara.'

For a few seconds I cannot feel the knots. For a few seconds this seems like a real possibility. I know I need to try and discuss what happened. I have spent so long building up to this session, determining to tell her. I take a deep breath.

'I slept with Sebastian,' I announce.

As soon as my words are uttered, the knots begin to strangle me again. I look up into Jill's face to try and gauge her reaction. I need some reassurance. But her expression does not change.

'Why?' she asks as calmly as if we were talking about the weather.

I don't reply.

'Are you attracted to him?' she pushes gently.

'No.'

She leans her head slightly to one side. 'Are you in love with him?'

'No.' I pause. 'It just happened. I don't know why. It shouldn't have. It all felt so strange. That's why I feel so guilty about it. There was no rhyme or reason to it. I have no excuse.' I look into Jill's calm blue eyes. 'My body just reacted. As soon as it was over I regretted it. As soon as I had time to think.' I pause. 'Now, I think of nothing else.'

107

Miranda

Trying to push the world away. Trying to push Sebastian away. Zara, you and Sebastian are home. I was beginning to feel better while you were gone, Zara, because you had taken him away. He is back and I am trapped. More trapped than ever. Like an animal in a snare. The pain of its teeth is getting worse – tightening together.

He is back at work, sitting next to me, and even though I'm not looking at him I sense his every movement. I feel his eyes on me. I chance a glance. I'm right. Flaming black eyes burn into mine. I give him a watery grin and pretend to continue to work. The words on the audit guidelines in front of me begin to dance and blur. The fist that had squeezed my heart once before grabs it again and wrings it more tightly this time. Squeezing it with a pulsating beat. The inky words in front of me are no longer words; they rise from the page like flies and swarm towards me.

I stand up and nearly collapse, holding on to the desk in front of me with one hand to steady myself, waving my other arm at the insects to discourage them, but they are relentless, buzzing towards my face, coming to bite me. The fist is churning, pulverising, liquidising my heart muscle. I can't breathe. I can't see. The insects are crawling all over my face, biting me, scratching their wings across my skin. The world dissolves around me. Everything becomes black.

The first thing I see when I come round is an accountancy journal being wafted from side to side across my face. The breeze it creates feels soft and delicious. But then I notice the hairs on the hand attached to it. Sebastian. The world surrounding me enlarges. I understand where I am. Lying flat on my back on the floor at work, a cushion beneath my head. Sebastian fanning my face with an accountancy journal. Nearby everyone else seems to be ignoring the situation and getting on with their tasks. My mind is blank.

After a few seconds I remember Sebastian's black eyes burning. The fist. The insects. Sebastian's eyes are glowing more softly now – embers after the climax of the fire. The insects have flown away. The fist has released its grip. I prop myself up on my elbows.

'What happened?' I ask.

'You stood up and collapsed.'

'And what about the insects?'

A brushstroke of a frown across Sebastian's forehead. 'What insects?' He pauses. 'What are you talking about?'

'The swarm. They were swarming at my head. That's why I stood up.'

'Miranda, there weren't any insects.'

Of course there weren't any insects. I've had a panic attack again. Sebastian is leering down at me with his cavalier grin.

Jill, help me please. Please help me again.

THE PRESENT

108

Sleeping in her cell in Eastwood Park prison, dreaming of Sebastian. He is so clear to her. So real. Dark wavy hair. Eyes trying to destroy her. She can taste his smoky breath. Touch his salty skin. Sometimes for a fragmented second she sees two people. Sebastian and Theo Gregson. In her dream she is running. Running away from him. The balls of her feet exploding against the pavement. Hot needles stabbing into her chest as she stretches for breath. Heart pulsating against her eardrums.

She wakes up in a cold sweat and sits bolt upright in bed, hands trembling. Without curtains, her cell is drenched in misty moonlight. Nothing is clear. Nothing tight-edged. That was the dream. Now for the panic attack. It has happened so many times. She lies back down in bed, pretending she is someone else watching from a distance, and holds her breath for as long as she can. When she exhales, the air splutters out clumsily, then she holds her breath again, and pushes the image of Sebastian away.

Somewhere in the small hours of the night she drifts back to sleep. But when she wakes in the morning, her heart and body are still trembling.

After breakfast – cardboard toast covered in something the caterers call margarine but is more like bicycle grease – she uses free-flow to go to the prison doctor. She can't carry on like this. She knows she needs to ask for help. She waits in the anteroom, locked in now, for almost an hour. No one to watch. Nothing to read. Just off-white walls glaring at her, making her blink.

At last the prisoner before her comes out of the doctor's room, looking wizened and diminished. Poor woman. Is she fighting cancer in prison? At last, the prison doctor puts her head around the consulting room door to beckon her in.

The consulting room looks pretty much like any other GP's room, except that it has no window and the furniture is bolted down. As if she is dangerous, about to lift a chair in the air and use it to attack. She weeps silently inside to be in an environment where she is judged in this way. The prison doctor is a pretty little woman with an oval face and oval eyes to match. A face of resonant shapes. She sits down in the consulting chair, opposite her.

'How can I help?' the doctor asks.

She takes a deep breath.

'I keep having panic attacks and however hard I try to control them, they're getting worse.'

She is almost in tears. Will this nightmare ever stop?

'Getting worse as your trial approaches?'

'Yes.' She pauses. 'I used to have them before I came to prison. I learnt to manage them. Now I just can't.'

Looking concerned, the doctor leans towards her. 'You had counselling in here before, didn't you? For depression. After your sister's funeral?'

'Yes.'

Kind eyes sparkle into hers.

'Did it help?' the doctor asks.

'Yes. I think so.'

'Well, I'll refer you back.'

So once again the psychotherapist visits her in prison. A man of about forty with a bald suntanned head, pinprick brown eyes, and a wide, wide mouth. Toned figure. Manicured nails. His aftershave smells like the tag end of a joint, heady and resonant. He smiles. A real smile that reaches his eyes.

He rubs the tips of his fingers together, slowly considering her, head on one side. 'I see from your medical notes that your sister suffered from panic attacks too,' he says.

Chest pain stabs into her as he mentions her sister.

'I really don't want to talk about my sister.'

He crosses his legs. Her chest pain increases.

'Would you like to talk about Sebastian?'

She does not reply.

He leans forwards, eyes shining into hers. 'Would you like to talk about him?' he repeats.

'I can't talk about Sebastian. Not yet.' She sighs inside. A long, slow, sad sigh.

He frowns a little. 'If he is the root of the problem, I think you're going to have to before too long.'

Her stomach knots. 'I wouldn't have come to see you if I had known you were going to bully me.'

He raises his eyebrows and his hands. 'I'm not trying to bully you, I'm trying to help you.'

'Nothing to do with Sebastian can possibly help.'

THE PAST

109
Miranda

'I didn't just sleep with him once. I slept with him, regretted it, and then he raped me.'

A sharp intake of breath. Jill's piercing blue eyes go cloudy. I try not to stare at her face. I cannot bear to watch her reaction, so I look at the wall behind her. At the photograph of her with her son on his degree day. He has a long face the shape of a rugby ball. A similar shape to hers.

'Did you report it?' she asks, her voice serrated with anger.

'Of course not.'

Her eyebrows rise. 'Why do you say of course not?'

'It's obvious, isn't it? I didn't want Zara to be hurt by what happened.' My voice sounds sulky. Teenage. Petulant.

'You could make a complaint and keep your identity secret.' There is a pause. 'It isn't too late to report it.'

Her words cut into me, and I feel the knots beginning to curdle in my stomach.

'Even with my identity secret, Zara would have been hurt.' I pause. 'She's vulnerable. She needs protecting, not exposing.'

Jill leans forwards, blue eyes darkening. 'If he's dangerous,

271

she'll be hurt in the end, no matter what. You could be protecting her by telling her.'

The knots are twisting and burning. 'I don't see it like that. If he hurts her in the end, she'll gradually realise what a bastard he is, and then she'll cope. If everything crashes now she'll go under, I know.'

'And what about you?'

I clench my fingers into a fist. 'That bastard's not taking me down.'

110

Miranda

'Sebastian, do you fancy lunch?' I ask.

A Jack Nicholson grin. My stomach tightens. 'I always fancy lunch with you.'

I fantasise about punching him in the face. I hear the crunch of his nose as it breaks. I feel the wetness of his blood.

But Sebastian and I stroll out of the office together, looking to the world like old friends going for a break. No one else will realise that my emotion towards him is fixed solid with hate. Not just when I am with him. I carry it everywhere, deep inside me.

'This is an honour, Miranda,' he says. 'Let's have a change. Can I entice you to Coffee Bombe? It's only around the corner. They do good sandwiches,' he says.

I nod and manage to muster a tentative smile.

Coffee Bombe. A typical Bristolian coffee shop: quirky, individualistic, fashionable. Painted bright blue and orange on opposing walls. Wrought-iron tables and chairs bolstered up with blue and orange cushions. Blue and orange pansies in the centre of every table. The waitress has dreadlocks and a nose piercing. Pink Floyd hums in the background.

'What do you think?' Sebastian asks.

'Nice change from Harrison Goddard,' I say politely, but I know that my voice sounds tight.

The waitress takes our order.

Sebastian leans back in his chair. 'Well Miranda, to what do I owe the pleasure?'

'I'm worried about Zara.'

He raises his eyes to the ceiling. 'You only ever want to spend time with me when you're worried about Zara.' A pause. 'Worried how?'

'You know how.'

A pirate's grin. 'Come on Miranda. Spell it out.'

My mouth flatlines. 'I love my sister. As you know I really, really, don't want her to know what happened between us.'

'I love her too. But I am different to you. I have a conscience. I think for the sake of our relationship, she deserves honesty.'

His pirate's grin widens. Maybe I'm getting a window here. At least he says he loves you.

I take a deep breath. 'But it will only hurt her unnecessarily. There's nothing real, nothing permanent between us. If you tell her, you're only telling her to make yourself feel better. If you really love her you must think about her.'

'Do you really think that's how it works?'

'Yes Sebastian, I do.'

The waitress interrupts with our coffee and sandwiches. Flat white, with beef on rye, for me. BLT and cappuccino, with a chocolate heart dusted on top of it for the young lovebird in front of me. The young lovebird with a twisted grin.

He takes a sip from his cappuccino, eyes slicing into mine. 'Thing is Miranda, I'm just an honest guy.'

'Who exactly are you honest with? Yourself? Your relationships?'

He licks some chocolate powder dust from his mouth. 'What are you accusing me of, Miranda?'

274

And I know I cannot cope with him. I do not know what to say to him. I feel as if I am about to fall off a precipice. Zara, what do you see in him? What do you see in this prig? I close my eyes and yet again I remember. The doorway to my bedroom. He is pulling me into his arms and kissing me. His grin is leering at me. I am sweating and trembling.

'Sebastian, all I'm concerned about is the wellbeing of my sister.'

'Is that what you were concerned about when you were climaxing?'

His words stab into me. But I stay calm. I repeat, 'Sebastian, all I'm concerned about is the wellbeing of my sister.'

The Jack Nicholson grin again. 'That's all I'm concerned about too.'

'Then leave it alone, please. It'll only hurt her. And I can't bear for her to hate me. Can you bear her to hate you?'

'Miranda Cunningham, I can bear anything for you. Especially when you beg.'

111

Sebastian

Jude, it's time to finally fragment the twins' relationship. Watch carefully now. It's about to begin.

112

Zara

Miranda and Sebastian are home from work. Sebastian only just cheerful enough: a slightly deflated version of himself when you are around. And you, Miranda, pinch-faced and miserable. I hate seeing you both like this. I know I have to find out about Sebastian's family. Is that what all this sulking is about, Miranda? Do you know something that I don't, and you can't bring yourself to tell me?

'I've made spinach and ricotta lasagne,' I announce.

I am trying to hold the atmosphere in this flat together. I decided to take a leaf out of your book and hope some home cooking would help. The lasagne has taken all afternoon to prepare. Cutting stems off spinach. Crushing pine nuts with a pestle and mortar. You do not reply. You take no notice of my catering achievement. Haven't you even noticed the scent of garlic and pesto wafting around the flat?

You walk through the kitchen area and sink into the sofa. You sit staring out of the window. What are you looking at? Passers-by? Weeds growing in the cracks between paving stones? Sebastian and I exchange a glance. He shrugs his shoulders. It is his *I told you she was difficult* shoulder shrug.

'I'll lay the table,' he says.

He proceeds to bang cutlery, mats and glasses noisily onto the table. Every time something bangs you raise your shoulders and wince, letting us know the noise he is making annoys you. We exchange another glance.

She's becoming impossible.

I try to appease you. 'After supper, would you like to go out for a drink? Just the two of us?'

'No thanks.'

I'm so sorry we are annoying you so much, Miranda. Soon Sebastian will have introduced me to his parents, and he and I will move out. Is that what you need? Your flat back to yourself? We're almost there. Sebastian has nearly saved enough for a deposit on a house.

113

Miranda

Jill's eyes are calm as a lake in winter, glacial and pale. She sits looking at me, hands together in her lap.

'That bastard's not coming between my sister and me. If he tells her we've made love I'll deny it,' I tell her.

Jill's eyes darken a little. Her fingers curl together. 'Sounds like a plan,' she replies.

Deny. Deny. Deny. A denial so deep the lie will become the truth in my mind.

The lie will be the truth in my mind.

The lie will be the truth in my mind.

THE PRESENT

114

Theo Gregson has come to visit her. They sit opposite one another in the conference room, separated by a grey plastic table, a difficult shade of grey that always looks dirty, however much it is scrubbed and cleaned. The prison heating has gone wrong. It's in overdrive. The thermostat must be broken. The heat is tropical.

'How are you?' Theo asks.

'Hot.'

He laughs. 'I know that.' There is a pause. 'We all are.'

Sweat pools above his upper lip. She wants to lean across and wipe it away. He leans back in his chair and crosses his legs, eyes melting towards hers. He is wearing jeans and a T-shirt, a leather jacket slung over the back of his chair. The T-shirt is white and has holes in. He really doesn't look like a barrister. He looks like a student. A student to hold hands with. To walk along Harbourside with. To walk to the pub with. In another life.

'How's it going – are you choosing to do anything educational now?' Theo asks.

'No.' I pause. 'I suppose I could if I asked. But just at the moment I can't concentrate.'

'You've got to hold it together. You'll soon be back to normal.'

'Yeah right.' She pauses. 'After a very constructive gap year?'

Another smile looking directly into her eyes. Not so fragmented this time – just full of sadness.

She pulls away from his smile by looking at the ground. She doesn't want his pity.

'Things are moving fast,' he says. She looks up. 'The trial's been set down for mid-February at Bristol Crown Court. I decided to deliver the letter in person.'

He bends to his side and opens his briefcase. He pulls out an envelope and hands it to her. Their fingers briefly touch. She feels his touch, like an electric current. The intensity surprises her.

She pulls her fingers away to open the letter and quickly scan it. The current that was pulsing through her, making her feel energised for a change, quickly fades. The notification of the dates of her trial. The actuality of the legal juggernaut about to crush her at last. Who will decide her fate? Who will determine her guilt? Her innocence? People who don't know her. People who've never met her. She feels like a piece of flotsam with no control of her life. Theo is watching her; she doesn't want his pity, but she is getting it. She knows it. She feels it. He leans across the table and he takes her hand in his.

'It'll be all right, I promise.'

The touch of his hand makes her feel warm inside. No electricity this time. Only reassurance.

'My mother used to say don't make promises you can't keep,' she says with a sad smile. 'It is not something that lies in your power to promise.'

'I mean it. I really do think that in the end everything will be all right.'

'If it's not all right it's not the end, sort of thing?'

'Something like that.'

They sit in silence. Comfortable silence. They are still holding hands, but it feels so right maybe they haven't noticed. After a while Theo cuts through the silence.

'I need to talk to you about your relationship with Sebastian. I need to show you something.'

Theo brings his briefcase and moves to sit next to her. He lifts his computer out and switches it on, then opens a file marked Sebastian. Two naked people appear on the screen, twisted together, making love. A leonine muscled man. With horror, she realises that the woman is her. The camera pans in to show her face contorted with ecstasy. She knows the man is Sebastian. She cannot watch any more. She sits with her head in her hands, eyes closed.

'Switch it off please,' she begs.

She does not want to look at Theo. She does not want to look anyone in the eye ever again. She remains sitting, head in her hands, trying to pretend she is in a safe place, in the dark, alone. That is all she wants – to be alone. He must have stopped the recording. The heavy-breathing soundtrack has gone.

'It was sent to me anonymously.'

There is a pause.

'Open your eyes, look at me.'

Another pause.

'This happens. More than you think. Open your eyes. We can deal with it.'

She removes her hands from her face, and opens her eyes.

'I don't think I can,' she says. 'Why would he want to film this?'

He puts his arm around her shoulders. 'You can. We will.'

His face is so gentle. So kind.

'We found a camera in your bedroom ceiling – and your sister's too.'

'But why?'

'We don't know that yet. What do you think he was playing at?'

Heat bubbles beneath her skin. 'He . . .' Her words skid to a halt. Then: 'I don't know what he was playing at.'

Theo Gregson is looking at her, totally unperturbed. As if they had been talking about football scores or the weather. Runny honey eyes soak into hers.

'I came here today to tell you that in court you must be honest about your relationship with Sebastian. So far you've brushed over what happened between you in your statements to the police. The jury are far more likely to understand the situation if you're honest.'

'I don't understand the situation, so how can I expect them to?'

'They need to try and understand. But without the facts, they can't.'

THE PAST

115
Zara

A day off work for Sebastian. A day off college for me. A day to ourselves. Early summer, gentle warmth floating in the air.

I wake early, before Sebastian, and lie listening to the rhythm of his breath. I hear the thud of the shower pump. Miranda, you are getting ready for another day at Harrison Goddard. You never use up your leave. You are rattling about in the kitchen. The front door clicks as you leave. Sebastian stirs. I kiss his forehead. He opens his eyes and my eyes fall into them. Dark, bottomless eyes.

'Zara, I love you.'

'I love you too, Sebastian.'

'I will never love anyone as I love you.'

He kisses me. Then he pulls away from me a little and we lie on our sides facing one another, eyes locked.

'I want our relationship to be completely honest. Completely open, always. What do you think?'

'You know I want that too. You know I'll be relieved when I find out more about your parents.'

He moves towards me and kisses me on the lips urgently. But I am getting wise to his moves. I think he is doing this to distract me. I close my mouth and pull away.

'Honesty should be the staple of any relationship. I completely agree,' I continue.

He grimaces. His face looks strange, unrecognisable.

'I'm not sure your sister would agree with that.' His voice and face are grey and stony.

'What's it got to do with my sister?' I ask.

'Quite a lot actually.'

I frown inside. What does he mean? What is he talking about?

'I've slept with your sister.'

I've slept with your sister. His words stab me like a sword.

'No.'

I can't have heard him right. He is joking. In a second he will grin and his eyes will convulse with laughter.

'No.'

But his lips don't move. His eyes are like granite. No. He doesn't love me, he loves you.

'Your sister seduced me.'

He doesn't love me, he loves you.

'No. Miranda wouldn't do that,' I say above the screaming that has started in my head.

'Don't you believe me? I'll show you. I've got it on tape.'

The screaming in my head increases. What has happened to my Sebastian? Where has he gone?

'Seduced you? What do you mean you've got it on tape?' I pause for breath. 'How did you manage to let her seduce you?'

'Let me explain.'

I am sitting on the bed next to him, head in my hands. He puts his arm across my naked back. I stiffen at his touch. My insides wince. My mind is rotating. I see you, Miranda, naked, moving towards him, smiling. He takes your hand. You lead him to your bed. He is on top of you and you are opening your legs. It doesn't take long. You don't waste any time with foreplay. He is inside you. He is thrusting. Your

285

head is back. I see your ecstasy. I see you climaxing and then I realise.

This is what you've always wanted. To steal my man. To destroy me.

116

Miranda

I am at my desk, trying to clear my mind. Sebastian is away today. A day off? A course? It is peaceful without him anyway. The new tax assessment I am working on needs to be submitted in a week, but I can't concentrate on compiling the facts. Now I know what you went through with A levels, Zara. Hellish, isn't it? I hope I was supportive enough.

I need to leave here. I need to get away from Bristol so much. The knot I have tangled in my mind is unwinding. I will look for a sponsored job in Hong Kong, where I can earn lots of money, and leave you with him. You will be all right. You are thirty years old. You've stopped cutting. You can look after yourself. Something snaps inside me. I feel free at last. Counselling has helped. I am strong again now. I can live my own life.

117

Zara

I feel the pain as intensely as if I have been sliced down my body with a knife. As if we were conjoined and you have been severed from me. All my nerve endings ache. Despite the severity of the pain, I feel weak and empty. Time stops. Everything stops. It will never start again.

'Leave. Right now. I never want to see you again.'

'You don't mean that, Zara.'

'I can assure you I do.'

His right hand strokes my back. I push it away and jerk away from him, still sitting on the bed.

'I love you, Zara,' he says. His words trip from his tongue, shallow and meaningless. I will never trust him again.

'I meant what I said. I want you to leave. I never want to see you again.' I am shouting, almost screeching. My words are high-pitched, uneven.

'But Zara . . . I just wanted to be honest.'

'Honest? There's no honesty in you.' My lips and chin are trembling. 'I don't know anything about you, or your family. Please Sebastian,' I beg. 'Pack your things. Go away.'

'If I go, I'll come back whenever you want me to.'

I push my eyes into his darkness. 'Sebastian, I will never want you back.'

118

Sebastian

Her words rotate in my mind. The look on her face when I told her. How can she take against me? She loves me. She'll forgive me. She will, won't she Jude? I guess within a fortnight. And I'll have achieved what I wanted. Pushed Miranda away. Then I can find the strength to tell her what happened. What I did to my family.

119

Zara

Sebastian has gone. I couldn't bear to look at him for another moment. The sight of him cuts into me and makes me feel sick. Miranda. I'm waiting for you to come home. My hand tightens around my knife. My Swiss Army knife. Mother gave us one each when we joined the Girl Guides. Do you remember, Miranda? You lost yours. I kept mine.

120

Miranda

I am walking home from work feeling calmer than calm, now I've decided what to do. The world seems clearer, sharper. For the first time in a long while, I register other people on their way home, on their way to the pub for the evening. A couple holding hands. An overweight middle-aged woman laden down by Tesco bags. I see the bus rolling past full of people getting on with their lives.

I am able to join back in now. Ready to get on with my life again. I am going to let you go, Zara, stop trying to protect you. I am going to move to Hong Kong, earn a shedload of money in a different environment. Leave you to sort Sebastian out yourself. Mother's harsh words no longer frighten me. She won't really want her money back. Deep down inside I know she only said that in a desperate attempt to make me stay and protect you, her precious. She will let you, her darling Zara, stay living in my flat forever. For as long as you want.

121

Zara

I am waiting for you, Miranda, knife in hand. You have destroyed me. I am waiting to destroy you.

122

Miranda

I text you, Zara.

Not working late tonight. Fancy a pizza and a chick flick?

123

Zara

Yes please, I text back, clenching my fingers more tightly around my Swiss Army knife. Once upon a time I used to cut myself to find release. Blood seeping out. Slowly at first. Then a line. A river. Oh the sweet, sweet release of blood. Once upon a time I cut Sebastian. I close my eyes and step back in time. I bite my lip. I move my razor blade towards his wrist. I touch it against his skin. I feel the skin separate. He inhales deeply. The inhalation of his breath, the way his lips part slightly, turns me on. I see the blood line. The seepage. Sweet seepage. Sweet, sweet seepage. Sweet release.

'Do you feel it?' I ask.

He closes his eyes.

'I feel it,' he whispers.

Miranda, this time I'm going to cut you. Too deep.

124

Miranda

Yes please, you text back.

Good good. What do you fancy seeing?

*Just get home and we'll talk about it. There are so many choices.
We need to talk face to face.*

125
Zara

I hear your key in the door. I hear your footsteps as you pad across the hallway. You call my name. I don't reply. The anger inside me is exploding. I cannot move. I cannot speak. It reaches its crescendo and I push through it. I'm moving through my bedroom, moving towards you. You are in the corner of the kitchen, putting the kettle on. You turn towards me, opening your mouth to tell me something. But I do not want to listen. Miranda, I will never listen to you again.

'How could you do it?' I ask, my voice skidding into a shriek.

You look at me, eyes wide. Are you pretending to be innocent?

'Do what?' you ask.

'Seduce Sebastian.'

My voice explodes. Your face fragments in front of me.

'Is that what he said?'

'Yes.'

'It wasn't like that.'

'What was it like, screwing my boyfriend? He's fucking fantastic isn't he?'

You shake your head.

'It wasn't like that.'

I don't believe you, Miranda. I will never believe you again. I carry on moving towards you, knife hidden in my right hand. I cannot see your face. It is out of focus. Covered by a cloudy mist. You are still standing in the corner of the kitchen, body straight. You must just be standing looking at me. You do not say anything. You do not apologise.

'I hate you, you bitch,' I shriek.

Still you do not move. Still you do not say anything.

And I am getting closer with my knife. Closer to cutting you. So close now that even though your face is out of focus, I can feel you. I can smell you. You smell of him. You smell of Sebastian. Of sweat. Of cigarette smoke. Of sex. Of testosterone. Of aftershave. I move towards your neck. Your smooth clear neck, to the place where I want to cut you. You try to step away now, but it's too late. I push my weight against you. You are pinned against the kitchen counter. You cannot move.

126

Miranda

I am light. I am happy. I am going to escape. Tonight I'm going to take you out, Zara, and spoil you. Tonight I am celebrating. I enter the flat. There is a strange quietness about it. No TV on. No music blasting from your bedroom. No one sprawling across the sofa.

'Zara,' I shout.

No reply. Perhaps you've just popped out to Tesco. I move towards the kettle to make a cup of tea. Just as the kettle starts to purr, I hear you scream, I hear you shriek. I turn around. You are powering towards me with a look on your face that I don't recognise. I have never seen you look like this before. Your eyes are wide and staring. Your chin is jutting. You look flushed, as if you have a temperature.

'How could you seduce Sebastian?' you hiss.

'I didn't.'

'Don't lie to me, you bitch.'

'Calm down, Zara. Let's sit on the sofa. Have a drink. Talk about it.'

'I hate you, you bitch. I will never talk to you again.'

You are pushing me. You are hurting me. Pinning me against the kitchen counter.

127

Zara

I am moving my knife towards your neck. Your soft sweet neck. Throbbing with arteries and veins. Throbbing as you panic. I smell your pain, even before I cut. I cut. I see the line. The release of blood. I cut deeper and deeper. Deeper and deeper, to make you feel my pain.

128

Miranda

'I'm going to kill you,' you screech. 'Fucking kill you.'

Your voice is no longer your voice. It sounds deeper, as if you are in a trance. You are lifting your right hand and pushing it towards the left side of my neck. What are you doing, Zara? What's going on? A glint of metal reflecting in the sunlight filtering through the window, and I panic. You have a knife.

'What are you doing Zara? Stop it.'

But your face is glazed, transfixed. You are not listening to me. You are pushing the blade of your Swiss Army knife towards me. I never realised how strong you are. I cannot move. You have pinned me against the corner of the kitchen counter, holding my hands together with your left hand.

I close my eyes to pray for strength, and as I do I feel a sharp pain in my neck. You are cutting me. You are stabbing me. I open my eyes and see raw hatred on your face. You lick your lips. Your eyes widen as you cut. You are lifting the knife, about to cut again.

For that split second, as you are in ecstasy, I manage to free my hands. I reach for the bread knife lying on the counter to my right hand. Hands trembling, I push your hand away from my neck and plunge the bread knife into your stomach. Up, up into your torso I push.

129
Zara

I have cut you. Your blood is spilling. I have cut and this time, for the first time, I feel no better. I do not feel the release. I back away a little. Your hands are free. I am looking at the waterfall of your blood as I feel my skin split. I feel wetness between my ribs. My heart judders. I can't breathe.

THE PRESENT

130

I lie on my bed in my cell, opening a letter. I know from the watermarked pale yellow paper and the franking on the envelope that it's from Theo. Yellow stationery, blue italic lettering. It's his chamber's stationery. I opens it, hands trembling. I feel his hand in mine as he tried to reassure me about the video tape. I see the kindness in his face. I feel so embarrassed I want to curl up and die just thinking about it. I want Theo to like me. To see a good side of me. All he ever sees is a contorted mess.

A few people, I suppose, are sexually thick-skinned. Exhibitionist. Otherwise we wouldn't have porn stars. Lap dancers. Prostitutes. In a way I envey them. They have a confidence about the intimate that I lack. To me sex is private. A totally intimate act. Having sex is a completely different experience from watching it. The two do not match. The sensation and perception of sex far transcends observation. In reality it is ethereal, unquantifiable. Watching it is purely mechanical. Thrusting and pumping. Moaning and lying back.

I can't believe that Sebastian has filmed me. A camera in both of our bedrooms. Filming his lips on my erect nipples.

Filming his pallid thrusting buttocks. What is the matter with the guy? What was he playing at? I feel degraded. Worthless. Humiliated.

I lie back on the bed and read the letter.

Dear Ms Cunningham,

Please do not let the tape pull you down. To me you are wonderful. A hero.

How can Theo be allowed to say that? He is my brief. We have a business relationship. He cannot mean this. He is just trying to cheer me up.

The letter continues:

Sebastian is a cruel, manipulative man. I've been looking into his background and it doesn't make for happy reading. I am developing new ideas about him. I think he deliberately contrived to tear you and your sister apart. Don't let him destroy you. Be bold. Be brave. Admit what happened to you. Come out from the shadow you're hiding under. Tell the world what your sister's boyfriend did to you. Tell the world the truth, Miranda. Please. I want you to be free. I want you to get out.

The letter falls from my hand. I sit up in bed. My life cannot sink any lower. I have reached my lowest point. I need to pull myself up. My name is Miranda Cunningham. I have been manipulated and raped by my sister's boyfriend. I need to face the shame of it. My name is Miranda Cunningham. I loved my sister. Miranda Cunningham will tell the truth.

131

The psychotherapist smiles his usual smile. His real smile that reaches his eyes. But I am shaking and trembling. My mouth is dry, and my chest and stomach are being stabbed a thousand times.

'Another panic attack?' he asks.

'No.' I pause. 'Well yes. But I've averted it. It's just that I want to talk about Sebastian now. It's time.'

132

I am locked in yet another cell, waiting for my trial to start. I'm not sure what time because the previous trial in my courtroom has overrun. I have been waiting in solitary since nine a.m. in a cell beneath Bristol Crown Court. Not sure how I feel, or whether I feel anything at all. After months in prison, part of me has closed down. I can't imagine this nightmare ever ending. I can't imagine I'll ever be free again. And even if I am physically free, I killed you, Zara, so how am I going to live with that? I should have just let you kill me. I often think about that. How much easier it would have been if I had died instead of you.

Closed windows. Stagnant air. Boredom and fear crippling me. Which one will destroy me first? Eventually, sitting on the wooden bench in my holding cell, I fall asleep. I dream I am standing in the sea with you, Zara. Young girls again, on the Costa Brava, where we went when we were seven. The waves are frisky and we laugh as we jump over them, Mother in between us, holding both our hands. Mother evaporates and now you and I are holding hands, walking through bluebell-carpeted woods.

I open my eyes to find myself sitting on the plank-like bed

in my cell, a guard standing in front of me rattling a pair of handcuffs.

'Your brief needs to see you before the trial. Come with me please.'

I slip off the bed, put on my shoes, and he cuffs me. He leads me along the corridor. He doesn't smile at me. He doesn't speak to me. He is a skinny man wearing a thick wedding ring, toes pointing slightly inwards as he walks. He unlocks a door and leads me into a cubicle with a bench to sit on and a glass barrier with a speaking hole. A cubicle, not a room. He uncuffs me.

'Your brief will be here soon.'

He leaves, locking the door behind him. I perch on the bench and wait, nose pressed against the glass. After a few minutes Theo glides in, gowned for court. He sits on the bench the other side of the glass and smiles. A half smile, full of concern. Eyes melting into mine.

'Just wanted to check you're all right.'

'Happiest day of my life.'

'You look nice.'

'I tried my best.'

'Your best worked.'

'I don't suppose what I look like will help.'

'Everything helps.' He pauses. 'I expect you know what I'm going to say. I've said it so many times.' Another pause, longer this time. 'Be honest. Be yourself. And it is very important you explain exactly what Sebastian did to you.'

At the thought of being interrogated about Sebastian, the panic and embarrassment that I am trying to contain inside me rises. I am trembling inside. I look into Theo's eyes.

I pause. I swallow. 'What if they show that film?'

'I've told you they won't – only to the jury in closed session and probably not even that if you tell the truth.'

'Where's my QC?' I ask.

309

'Going through the trial notes.'

'So late?'

'She's very familiar with them, and very experienced. I just mean going through them *again*.' He smiles. A wide, reassuring smile. He touches his hand against the glass as if he is trying to touch me. 'Everything's under control, Miranda. I promise. I just wanted to see you to check that you were OK.' Honey eyes run into mine. 'I wanted to wish you good luck.'

'If everything's under control, why do I need luck?'

'Everybody needs luck.'

One last smile, which starts as a grin and then expands, and he is gone, robes streaming behind him.

Back to my cell with the guard. Two more hours until I am called. Two more hours to relive what I have done. Memories of you, Zara, running through my head. You and me on the beach together, two schoolgirls walking into the sea. You are crying. A wall of tears blankets your face. I pull you towards me and hold you against me.

'I can't do my exams. Please help me,' you beg.

My mind jumps to Bristol.

'I've met someone,' you announce, face flushed, eyes shining. I remember the metallic taste of the chicken tikka ready meal I ate the first night you went out with Sebastian, leaving me in our flat alone.

I am back lying on the rug in front of the TV. We are on our stomachs, Zara, facing each other. Your golden eyes sharpen beneath the electric light of the wintry evening as you light the spliff and take the first drag. You inhale deeply, as if you are sucking the elixir of life itself into your very being. A passing frown as you concentrate. Holding in. Release. The musky aroma of cannabis spreads thickly around us. Clinging. Sickly. Sweet. You pass the spliff to me. The same routine: holding, holding, release.

'I worry about how much I love Sebastian,' you say. 'I worry I love him too much.'

The cannabis is making me feel floaty.

Zara, that was true. You loved him too much.

And I am back hearing him grunt in my ear like a stuck pig as he climaxes. I vomit in my mouth and swallow it. He pulls out of me. The burning pain he was causing me increases. It is almost unbearable. I try to breathe deeply to cope with it, but that is impossible with my head stuffed into the duvet. I cannot bear to turn around and look at him. I hear him moving about my bedroom. I presume he is gathering his clothes. What can he be thinking? Is he pleased with himself? I hear the bedroom door open and close. I move my head a little so that I can breathe.

'Please Sebastian,' I say. 'You're making me ill. Please promise me you won't tell Zara what happened between us.'

He puts his hand on my arm. A Jack Nicholson smile. 'It turns me on when you beg.'

I feel the slippage of skin. The resistance. The wetness. I see your clammy staring eyes. Your blood-mangled body. Your hair splayed across the white floor. I feel your alabaster stillness.

In court at last, I sit next to the skinny, silent guard. Behind the floor to ceiling wall of glass, protecting the public from me. I am not cuffed. But he insists on making me aware of the cuffs' presence. Where does he think I'm going to go? The court is coming to life in front of me. Barristers and solicitors arriving. Robed court officials pacing. Why are they always pacing so self-importantly? Is it because they are bored?

Theo's wig looks ridiculous. It only just perches on the top of his head as if it doesn't fit him. It certainly doesn't suit him. Mr Mimms, Theo, and my QC are sitting in a row of wooden benches in the middle of the court. Leaning their heads together and chatting from time to time. Shuffling papers in front of them. Theo turns around to look at me.

'Are you all right?' he mouths.

I nod my head. All right? Am I all right? Will I ever be all right again? At least he cares enough to ask.

The prosecution lawyers are bustling in carrying their bundles. My lawyers smile and greet them politely. To me they feel like the enemy. People here to end what little is left of my life. Maybe the outcome of this trial makes little difference to me. My life is over anyway. Without my sister I do not have a life.

Three prosecution lawyers. A QC, a junior and a solicitor. I look across at them. So many people against me. What chance do I have against them? The silk, the one with a larger wig, looks a bit like Stephen Fry. Large and substantial. Not handsome but something commanding about him. Slightly pock-marked skin. Slightly bulbous nose.

I look across to the public gallery. I see my mother entering and settling on the front row. Her shoulders look rounded, in a way they never used to be, as if she is starting with osteoporosis. Weaker, thinner somehow. She turns around. As soon as she sees me her jawline sags. A shadow of an expression. I twist my lips into a ragged smile that is supposed to say, *how has our life come to this?* Mother replies with her eyes. *Don't worry, we'll come through it.* I know she is only just about holding it together. I weep inside.

The judge enters. The court stands and bows. A female judge. Bleached blonde hair sticking out from the front of her androgynous wig. She would be pretty if she didn't have such ferret-like eyes. She is wearing bright poppy-red robes. Blood red, shrieking of authority.

Entrance formality over.

'Bring in the jurors,' she requests.

A court clerk scurries off to fetch them, head bowed in

312

respect. After a while they come in, one by one, jaded already, overwhelmed by procedure, unsure of themselves, aware they are being watched by lawyers and the public. Twenty-four people on jury service, waiting to be called.

I drink in these people on whom my life depends. Thirteen women. Eleven men. Two look as if they are over forty. One black, two Asian. Everyone else white. No one particularly smartly dressed. A Sikh man wearing a turban and round glasses. A young white man with a heavy brown beard. A man with a beer belly so large he could be about to produce twins. A woman wearing fuchsia lipstick which clashes with her dress. A woman with silky lashes and a gouged earlobe. She's the prettiest. Pity she's stretched her earlobe so much. Three people so seriously overweight they can hardly walk. They all hover close to the door they entered through, which is to the right of the dock. To the right of the court at the opposite side to the entrance for the lawyers and the public.

A clerk of the court draws twelve names at random and one by one my jury take their seats. One by one I take note of them. One by one I try not to stare at them. One by one they take a sideways glance at me. The three seriously overweight are picked. They all sit next to each other. The Sikh man with the turban. A bald man. A bearded man. The girl with the lashes and the earlobe. A girl who looks a bit like a pixie. Short hair. Big eyes. Big pointed ears. A middle-aged woman with curly hair. A cross-dresser. A man in a lumberjack shirt with greasy hair. A young man with foppish blond hair – a Hugh Grant in his heyday look about him as he pushes his hair from his eyes.

They take their oaths individually. I watch anxiously, analysing the timbre of every voice. But the only voice I really hear is yours, Zara, saying, 'I'm going to fucking kill you, you bitch.'

Zara: it worked. You fucking did.

133

In court again. Court dominates my life. A respite from prison. Or is it? I suppose it is a window to the world for a while. More colour, more variety than my usual cell. I cannot complain of being bored. But the fact that so much hangs on every word spoken, the heavy sense that this may be my last glimpse of the world for a long time, does not make me feel relaxed. It makes me feel clinging-at-straws desperate, constantly suppressing a panic attack.

I see the public come and go, not always sure who they are, or why they chose to come. Are they law students? Journalists? I envy them their freedom from the bottom of my heart. I envy everyone. Every clerk, every solicitor, everyone – even those who just seem to do the photocopying.

The Stephen Fry lookalike, aka the prosecution barrister, Paul Early-Smith, is opening my case, standing to address the jury. He coughs. His wig slips a little to the right of his head. He pushes it back.

'Miranda Cunningham, a thirty-year-old accountant from Bristol, is charged with the murder of her sister.' He pauses. 'Zara Cunningham.' His voice is overeducated. He punches his words into the air with force. 'She is pleading not guilty,' he continues. 'Her defence is self-defence.' He stands facing the jury and opens his arms, wide, like a bird's wings. 'Let me outline the prosecution's case.' He pauses to look down at his notes. He adjusts the angle of his glasses.

'The evidence will show that Miranda Cunningham has *serious* mental health issues.' I stiffen inside. How dare he say this? 'She became besotted with her sister's boyfriend, Sebastian Templeton, fixated by him in fact to the point of infatuation.'

I was told he was going to say this, but hearing the words actually spoken in court in front of the jury is too much.

'She pestered him for sex so frequently that Sebastian Templeton decided, perhaps unwisely, to acquiesce, in the hope she would then leave him alone. I say, perhaps unwisely, because Sebastian was deeply in love with Zara.'

The words float away from me and I am back, lying on the bed, head pushed into a pillow. He is entering me. He is hurting me. I am crying with the pain.

Mr Early-Smith takes a long melodramatic pause, where he stretches his neck and lifts his bulbous nose in the air. 'But Sebastian's desperate attempt to get Miranda to leave him alone didn't work. It made her behaviour worse. After their one-time sexual liaison, Miranda became even more besotted with him, and proceeded to murder her sister with a bread knife in the desperate hope that she could then have him to herself.'

I sit shaking my head, tears rolling down my face.

134

Pre-court briefing. Sitting in the meeting room opposite Theo. He briefs me first thing in the morning before court starts, as soon as the morning session is over, and as soon as the afternoon one finishes.

'Sebastian is being called as a witness today,' he says.

Suddenly I think I might vomit. I put my head between my legs, hand over my mouth, and retch, but nothing comes out. He leans across and puts his arm across my back. Slowly, slowly, I lift up my head.

'Why didn't you tell me sooner?' I ask.

'We didn't know. The prosecution found him hard to track down. He's been living abroad apparently.'

'I wanted to explain. To ask him to forgive me.' I pause. 'Maybe if he was abroad, that explains why he didn't visit me, when I asked.'

Theo's eyes darken. His face softens, as if he feels sorry for me. 'Maybe,' he replies.

'Why are they calling him?' I ask.

'Give you three guesses.'

'To discredit me of course.'

A headache is beginning to crack along my jawbone and pulsate against my temples.

'What will he say?' I ask.

'Whatever lies first come into his head I should think.' He pauses. 'Don't worry about it. I've got plenty of good witnesses who are going to be very helpful. Whatever Sebastian says today, by the end of the case he's going to end up discredited – not you. It's not just going to be your word against his.'

'How can you be so sure?'

'Trust me, Miranda.'

'I do, Theo. It's just I sometimes worry, is trust enough?' I pause. I bite my lip. 'I've always felt happier with knowledge.'

I feel empty inside. He squeezes my hand.

'Trusting me is enough, I can assure you. I've got to go now. See you in court.'

The guard takes me back to the dock. Court is gathering. The usual. Lawyers and clerks arriving, the public slipping in. My mother is here every day, woebegone in the front row. The sight of her looking so broken is tearing me apart.

My heart lurches. Sebastian is here, being escorted by a clerk to sit on a bench near the witness box, to wait to be called. I have not seen him since he burnt me with his acid eyes at your funeral, Zara. The sound of his voice haunts me.

'Miranda Cunningham, I can bear anything for you. I love it when you beg.'

The fist that grabs my heart all too often tightens. Pins and needles stab down my left arm. I am sweating; sweat pours off me like a waterfall. He is looking at me from the other side of the courtroom with empty hollow eyes, as if I'm not here. Looking straight through me, as if I'm invisible. He has lost weight. His craggy face is craggier than ever. His hair is shorter, more conventionally cut. Why did you tell her, Sebastian?

317

What's wrong with you? What do you want? What did you ever want?

The judge enters the courtroom and all eyes turn towards her. Theo turns to check on me, as he rises to stand. My eyes meet his.

'OK?' he mouths.

'OK,' I mouth back, as I rise and bow to the judge, even though I am not OK. The judge calls for the jury who are brought in. They sidle in looking bored and despondent. No one even looks across at me. That's good. I don't want them to. I don't want them analysing my inner conflict. When they have settled in their seats, the session starts.

'Good morning,' the judge says in a headmistress tone. Jovial. Assertive. 'Today we begin with witnesses for the prosecution.' There is a pause. 'Mr Early-Smith, please proceed.'

Paul Early-Smith aka Stephen Fry lookalike stands up. Slowly. Grandly. Adjusting his robes around his body. Right hand clinging to a few notes.

'Sebastian Templeton please.'

Sebastian stands, eyes towards the judge now, and the clerk of court leads him to the witness box. The clerk of court hands him a Bible. He puts his hands on the Bible and swears: 'I swear by Almighty God that the evidence that I shall give shall be the truth, the whole truth and nothing but the truth.'

Does Sebastian even know what truth is?

I close my eyes. A kaleidoscope of coloured shapes spins in front of me. Even though I am sitting down I feel dizzy. I put my hands on the bar in front of me to steady myself. When I open my eyes again the room is swaying gently, like a ship at sea. Theo turns around again. His runny honey eyes push into mine. Runny honey eyes to push Sebastian's eyes away. But I can't push his eyes away today. I have to look at him and listen.

'Please explain to the court how Miranda was sexually harassing you,' Paul Early-Smith asks.

Sebastian smiles sadly. As if his life is a torment.

'She wouldn't leave me alone. Always sitting too close to me. Putting her hand on the top of my leg.'

'Did she ever attempt to kiss you prior to the night you had sex?'

'Yes. She tried to kiss me on a number of occasions. At the Christmas party we held in her flat. On New Year's Eve. Several other times I think. So often that I can't remember all the details.'

I am so angry. Solid with anger. How can this be? How can he be allowed to stand there and lie? I shake my head in disbelief. He is describing exactly what he did to me.

'How did you respond?'

'I pushed her away. I tried to explain that I was in love with her sister and I didn't want to mess around, but she was infatuated with me and wouldn't listen.' He pauses for breath. 'After that her behaviour became worse.'

Early-Smith flaps his robes and opens his arms a little. 'Tell me, Sebastian, what happened the night you had sex?'

Now I wish I was anywhere but here.

'I think she put MDMA in my drink.'

I breathe in so sharply, my breath makes a sound. The barristers, the solicitors, the officers of the court are all turning to look at me. So far Sebastian has been turning everything around – making out I did to him what in reality he did to me. I am so shocked. MDMA. Is that what happened? Did he put MDMA in my drink? That would explain why I felt so weird when I'd only had one G&T. Why I suddenly wanted to go to bed with him – it must have softened me up, made me feel compliant. It would explain everything. And I have been tormented by guilt for sleeping with him.

319

Zara, how did you fall in love with this deceitful lying bastard? How did I ever let him live in our flat?

'What makes you think she might have put MDMA in your drink?' Paul Early-Smith asks.

'She was at the bar for a long time. And my drink tasted a little funny.' He pauses and looks straight across at me. 'And I so didn't find her attractive. Never have.' He is looking straight at me. I pull my eyes from his and look at the floor. 'I reckon she must have used something to lighten my mood, otherwise I wouldn't have been able to get it up,' he continues. 'I didn't even want to go and have a drink with her. My girlfriend Zara was keen to try and push us together, for us to be friends. I only went for a drink with Miranda to please Zara.'

Paul Early-Smith clears his throat. 'Let's move on to the seduction.'

Seduction. My blood boils.

'She came on to me as soon as we got back to the flat, after our drink. And because of the MDMA I managed to make myself shag her.' He laughs. His Joker in an old *Batman* film, corny laugh. 'She wasn't the sort of girl who usually gave me an erection, so I had to fantasise that I was doing it with someone else.' A dramatic pause. 'I made myself do it. I thought if I shagged her she might be satisfied she'd had me once and then she'd leave me alone.'

'But it didn't work like that did it?' Early-Smith asks looking smug. 'Can you confirm that she requested intercourse again in the morning?'

Sebastian smirks. 'Yes. She was really hot for it. Rampant.'

I am so embarrassed. So angry. I feel hot, and I know I am blushing. I daren't look across at the jury to see how they are reacting. I keep my eyes on Sebastian. I can't believe what he is saying. What is the matter with him? Why does he hate me so much?

'And she carried on pestering you behind her sister's back for months and months, didn't she? Could you give us a few examples?' Early-Smith continues.

Sebastian continues to spout nonsense about my alleged behaviour. My mind closes down. I am no longer listening. I sit looking at my feet. At the flat leather pumps I wear to court every day. I need to polish them tonight. When I manage to look up and re-engage, Mr Early-Smith has finished his questioning. He is sitting down looking inordinately pleased with himself. I dare to take a quick glance across at the jury now. They are sitting expressionless. Straight-backed. Straight-faced. Waiting for Ms Little to start cross-examining.

She is standing up. Bandbox as usual. Immaculate blow-dried hair shining out from beneath her wig which she adjusts a little before she starts.

'Mr Templeton, we've all read your statement, and listened to your evidence.'

I haven't read his statement. I flick through the file in front of me nervously. It must have been added late last night. I find it attached with a paperclip at the front. The words on the page merge together and swim in front of me.

'I've just got a few questions arising from what you have said, before we move on to CCTV evidence.' She pauses. 'If Miranda had to spike your drink with MDMA for you to be willing to have sex with her, how did you manage to have intercourse with her in the morning when the effects of the drug had worn off?'

Sebastian doesn't look so cocky now. His eyes dart a little from side to side. He looks flummoxed. He doesn't reply.

'Please answer the question,' the judge says, in a sharp voice.

'I just made myself. I had to do something to stop her pestering me. I thought if I gave it to her twice, she would stop pestering me.'

321

'But Mr Templeton, you specifically said under oath that you didn't think you would have been able to "get it up" for sex with Miranda Cunningham without "help", and that is why you think she put MDMA in your drink. So I repeat the question, if that is the case, how did you manage to have sex a second time?'

'I don't know.'

'Is it possible that you were not under duress at all, and you're not telling the truth?'

'I'm under oath so of course I'm telling the truth.'

'The facts don't add up, Mr Templeton.'

'She was pestering me. I had to do it.'

'So moving on then,' Ms Little continues. 'Can you explain in what way she was pestering you?'

'I have already explained.'

'Let's just run through it again.'

'She fancied me like mad. Whenever Zara wasn't around she was sitting next to me on the sofa, putting her hand on the top of my thighs. Following me to work, making sure she was sitting close to me.'

'Mr Templeton, let's look at some CCTV.'

Ms Little presses the controller in her hand and a screen lights up in the corner of the court, to the left of the witness box. The picture is clear and sharp. It shows the middle section of our desk at work. CCTV? At work? I never knew they were filming us – 9:30 a.m, according to the timer on the right side of the screen.

I walk across the screen, sit in my usual seat, switch on my computer screen and start to work. She fast-forwards all the empty sections. One by one a few other people join me. At 10:30, Sebastian saunters into the office and sits next to me. He folds his arms and legs and sits, not working, staring straight at me.

'Like this do you mean, Mr Templeton?' Ms Little QC asks.

'Ms Little, I can assure you that's a one-off. Is that all you can find for your files?' Sebastian replies.

'I have a few more recordings at a high enough standard to be shown in court,' she says with a smile. 'Let's get on with the next one shall we.' She presses the controller again. Once again the screen lights up.

'Did you know there was CCTV on Park Street?' Ms Little asks.

Sebastian doesn't reply; he is too busy looking at the screen.

This time, I am rushing up Park Street. Sebastian is also rushing up Park Street, behind me. He breaks from a fast walk into a jog, looking towards me all the time. He catches up and puts his hand on my shoulder. My body jumps, as if him catching up with me wasn't what I was expecting.

'Last tape, apart from the one you've seen in closed court. May I proceed, My Lady?' Ms Little asks the judge.

She nods her head. 'Of course.'

This tape shows Sebastian and I walking into the coffee area. He puts his hand on my bottom. My fingers whisk his hand away.

'Mr Templeton, is this another one-off?'

'Ms Little, the jury will have to make their own conclusions. I have nothing to say.'

'Finally Mr Templeton, there is a tape of you and Ms Miranda Cunningham making love.'

My heart stops.

Ms Little continues, 'You must know about it. We assume you took it. Cameras were found in the lights in the ceiling in both girls' bedrooms. It is alleged that you filmed Miranda so that you could compromise her. You sent the recording to us – to embarrass Miranda. We have shown it to the judge and the jury in closed session. Was this a time when you considered that you were being forced? Or was it all because of the MDMA? We have had the tapes examined very carefully. According to our expert, you appear too energised to be on MDMA. I refer the court to page seven of the second bundle.'

At the end of the session, I am taken, as usual, straight to meet Theo. I am so exhausted. I feel as if I have just been dragged through an assault course. My shoulders and muscles ache. Theo is there first. He has taken his wig and robes off when I arrive, and is running his fingers through his gown to smooth the creases out. As soon as he sees me he smiles.

'Are you OK?' he asks, as I sit down opposite him as usual.

'Of course not,' I reply, trying not to burst into tears. 'It's so frightening listening to such a strange contortion of the truth. I felt so helpless sitting there.'

He reaches across the table and takes my hand. 'It went swimmingly though. Ms Little really caught him out.' He pauses. 'And we'll soon get our turn to push back. You'll come across well.' He squeezes my hand. 'Really well.'

'But . . .' I splutter, 'he's lied about so much, can anything he's ever said be believed?'

His amber eyes melt into mine. 'His lying is serious. He's an unreliable witness.' He pauses. 'But Miranda. I'm onto him. Big time.'

I look at Theo and wish I could ask him to hold me. Just for a minute. I wish I could place my head on his chest and feel his warmth.

135

Sebastian

Ms Little is a real bitch.

She thinks she's so clever, almost catching me out, but all she is, is an overeducated, cardboard cut-out of a woman, who's never experienced real life. Her voice is so moderated, it sounds as if she has a large stone in her mouth. You know the sort of thing: lips hardly move when she speaks. I expect it's missionary position, eyes closed, if she ever condescends to fuck. She's the sort of woman who thinks she's pretty, but is best viewed from a distance. Teeth, hair and make-up. No real looks.

And the legal system's a bitch.

Everyone who's familiar with it always says that. How dare she infer I was lying? I'll sue her for defamation of my character, as soon as this case is over. I'll discuss it with Early-Smith. Not believing me about how much Miranda was coming on to me? Miranda has been a flirt and a minx right from the moment I met her, sidling up too close to me on the sofa. Contriving to arrange to meet. How dare she infer I'm a pervert because I had a camera in the bedroom? Lots of people like to watch replays of themselves having sex.

But Miranda is the biggest bitch. Killing my soul twin. The

only thing that's keeping me going right now is thinking about what's going to happen to her. She'll go down for life. She'll never get out of prison. Ms Little won't win. If the police don't get enough evidence against her I will. I will catch her client out. Jude, I'll follow her everywhere at the courthouse, double-check her every move.

I have already made my own crime board on the kitchen wall at home, based on every piece of press coverage I can get my hands on. I will document every person she talks to in or around court. When her transport van arrives, and when it leaves. How long she spends in the lavatory. I will note every minute she spends with her barrister, and with her QC. Theo Gregson has the hots for her. I know from the way I saw him looking at her at my beloved's funeral. He must be an idiot. Can't he see that she's a cold-blooded murderer? It really made me sick when I saw her at Zara's funeral, pretending to look upset. She's murdered the woman I love.

She doesn't deserve to exist.

136

'And now today,' Theo tells me, 'it's our turn to defend. This is when the case will really get going. When you'll really come into your own.'

We are standing by the table in one of the court meeting rooms. He leans towards me. I lean towards him a little. I would so like him to hold me in his arms. Just for a few seconds for reassurance. Our lips almost meet. He looks embarrassed and pulls away.

'Sorry,' he says, stepping back. 'Invaded your personal space.'

We remain standing by the grey plastic table a little longer. He really is too good-looking to be a barrister. Why has he chosen such a depressing career? Slowly, slowly, he moves away and sits on the other side of the table as usual. I sit opposite him.

'We need to talk about today in court,' he says, adjusting his wig.

'OK. Fire away.'

'As you know Ms Little is putting you on the stand today. She will ask you a few questions and then the prosecution will cross-examine you. It won't be easy.' Theo taps his fingers on the plastic table. 'Remember we have good witnesses to call later, who will support your case. You have nothing to worry about. Whatever happens today, you must relax, take it in your stride, and tell the whole truth.'

'Relax?' I pause. 'I'm not very good at that when I'm in court charged with murder.'

'Maybe that's not quite the right word. Maybe I should have said that whatever happens today I know you will cope. I know you'll get through it.'

Honey eyes melt into mine, and I wish I had met him in another life.

137

Theo has escorted me to the dock. I am sitting trying to numb myself to the situation by pretending I am not here. Trying to remember the feeling of air on my face as I walk in the countryside, inhaling the scent of freshly mown grass. Trying to remember the distant sharpness of the stars shining down from another universe. Trying to remember the sight of a sunset, a dozen shades of orange melting slowly into the horizon. Trying not to watch court society beginning to gather. Lawyers. Clerks. Press; trying not to imagine what they might be writing and saying about me. Members of the public with nothing better to do. Pretending not to see Mother arriving, looking bereft. Forcing myself not to stiffen as I see Sebastian taking the seat behind her.

I was hoping he wasn't going to come and watch the trial after giving his evidence. I was hoping he was going straight back to his new life in another country. Just looking at the back of his head makes my jawline go tense and a headache start to throb at my temples.

The judge arrives. She looks a little flustered today as if she's been rushing. It's difficult to imagine that she lives a life outside her professional one. Flustered makes her look more normal. More like the rest of us. We stand and bow, and she calls for the jury, who arrive in their usual lumbering, semi-disinterested fashion. I want to shake them. I want to shout at them. This is my life. What happens in here really, really matters.

Ms Little QC stands. Polished and painted. Botoxed and airbrushed.

'We call the defendant, Miranda Cunningham.'

What I have dreaded for so long is happening now. The guard sitting next to me is opening the locked door of the dock. The court clerk is walking towards me to take me to the witness box. I am stepping into the court. The air in the court feels different to the air in the dock. Heavier somehow. I hear my footsteps resonating on the ground as I walk. I feel the eyes of the court on my back. I step into the witness box, raise my head, and try to smile, but my lips don't move.

The clerk hands me a Bible and asks me to repeat after him, the truth, the whole truth and nothing but the truth spiel. I feel hot. My hands are trembling. I look across at Theo. He nods his head encouragingly. I repeat slowly and carefully. I manage it.

'Did you have sexual relations with Sebastian Templeton?' Ms Little asks gently.

A stone rotates in my stomach, heavy as lead. I take a deep breath. I exhale slowly. 'Yes.' My voice ricochets around the court, thin and stretched.

'How many times?'

My heart is racing. I inhale and exhale slowly to try and calm myself. I take too long to reply.

'Answer the question, please,' the judge pushes.

'Twice.'

'Can you run me through what happened?' Ms Little asks, concern brimming in her eyes.

I inhale deeply, to try and calm myself. 'He had been coming on to me behind my sister's back ever since I met him in October last year.' I pause for breath. 'He had even touched me inappropriately at work. I didn't do anything to encourage him, until that night. I didn't want to have a relationship with him. My sister was in love with him.'

'Did you find him physically attractive?'

'No.'

'So what happened that night?'

'We saw my sister off at the station. She was going away for the weekend. Then we went to the pub for a drink. I only had one gin and tonic. When we got home he tried to kiss me as he has done so many times before and this time I kissed him back and we ended up having intercourse.'

'Do you know why you changed your mind? Was it possible he spiked your drink?'

'He could have. He had the opportunity. Contrary to what he said, he went to the bar not me. I only had one glass of G&T and felt dizzy.'

'In his witness statement he accuses you of putting MDMA in his drink. Do you think it could have been the other way round?'

'Easily. I couldn't have put MDMA in his drink. I don't even know where to buy it. It was Sebastian and Zara who used to take it. Although I didn't realise my drink had been spiked at the time, I did feel very spaced out and very strange. I think that must have been why I allowed him to have sex with me. Up until that point I didn't even like him. I had never found him attractive.'

'Have you ever had ecstasy, or MDMA before?'

'Once, that's all. I took an E at our Christmas party. I was light-headed then as well. It made me very friendly. Wanting to dance and chat with everyone.'

'Did you feel a bit the same the night you made love to Sebastian?'

'Well, not quite the same. The night I had sex with Sebastian I felt much more spaced out.'

'Thank you Miranda.' She pauses. 'Moving on. How did you feel after you had sex with Sebastian?'

'As soon as we had finished, I fell asleep. When I awoke in the early hours, I bitterly regretted it. I left him asleep in bed and showered. After my shower, I went back to the bedroom to fetch some clothes. I didn't know whether I loathed myself, or him, more. I wanted to get dressed, leave the flat and get away from him. But he was awake, waiting to pounce.'

'Waiting to pounce? What exactly do you mean?'

'He was erect. Grinning at me. He told me he wanted to do it again. I said no. I told me very clearly that I didn't want a relationship with him. That I had made a terrible mistake. That I didn't want to hurt Zara and that she mustn't find out about what had happened between us, because it would hurt her too much.' I pause. 'And that it would never happen again.'

Overcome by unpleasant memories, I stop speaking. I am biting my lip to push back tears.

'Please continue, Ms Cunningham,' the judge says softly.

'Because I wouldn't go with him again voluntarily, he raped me. Restrained my arms, threw me onto the bed and entered me from behind.'

'How has what happened affected you?'

'Very badly . . .'

I forget I am in court. I tell them all about how difficult I found it – at home and at work. How worried I was about hurting you, my beloved sister. How guilty I felt.

When I have finished my emotional outpouring, Ms Little smiles at me encouragingly.

'Thank you very much, Miranda,' she says. 'Now let's move on to the next topic.'

Next topic. My sister's death. The stabbing. My sister's dead staring eyes pushing towards me. Eyes that will never go away. They follow me every day, coming to me at odd times when I least expect them. As I clean my teeth. As I shuffle along the prison corridor to the canteen. I see them now as I stand in court, moving towards me, closer and closer. I am shaking, drenched in sweat, tears welling behind my eyes.

'Are you all right to continue?' I hear the judge asking somewhere in the distance of my mind.

Sebastian looks across at me, eyes burning, and a little strength builds within me, to push back, to not let him destroy me. I swallow my tears.

'Yes,' I reply.

We have been through this so many times. Once again, Ms Little runs through what happened with me as gently as possible, but still I relive every second, every expression on your face. The feel of the knife. Finally she says, 'That will be all, thank you,' and sits down.

'Let's take a break. Court rise.'

138

Back in the court meeting room with Theo, still drenched in sweat, still trembling after what I have been through. Theo is also perspiring. He takes his wig off and puts it on the table, and walks across the room to open the window, the full two inches it can be opened. He fetches us both some chilled water in plastic cups and sits down opposite me. The cup shakes in my hand as I take a sip.

'You did well,' he says, amber eyes dissolving in mine.

'I'm not sure I can cope with Early-Smith's cross-examination,' I say. 'I just can't bear to continue to relive it.'

Amber eyes harden a little. 'You can. You must. You will.'

'Please Theo, I need someone to hug.'

We both stand up, and meet somewhere at the side of the table. I am so keen for physical reassurance I do not notice where I melt into him. He body is so strong, so reassuring. His energy pulsates towards me and builds within me. When he holds me against him I can cope with the world. I want to stay like this forever, but we cannot stay like this for long. All too soon, he pulls away and straightens his wig. Time to go back to court.

139

Early-Smith is ready to cross-examine me. I shudder and look down at my hands. They are trembling so much that I clasp them together and put them behind my back, hoping no one will notice. Early-Smith. Ugly. Heavy. Well educated. Condescending. I stand looking at him, trying to remind myself that I was well educated, once, in another life. Now I am a criminal. Innocent until proven guilty. But it seems like the other way round. A criminal stuck in a world I never dreamt of. A world I will never escape.

Paul Early-Smith is standing in front of me, determined to make sure of that. He clears his throat to warn everyone he is about to speak. His bulbous nose seems even more bulbous than usual. His eyes are bulging like a frog's.

'Do you really expect the jury to believe that you were raped, when you have only recently mentioned it?' he says, a snarl in his mouth and in his eyes. 'Why didn't you report it immediately?'

'I was traumatised and embarrassed.'

'Do you really expect us to believe that an educated professional woman like yourself would be too afraid to speak up?'

He pauses and looks across at the jury. He adjusts his robes a little and turns back to eyeball me. 'How exactly are you intending to prove that you were raped?'

'I haven't been focusing on anything lately, let alone getting proof about being raped. It has all been so awful, losing my sister.' I swallow hard to try and stop myself from crying. 'It was very difficult for me, Sebastian being my sister's boyfriend, and Zara being so in love with him.' I swallow again before I am able to continue. 'But I became so low afterwards, and had such unpleasant symptoms that Zara took me to see a doctor.'

Early-Smith and his solicitor exchange an anxious glance. They didn't know about this. I have only had the courage to submit this evidence so recently that my written submission must only just have arrived at court.

'Which doctor was that?' Mr Early-Smith asks, skimming through his notes and frowning.

'My local GP – she asked me whether I'd been raped. She said my symptoms were consistent with rape.'

Mr Early-Smith's face closes. He doesn't want the jury to hear any more of this.

'Thank you, Ms Cunningham. That's all on that subject. Let's move on and deal with the actions that led to your sister's death in more detail.'

In more detail. My mind feels numb. How is more detail possible? I have told Ms Little everything. The more I repeat it all, the more it haunts me, the more I want to forget. But I know I cannot. I close my eyes. Not long to go now. Not much more. I must just keep calm and soldier on.

'Let's start with when you got back to the flat. Were you angry with her?'

'No, as I told Ms Little, I was looking forward to seeing her. We were texting one another, planning to go out for a movie and a pizza. It was the other way round. I didn't realise as I headed back to the flat that she was so angry with me.'

'Talk us through it again.' Early-Smith smooths and flaps his robes. I look at him and I feel so tired.

'So you came back into the flat?' he prompts.

So very tired. My legs go weak. I lean on the stand in front of me, to support myself.

'Yes. I came home from work,' I reply.

He leans forwards a little, a frown rippling across his face. 'Tell me your exact movements.'

Exact movements. What is he playing at? I have just been through all this with Ms Little.

'Even though we were arranging to go out later I knew I had time for a cup of tea, so I went straight into the corner of the kitchen to put the kettle on.'

'What time was that?' His voice is harsh. Staccato.

'It was about six o'clock.'

'When did you first see your sister?'

I have been through this so many times, but now I don't remember. I don't remember exactly. I close my eyes and try to picture it, where she was when I entered the flat. I open them to find Early-Smith's bulging eyes raised to the sky impatiently.

'Well, Ms Cunningham, are you able to continue?'

I open my mouth to reply, but no words come out. Paul Early-Smith QC glances across at the judge to gauge her reaction.

'Yes. Yes,' I finally manage.

'When did you first see your sister?' he repeats lancing me with his eyes.

'About the same time. I'm not sure where she was. It all happened so quickly.'

'Did you greet her?'

'I suppose I must have.'

'You suppose?' There is a pause. 'So you don't remember whether you greeted her, yet you expect us to believe you remember she was about to kill you?'

My insides tighten. My pulse is racing. 'I can't remember where she was when I first came home. All I remember is that she came at me. She was so angry. I have never seen her like that.'

'When did you first realise that she had a knife?'

'When she came at me. She had her Swiss Army knife in her hand and she stabbed me in the neck. She was going to kill me, to stab me again. So I . . . So I . . .' I am crying now, tears streaming down my face.

'Please continue, Ms Cunningham.'

'I grabbed the only thing I could – the bread knife from the kitchen counter, and stabbed her in the stomach.'

Early-Smith's lips stretch into a disbelieving smile. 'Had you ever seen your sister this angry before?'

'No. Never.'

'Had your sister ever attacked you before?'

'No.'

'Not even when you were children?'

'Maybe. I can't remember.'

'There seem to be a lot of things you can't remember. Is that convenient?'

I don't reply. He gives me a short, contrived smile, a sideways glance to the jury, and turns his head back to me.

'Tell me, Ms Cunningham, to the best of your knowledge, has your sister ever attacked anyone else?'

'No.'

'Had she ever shown any signs of violence at all?'

'No.'

'So how were you so sure she was about to kill you?'

'She accused me of seducing Sebastian. He'd told her we'd slept together. She loved him very much. She was so, so angry.'

'But how were you so sure?' He pauses. He raises his hands in the air. He looks across at the jury again. Not a sideways glance this time, a full-blown triumphant stare. 'To kill someone but rely on self-defence, Ms Cunningham, you have to be sure.' The end of his knobbly nose looks as if it is pulsating. He shakes his head a little. 'Tell us all, Ms Cunningham, were you sure?'

I do not reply at first. Two can play this game, Early-Smith, pausing for dramatic effect. Then: 'Yes, Mr Early-Smith. I was sure. Very sure. I loved my sister very much. I would never have stabbed her unless she was about to kill me. I didn't intend to kill her. I just needed her to stop.'

140

'That's it. It's over. I'm going down,' I tell Theo.

'It isn't over,' he replies, eyes hard and definite. He reaches across the table and takes both my hands in his. 'Prosecution counsel always treat the defendant like that. The forensic and medical evidence completely verifies what you say.'

Tears in my eyes. Knots in my stomach. 'I hate the man. He makes me feel dirty.' I pause and clench my fist. 'But not as much as I hate Sebastian.'

His hands stroke mine. 'Calm down. I know it's difficult to handle but Early-Smith's only doing his job. Everything went just as expected. It's our witness evidence tomorrow. I promise you, everything will be fine.'

'It feels as if nothing will ever be fine again.'

He lets go of my hands. He moves his right hand towards my face. Gently, softly, he touches my chin and lifts it a little, pressing his eyes into mine, eyes that are softer now. 'Not long to go now.'

141

Ensconced behind my wall of glass, another key day is starting in court. Witness evidence. The first witness to be called is the forensic expert – Professor Holywell. I see him waiting on the benches to the left of the judge's area. He has thin white hair around the edge of his pate that seems to be sticking up with static, staring eyes and round glasses. He is wearing crumpled cords, and a threadbare tweed jacket with leather pads at the elbows. Rummaging through a pigskin briefcase as if looking for a document. His shoulders widen with relief as he pulls out some papers and starts reading them. Despite his thick glasses he still has to hold the notes at the end of his nose, frowning as he reads.

The morning court gathers as Professor Holywell continues to read his report, oblivious to the movement around him. All the usual. Barristers. Court officials. Jury. Rising for the judge. And now Professor Holywell is taking the stand, being sworn in, and Ms Little is standing up to examine him.

'Let's not waste the jury's time and just cut to the quick. Tell me Professor, does the evidence that you have examined regarding wound size and shape, and force used, corroborate the defendant's evidence?' Ms Little asks.

'Undoubtedly yes. Without question. Entirely and completely.'

Theo turns around and smiles at me with his eyes. Eyes that say *I told you so*. Mother turns around and smiles. My insides flood with a warm sense of relief. Ms Little sits down and Paul Early-Smith stands up. Paul Early-Smith does not look pleased.

'On page seven of your report, you discuss blood splatter evidence. According to the defendant there was only a few seconds between the two stabbings. Allowing for margin of error, could the order of stabbing have been the other way round?'

Early-Smith is standing, shoulders wide, bulbous nose raised. Pleased with himself. I do not like the way his smile plays on his lips. Professor Holywell runs his fingers through his hair. He leans forwards to address Early-Smith. 'No. On every occasion where there is overlap, the blood that soaked into the underlying fabric was always Miranda's.'

Theo turns around to look at me. *I told you so*, his eyes tell me once again.

142

The second witness to be called today is my GP, Dr Dale. I do not want to listen to this, but I have no choice. What is she supposed to say? I never even told her what happened. But Theo and Ms Little have insisted she is called. She is standing in the witness box, fine-nosed and smartly dressed. Navy blue perfection edged in white. Hands brandishing matching shellac.

I am sitting here dying inside, trying to keep calm. Trying to do my best. I feel empty and limp. As if my body is no longer my body, but a sack of skin with no tissue or bones to inflate it.

'I understand from your statement that you have been a GP for twenty years and that you are specifically trained to deal with rape victims. Is that correct?' Ms Little asks.

Dr Dale nods her head. 'Yes. Dealing with rape victims has always been one of my specialisms.'

'Is it correct that you believed the defendant, Ms Miranda Cunningham, had been raped, around the time she now alleges the incident took place?'

'Yes.'

'Even though she never actually told you that she had been raped?'

Dr Dale gives Ms Little a slow purposeful smile. 'Yes. It's common for people to be secretive after such a *terrible* experience.'

Her voice stalls on the word *terrible*, as if she is in pain herself. Early-Smith stirs uncomfortably.

Dr Dale continues, 'She had developed a severe burning pain in her vaginal area that wouldn't go away. Once investigated this couldn't be explained by a physical cause. The cause of this psychological symptom is invariably rape.' There is a pause. 'She seemed very distressed, but wasn't willing to talk about why. When I asked her whether she was in a relationship she became tearful.' Dr Dale pauses again. 'Miranda most definitely exhibited all the warning signs of rape. I documented it fully in her medical notes, which I made at the time, and are being distributed by the clerk right now.'

143

Sebastian

Dr Dale. Yet another condescending woman full of clap-trap. Rape? Miranda was gagging for it. Desperate. She hadn't had sex for over three years. Zara had spilt the beans to me about that. I know I put a little something in her drink to warm her up, but she needed me to do that to help her relax. Once she was relaxed there was no stopping her. You should have heard the scream of her climax.

144

More witnesses today.

Ms Holt is approaching the box. I don't know who she is. I didn't know she was being called. A slightly overweight blonde of a similar age to me. Quite pretty, wearing a short red woollen sweater dress and black boots. I flick through the bundle to try and find out about her. Nothing here. A clerk is walking around court with a pile of photocopying. He passes a sheet to my guard, who passes it to me. Ms Holt's witness statement. A last-minute addition to today's list. I don't have time to read it, or even skim it.

Ms Little is starting the questioning.

'I understand, Ms Holt, you are here because you are suggesting that Sebastian Templeton raped you.'

Another rape. The bastard. My heart skips a beat.

'That's correct.'

'Could you explain what happened please?'

Ms Holt begins to speak. She has a calm, clear voice. I don't want to listen to this. Her words move in and out of focus. Words and feelings and memories all jumbled. I see him sitting next to me at work again. I hear his voice. *I know what you like. Remember, Miranda.* And I feel him entering me again. I see your face, Zara, the face I loved so much. I want to speak to you. I want to touch you. Hold your hand and tell you how sorry I am.

I push my memories away. The court comes back into focus. Ms Little has finished questioning. Ms Holt has finished speaking. Mr Early-Smith is standing up to cross-examine her.

'You are accusing Mr Templeton of raping you, but this was two years ago and you never brought charges – can you tell us why?'

She flicks her hair from her eyes. 'He threatened to hurt me if I reported it.' She pauses. 'He said no one would believe me anyway.' Another pause; she almost cries. 'Also I was applying for a job as a nursery school teacher and I thought being involved in a rape accusation would make schools feel uncertain about me. I felt tainted by what he had done to me.'

Mr Early-Smith smiles. A knowing smile, as if he thinks he is about to trap Ms Holt.

'Surely if he really had done this you had a moral responsibility to report him immediately, to protect other people?'

She doesn't reply. She is fighting back tears and looking at the floor.

'Why are you speaking out now? What was your trigger? Why not last month? Last week?'

She looks up. Head high and proud now. 'Theo Gregson came to see me and explained what had happened to Miranda. He seemed to know I used to spend time with Sebastian Templeton. He explained the situation and I agreed to help. His behaviour almost ruined my life. I don't want it to ruin anyone else's. Surely, Mr Early-Smith, this is the perfect time to speak out?'

Mr Early-Smith frowns over the top of his half-moon glasses. His termination look. 'Thank you, Ms Holt. That will be all.'

Ms Holt looks across at me and nods, purposeful rather than intimidated now, as she leaves the stand and goes to sit at the side of the court. Her shoulders are wide. Her head is raised. Her eyes shine. Pleased with herself. Proud she has fought back.

145

Sebastian

So, Miranda Cunningham, Caroline Holt, where do you think you are going with this? You say I raped you, so why did neither of you report it? You wanted it, both of you. You were desperate for it. A man like me always knows what a woman wants.

146

Ms Little. On her feet again. Adjusting the angle of her glasses, checking her notes. She calls Ms Phipps. Our English teacher from school and close family friend of many years. My godmother. Your godmother too. Almost sixty now, approaching retirement age. Over a year since I last saw her. She has lost weight and grown her hair; it tumbles onto her shoulders and softens her face.

Ms Little leans forward eagerly. 'It has been alleged by the prosecution that Zara and Miranda were rivals. That Zara was lively and pretty, much more popular than Miranda. Apparently Miranda was jealous of her.'

'They are so wrong. Both girls were very popular in their own way. Zara had a more lively social life than Miranda. But Miranda was very popular too. It was just her choice to live a quieter life. Miranda was more academic, but Zara was very artistic. They complemented each other perfectly. They loved each other intensely. They were inseparable. I should know. I am their godmother. I have known them all their lives.'

I watch Mr Early-Smith, sitting at his bench. He shrugs his shoulders condescendingly, and raises his palms.

147

I am with Theo Gregson in our court meeting room, again. This morning he has shaved roughly and cut himself, a little bit of blood on his chin. My fingers itch to clean him up, to wipe it away. And he looks as if he hasn't slept. Pale skin. Bags beneath his eyes. Is he worried? Does he think we are going to lose the trial?

'Summing up today,' he says. 'Most important day.' There is a pause. 'Apart from the verdict.'

My stomach coagulates. 'Not that you're trying to make me feel nervous or anything?'

'Would I do that?' He manages half a smile.

'How many things could go wrong?'

'Hard to say.'

'You're usually more encouraging.'

He shrugs. 'Nothing to worry about. I'm always like this on the last day.'

148

The court has moved to a new level of seriousness. No interim buzz of conversation between the clerks, between the solicitors and barristers. The members of the public sit forwards, stiff like dummies, hands in laps. The judge arrives, brow furrowed, and everyone stands. The jury return and the air around me tightens. My mother looks around and catches my eye anxiously. Sebastian doesn't turn around; his eyes are firmly fixed to the front. Theo doesn't turn around either but I know he is rooting for me.

Paul Early-Smith stands up and I feel weak. He stands and gives the jury his *I'm an officer of the court* look. The one I suspect he practises in his hallway mirror every morning. Folded brow. Dimpled nose. You don't need to try, Paul Early-Smith. You already look intimidating enough. He coughs to clear his throat.

'Miranda Cunningham murdered her sister in cold blood.' He pauses. 'In cold blood,' he repeats in a thunderous tone. My insides quiver. 'Because she was infatuated with her sister's boyfriend, and wanted her sister out of the way so that she could have him to herself.' He waves his right arm dramatically towards the jury. 'The sex tape has shown us all the level of enjoyment she had with him.'

The sex tape.

I feel sick whenever anyone mentions it. I feel my face reddening. I look across at the jury and hope they are not watching me. But two of them are. The girl with the weird ear piercing, and the man in the turban, are both looking my way. My face becomes hotter as they gaze at me. The man in the turban has a sneering, twisted face. The girl's expression does not change. I pull my eyes from them and stare back at Mr Early-Smith. I stare at his profile as he addresses the jury and I hate him for the way he is twisting me, twisting my life.

'She had been pestering and cajoling Sebastian Templeton ever since she met him,' Mr Early-Smith continues. 'After being envious of her more attractive, outgoing sister for years, she finally took revenge on her.' He pauses for dramatic effect, shoulders and nose raised, making him look increasingly pompous, making me resent what he is saying even more. 'Over the relevant period, Miranda Cunningham became increasingly unstable and now, for her own safety and that of the larger public, she needs to be incarcerated as soon as possible.'

It's not true, I want to shout. But I am not allowed to speak. *It's not true,* I shout in my mind, body stiff with anger.

The conniving bastard otherwise known as Mr Early-Smith, sits down with a flourish, the jury still transfixed by him, still watching him. My heart stops for a minute. I put my arm on the shelf in front of me to steady myself. I breathe deeply until everything calms, until my heartbeat comes back.

I watch Ms Little rising from her seat. Smooth. Cool. Confidence rippling across her skin. She moves slowly, with certainty. She turns to face the jury.

'I want you to understand that Miranda Cunningham loved her twin sister more than anything in the world and grieves

353

for her every day.' Silent tears run down my face. 'That grief is painful to watch for anyone who knows her.' Theo turns around to check whether I am all right. My eyes melt into his. My tears continue.

Ms Little's words are cascading over me somewhere in the distance of my mind, but I am not sure whether I am hearing them or whether they are just an echo. 'Miranda Cunningham is the last person in the world who would cause deliberate harm to her sister Zara. We can see this both through testimony, and observation of her loving nature.' Ms Little pauses. 'What has happened here is a travesty. A man playing around with twin sisters, attempting to pit one against the other. Manipulating both of them.' A long pause just as dramatic as Early-Smith's. 'What motivated this man remains a mystery. What is clear is that he was a man with no love for either of them.'

149

Sebastian

'What is clear is that he was a man with no love for either of them.'

Ms Little QC's words sear into me. I am so angry, my lower lip is trembling. My head feels as if it is exploding. I loved Zara so much. What does Ms Little know about love, or loss? Oh how I have loved and lost. I would die for those I love. I will kill for those I love. Just watch.

My fist clenches and I hit the back of the bench in front of me so hard I fear for a second I have broken my hand. Two guards are on me, restraining me, dragging my arms behind my back and cuffing me. Big brutes, chests built of brick. I try to bite one of them but my mouth doesn't quite reach. They bundle me out of court, frisk me, and lock me in a holding cell in the basement of the building, to calm me down. I am trembling with anger.

I love Zara so much I will never calm down. Miranda will not get away with this.

150

Members of the jury exchange glances as Sebastian is escorted from court. I see Ms Little exchange a glance with Theo. Theo turns to me and mouths to ask if I am all right. I nod back, pretending I am OK. But I do not know whether I am OK or not. I feel light-headed, as if I am in a vacuum.

'Please continue, Ms Little,' the judge intervenes.

'Miranda's sister, in a rage of hate and jealousy, knowingly brought on by that man, tried to kill her. Miranda acted reasonably in self-defence. She loved her sister and is devastated by what has happened.' There is a pause. Ms Little gesticulates in my direction. 'Look at her. Look at what this is doing to her. She needs to go home to her bereft mother. They need to have time to rebuild what is left of their lives. They need to be together in privacy and peace.'

I do not see anyone looking at me, except my mother, who has turned her head towards me, tears streaming down her face. I long to touch her, to hold her, pain rising inside me.

Ms Little sits down. Time stops. The court seems to have frozen around me. Nobody speaks. Nobody moves. Then slowly, slowly, the judge starts to address the jury.

'To convict this young woman of murder, you must be sure, beyond any reasonable doubt that Miranda intended to kill her sister – that it was a deliberate act, and not one undertaken in reasonable self-defence. I have no need to tell you that this is a very serious case regarding an intelligent young woman, with no previous record of violence or indeed any criminal conduct. A young woman whose behaviour and achievements until this point in her life appear to have been exemplary. A woman who may have been raped. Please now retire and deliberate upon your verdict.'

Theo turns to look at me and nods his head. The softness in his eyes tells me he is pleased with the summing up.

151

I am taken to a holding cell beneath the court to wait for the verdict. I look at my watch. It is midday. At four-ish, Theo has told me, the judge will talk to the jury. If it looks as if the jury won't reach their decision today, I will be taken back to Eastwood Park prison. Difficult as that will be, because it will mean the jury are divided, at least I'd be able to see Jane – my favourite listener. But if their decision is taking that long, I'll need to see Jane, not just want to. Jane has been so good to me, encouraging me to carry on through my darkest patches.

The guard who is looking after me today, a swarthy man with large brown eyes and a beard, is trying his best to be kind. He has brought me a cup of coffee, a block of chocolate, and three lifestyle magazines. Lifestyle. Will I ever have a life again, far less a lifestyle? After so long in prison the concept seems frivolous. Sitting in my cell looking at lifestyle magazines doesn't help me pass through time that has stopped. It pushes me back. Uncertain of my future, all I can do is dwell on the past. Snippets of the past race through my mind like a film montage.

My very first memory of you, Zara. Two years old, holding

hands as we ran across the beach. Barefooted. Grains of sand sticking between our toes. Running. Running. Running.

Later, running across playing fields, towards your netball changing rooms. People staring. Whispers on the wind. Zara. Zara Cunningham. They called the ambulance and the police.

The doctor walking towards me in the hospital corridor.

'Zara is stable. She has regained consciousness. All the neurological tests are positive.'

Stable. Positive. Neurological. Words tumble in my head and for the first time in hours I stop having to concentrate to breathe.

And now you are home from hospital and we are lying on the floor together in my bedroom, sharing a joint.

'Miranda,' you say, 'stop beating yourself up. It wasn't your fault.'

I wish you could say that to me now, Zara. I wish that was what you thought.

Again and again I see you bursting through the door of our shiny flat in Bristol, skin slightly flushed.

'I've met someone,' you say.

Emphasising *someone*, Zara. So many people, but never 'someone' before.

A portfolio of photographs of Sebastian, spilling from Mother's hands across the coffee table in our flat, and I hear you telling me, 'I never knew I was alive until I met Sebastian. I love him so much.'

You step towards him, put out your hand and stroke his cheek.

And now Sebastian is pulling me into his arms and kissing me. His tongue is in my mouth. And now Sebastian is shoving me face down into the duvet and penetrating me from behind. It hurts. It really hurts. A burning pain in the walls of my vagina. The pain is rising, engulfing me, and I am telling the psychotherapist I do not resent my sister. Tears are rolling down my face. Sebastian's face is moving towards me. I feel his heat. I taste his breath.

'I like it when you beg.'

He puts his head back and laughs his hyena laugh. Sebastian's face disappears. I see your beautiful face, Zara, riddled with anger.

'I'm going to kill you, fucking kill you,' you shout at me.

I feel the slippage of skin. The resistance. The wetness. And I am walking behind your coffin at the funeral, Sebastian's eyes searing into mine. Sebastian's eyes soften. They become Theo's. Seeing Theo's eyes in my mind soothes me. The images disappear. I begin to breathe gently again.

152

The jury are ready to return their verdict. The court buzzes with anticipation. Mr Mimms, Ms Little and Theo are heads together, conferring. Early-Smith and co. are huddled together looking smug. Can they tell anything? I've not even been sent back to Eastwood Park, their decision is so quick.

Court officials are laughing and chatting, an air of relaxation etched across their faces. As if they are about to get an early break. Mother is sitting at the front of the spectator gallery, hands together on her lap. The press. Sitting watching me. Watching my reactions like gannets ready to dive for prey. Probably already ready with two different stories, depending on the next five minutes. Some in the seats to the left of the witness box. Some in the upstairs gallery. Gannets. Crows. Vultures. Rooks.

Sebastian is here. Sitting behind my mother as usual. My mother never talks to him. He always ignores her. He always ignores me. He never tries to talk to me, not even when I pass him in the corridor attached to my guard.

Theo turns to look at me. His eyes glisten towards mine. I've just seen him in the meeting room. I wasn't sure he would brief me today. What is there left to say? Good luck? But he did, and instead of talking much, he held me against him in a special bear hug. He smelt musky and reassuring. Like when I asked him, before. Except I didn't ask him this time. It just happened.

'Miranda, we know you're innocent. If you're not released today, we'll appeal,' he said.

He tells me that again now with his eyes, before he turns away.

The judge enters through her doorway at the back right of the court, a pile of papers in her hand. As soon as she arrives, the court quietens and everybody stands. She tells a court official to fetch the jury and I tremble inside. Is the entire course of the rest of my life to be determined by a single act of sex, instantly regretted?

The jury arrive, far more perky than normal. Maybe the sniff of release from their duty has energised them. As they enter the court the young woman with the silky lashes and the stretched earlobe looks across at me. I sit looking across at them, these people on whom my fate rests. These people whom I know nothing about. These people who know nothing about me. They might think they do, because of the court case; but sex, blood, knives and grief — is that really me? Or just what has become of me?

The three jurors who are severely obese hobble towards their seats. How did they become so fat that they can hardly walk?

The Sikh man with the turban. Is he shocked by my sexual behaviour? Will that count against me? The bald man. About forty. The bearded man. About twenty. What do I know of their attitude?

The girl with the lashes and the earlobe. Do her glances demonstrate empathy? Maybe. I like to think so. The girl who looks like a pixie with short hair and big eyes. A modern girl.

Or at least that's how she presents. Might she understand what I've been going through? What it feels like to be raped? She looks so well groomed, so innocent. Will she have empathy for someone who plunges a knife into their sister? Does she have a sister she loves? Does she know what it feels like to love, and be loved back?

Once again I feel the slippage of your skin, Zara, the resistance, the outpouring of your blood. The stench of blood. Heady, heavy like the stench of a butcher's shop. The stench of blood fills my nostrils and for a second I fear I will vomit. I sit, head down, cup my hands across my mouth and swallow to push the nausea back.

Calm again, I lift my head, my eyes back to the jury on whom my life depends. I see a middle-aged woman with curly hair. She looks kind enough. But what do I know of her? The cross-dresser. Hopefully a broadminded thinker. Next up, a man in a lumberjack shirt with darting eyes. And finally the Hugh Grant lookalike. Foppish blond hair constantly pushed from his eyes. Hugh Grant, did you support me? Or did Sebastian's tale of being hit on by women resonate with your own personal experience?

Enough of this. I cannot cope with this petty analysis any more. I pull my eyes from the jury and rest them on the floor. Nausea wells inside me. Urgently this time, pushing into my throat.

'I need to go to the bathroom,' I tell my guard.

It is like Chinese whispers. The guard whispers to a court official, who whispers to the judge. The judge whispers to the court official who walks across the court and whispers back to the guard.

'Permission granted, but please be as quick as possible.'

As quickly as possible, the guard takes me to the lavatories for prisoners in the bowels of the building, near the cells, deep below the court. Once inside the dated lavatory cubicle with cracked grey tiles and mould in the grouting, I lift the toilet lid and vomit profusely. A sea of soupy pink vomit, slippery with grease. It smells like cow dung. The smell of it makes me retch and vomit again. Sickness expunged, I shake and shiver, covered in goose bumps.

Then my body calms and at least for the time being I feel much better. I stand up and flush the toilet. I wash my hands, splashing my face with cold water. I clean my teeth with my finger and a nugget of liquid soap from the hand dispenser. The detergent froths across my teeth. It tastes sharp. Some slips into my throat and makes me cough.

In the lift on the way back to court, the guard holds my trembling hand.

Back in the dock. All eyes are on me. Eyes making me feel sick again. But even if I vomit all over myself, all over the dock, I cannot leave again. Theo turns to look at me. For a second the sickness evaporates.

The judge stands. The court quietens.

'Jury, have you elected a foreperson?'

The jury nod, and mutter yes.

'Will that person please stand.'

The bearded man of about twenty stands. Fancy electing someone so young. Perhaps he is older than he looks.

'Have you reached a decision?'

'Yes.'

'And is it the decision of all of you?'

'Yes.'

'Do you find the defendant guilty or not guilty of murder?'

'Not guilty.'

I exhale with relief. And Zara, if only you were still alive I would shout for joy from the top of the highest mountain I could find.

Not guilty.

Not guilty but still sentenced to spend the rest of my life trying to forgive myself. Trying to get on with my life. But at least I will have the freedom to try.

153

Sebastian

She looks so relieved. She steps out of the dock, towards the insipid Theo. I can't believe what's happened as she falls into his arms. I can't believe the jury let her go. How did they fall for her lies? Her cunning? Can't they understand, Zara's the victim here? Were they bribed? Threatened? Pushed? No one notices me slinking away. No one sees me slip into the side street across the road from court, to watch and wait. Miranda Cunningham cannot be allowed to live.

154

The guard is releasing me, letting me out of the dock. My limbs are so stiff I can hardly walk. I am in a daze. After so long incarcerated I can hardly take in what has happened. I look across at the jury gratefully, but they are filing out, unperturbed, probably in a hurry to get home. I am out of the dock. Standing in court as free as the next person. Free to go anywhere I want. Free to go home. But somehow freedom stifles me and I can't move at all.

Before I know what has happened I am in Theo's arms. He pulls me towards him and holds me against him as if I am precious. As Theo lets me go, I see the back of Sebastian's head as he skulks out of court, and a shadow darkens across my heart.

Ms Little steps towards Theo and me. *Too friendly Theo, too friendly,* she tells him with her eyes. She puts her hands on my shoulders, holding me primly from a distance, showering me with wafts of her flowery perfume, and telling me how very pleased she is. Mr Mimms shakes my hand and nods his head. A shake and a nod. Friendly for Mr Mimms.

'Thank you so much, Mr Mimms,' I manage.

And Mother is here, moving towards me. Crying. Smiling. Laughing. Trembling. Loving me. Holding me in her arms.

'Come on,' Mother says, 'let's get straight in the car and drive back to Tidebury tonight.' Tears are streaming down her face. I step back from her a little.

'Please Mother, I just need a little time on my own.' I pause. 'I want to go back to the flat, to try and face what happened.'

She is looking at me, eyes riddled with concern.

'I was taken away from the flat immediately and I haven't been back since,' I continue. 'I need to be there with my thoughts for a few days first, before I come home.'

For a second Mother looks crushed. Devastated. Then she composes herself. Her eyes soften a little. 'OK. I'll wait. I'll stay a bit longer in the hotel.'

'I won't keep you waiting long, I promise.'

The world moves around me, slow and unreal, as Mother and Theo escort me out of court, into the lobby. Somehow, from somewhere, I seem to be carrying my prison possessions in one of those weird perforated bags.

Standing in the middle of the lobby, Mother and I stare at each other.

'Are you sure you want to go back to the flat tonight?' Mother asks.

'Yes.'

'Are you sure you'll be all right? Why not wait until tomorrow?'

'Yes Mother, I'm sure.'

Mother hovers around in the lobby for as long as possible. Eventually she tears herself away, reluctantly. So reluctantly. Walking away as slowly as possible as if she can't bear to leave me. Turning in the doorway for a last concerned look. Now not quite so stooped as in court, but still only a shadow of her former self. As soon as she has stepped outside I am flooded with relief. I have enough guilt to carry. Her pain increases it.

Theo and I stand looking at each other in the lobby.

'Thank you so much for everything,' I say.

'Can I give you a lift to the flat?' he asks.

'No thanks. It's no distance. I can easily walk from here.'

His eyes, like my mother's eyes, brim with concern.

'I really do need a little time to myself.'

'I understand,' he says face stern. There is a pause. 'Well, bye then. Good luck.' His feet shuffle a little from side to side. 'You've got my number if you need it. Call me anytime.'

'Thank you.'

He walks away slowly. I feel lost.

Dragged down by the weight of my large plastic bag, I move through the Crown Court exit onto the street. A dark February afternoon, cold nipping at my fingers and my face, and I realise I don't have a coat. Where is it? It could be anywhere after all that has happened: the prison, the police station. At the bottom of the large plastic bag I am carrying. Did I even have it with me in the first place? If I've lost my coat it's nothing. Nothing in the scale of things.

How long will my perspective stay like this? A year ago I'd have beaten myself up if I'd lost my coat. But then I had not lost my sister. Pain and death push irrelevances out of you, at least for a while. Maybe the world needs some trauma to keep it balanced.

Without my coat, I rush home pinched with cold. Past the theatre. Past the restaurants and bars of Harbourside, people sitting outside beneath heaters, drinking, smoking, chatting. The evening lights reflecting and shimmering across the water, making everything look more mysterious. More glamorous. I had begun to think I would never see this again, or at least not

369

until I was too old to enjoy it. But without you, Zara, I am not sure I will ever enjoy it again.

Five minutes later I am standing outside my flat. So close to the Crown Court. So close, and yet when I was incarcerated there it seemed so far. I stand outside the flat, heart thumping. I put the key in the lock. I turn and push. It is a little stiff. It needs some WD-40. But I push and twist and it releases. It allows me in. Into my small hallway.

Two steps into the living room with its two leather sofas, shiny granite kitchen nestled in the corner. I see your body there, Zara. Will its bloodied alabaster tangle ever go away? I walk past your ghoulish image, still smelling your blood.

Towards my bedroom. I open the door slowly. My bedroom, but not my bedroom. Mother has tidied it. She told me in one of her visits how she had scrubbed and cleaned the flat. It was tidy anyway but now it is almost empty. I stand looking across my bedroom. The bed still shouts towards me. The bed where Sebastian and I had sex. The bed where he raped me. I can't bear to look any more.

I go into your bedroom, Zara. Again antiseptically tidy. But traces of you still stab me. Mother has left a few of your possessions in place. Your favourite perfume. Your make-up in a bowl. Your hairbrush containing a nest of perfect golden brown hair, waiting for you to return. As if Mother couldn't bear to throw them away. My heart stops. Why did I want to come back?

The landline rings. I rush back into the living room to pick up.

'It's Mother. Are you all right?'

My stomach tightens. I want peace. I want space. I want to be left alone.

'I'm fine,' I lie. How will I ever be fine again? 'I'm just going to watch a bit of TV and go to sleep.'

Silence reverberates down the phone line, pressing against my eardrum.

'All right,' she says eventually. 'I'll ring again in the morning.'

'Thanks Mother, love you.'

'Love you so, my darling.'

Her voice is overly intense. Her words curl around me and strangle me. What doesn't she understand about me wanting to be on my own? Not just want, need. I need to be alone, with a feral intensity. I sigh with relief as I put the phone down.

I flick the remote and the TV comes on. Images flicker across the screen in front of me but I am not watching it. I have not had alcohol in so long. Suddenly I want a drink. Maybe some alcohol will relax me, make me feel better. I walk across to the cupboard in the kitchen area to see if there is any in the flat. I open the cupboard door. Everything is in a jumble just as we left it. My heart stands still. I see a bottle of Rioja at the back. Rioja, Sebastian's favourite.

And I am back. Back to the first time you brought him to the flat.

Sebastian Templeton. Dark and swarthy, needing a shave. Wearing designer jeans: pale blue, with carefully placed rips. Well-worn brown suede boots. Black cashmere round-neck sweater. A black stud in his left ear – subtle but quirky. Designer stubble cutting into me as he kisses me. The smell of mint. He had just cleaned his teeth.

I remember pouring us a glass of wine each, sitting in a row together on our sofa to drink it, Sebastian in the middle. The bastard. The damage he has caused us. Hands trembling, I reach for the bottle from the cupboard. I open it and pour myself a tumbler full. No half measures tonight. I knock it back almost in one, too quickly to taste it properly, and then I go and lie on the sofa, letting the images from the TV in front of me slide across my mind and anaesthetise it.

155

Sebastian

I see her silhouette through the window blinds. Drinking wine. Typical. She always drank too much wine. I know she is alone. No one else has entered the flat, and I have been watching the flat for hours. I look at my watch. Now is the time. Time to pay her a well-deserved visit.

156

I must have fallen asleep. Suddenly I am awake, head a little fuzzy, aware of the doorbell ringing. The sound drills into me like an electric shock. Who knows I'm here, except Theo and Mother? Is it Mother, so super worried that she is paying an impromptu visit? I walk through the flat to the front door.

A mass of black hair greets me through the crusted glass window of the door.

Sebastian.

Sebastian come to talk to me.

At last.

I open the door and he is here, standing in front of me. For a second I forget what has happened. For a second I forget you are dead, and I expect you to be standing behind him. Then I remember, and my blood runs cold with dread. Dread of the past. Dread of the future. Pure, unadulterated dread.

'May I come in?' he asks.

'Yes,' I reply. 'We need to talk.'

He steps into the hallway. He pushes his dark eyes into mine. They do not simmer like they used to.

'Not exactly like the old days is it?' he says.

The pain of what has happened solidifies in the air between us. I don't reply. I step through our compact hallway. He follows me. He flops onto the sofa and crosses his legs, not as flamboyantly as he used to. I sit on the sofa opposite him.

'Why didn't you come and see me when I asked?'

His face stiffens. He shrugs. 'Why did you want me to?' he asks.

'I wanted to explain what happened,' I continue. 'I wanted you to forgive me.'

His eyes solidify. 'I will never forgive you.'

His words sear into me. Is that what I really wanted – his forgiveness? Most of this was his fault. Maybe I wanted to castigate him, to blame him, and assuage my own guilt.

'I will never forgive you,' he repeats.

We sit in silence for a while. A silence louder than sound, that burns against my skin. I cut through it.

'You shouldn't have told her.'

He smiles his slow, Machiavellian smile, without moving his eyes. I watch him slowly, slowly put his hands together on his knee and intertwine his fingers. I watch restless fingers doing a slow dance together, stroking, playing, like they once played with my body.

'You're in denial if you think Zara's death was my fault,' he says.

A scream is rising in my head. I breathe deeply to push it away. 'I begged you not to tell her. That's what set her off. That's why she nearly killed me,' I say through clenched teeth.

'I wish she had killed you,' he hisses.

His words stab into me. 'This isn't about me. You broke her heart. That's what I wanted to stop.'

'I loved her, you know. More than anything.'

My body aches. Pain upon pain. Pain of mind and body, interlinked. 'Then why did you play around with me?' I ask.

'I wanted her to be free of you.' His eyes, his body, spit with hate. 'I wanted her to kill you. Then she and I would be free.'

'Free how?' I ask, body trembling.

'Free of you, you bitch.'

'But, but . . .' I splutter, '*if* Zara had killed me she would have gone to prison.'

His eyes are mad. His eyes are wild. His fists are clenched. 'Why? You haven't.'

'But I didn't attack her.' I pause. 'She attacked me. That's why I haven't gone to prison – because I was innocent.'

He grins, lips laced with acid. 'Such faith in the legal system is touching. Don't you think there might be an appeal?'

'Theo would have warned me about it,' I snap back.

'Theo. The effeminate angel Gabriel who's looking after you.' He is mocking me with his voice. With his eyes.

'Let's keep Theo out of this,' I say.

'The guy's mad. He's been following me for weeks. Thinks he's one step ahead of me but he's not.' He pauses. His eyes are so hard, so dangerous. 'So where were we? Ah yes. I remember. Zara should have killed you.'

'Thanks,' I whisper. I sit with my head in my hands, feeling weak inside.

'She had nothing to worry about. I would have got here and set up the crime scene to make it look like self-defence; hurt Zara a bit with gloves on, and then covered my assault weapon with your prints.'

'What you're saying is ridiculous.'

'No it isn't.' There is a pause. 'Two can play your game, Miranda.'

'But I wasn't playing a game, Sebastian, I was telling the truth.'

'All truth is relative, Miranda. Surely you know that? You were so infatuated with me I could have done anything to stitch you up.'

'You're wrong, Sebastian. I wasn't infatuated with you; I tolerated you to please Zara.'

'So infatuated with me, you went to great lengths to kill her. The prosecution were right, weren't they?'

'No.'

'You are still in love with me.'

'No.'

'You were the unstable one. Crying in bed. Panic attacks.'

His face is blurring in front of me. I cannot see him but I can still hear him.

'You still want me, don't you?' he taunts.

I know I must walk away.

'I remember you groaning with pleasure beneath me.'

'Be quiet, Sebastian, please.'

Tears are rolling down my cheeks now. My whole body is trembling and I know I must get away from him fast. I walk quickly towards the door of the flat, trying not to panic. I turn my head back.

'I don't want you, Sebastian. I never did,' I tell him.

He rushes towards me and grabs me. I struggle to get away from him but I'm powerless. He drags me to the corner of the kitchen counter where I was with you, Zara. He has my hands clasped behind my back with his left hand; in his right he has a knife – I see the glint of its blade in the electric light.

'Let me do what Zara should have done.'

My hands are seconds away from the carving knife in the drawer behind me. I know it's there. I know I can kill him, this man I hate. This man who I have dreamt and fantasised about killing. I can finish him forever, right now, if I struggle, if I fight. My hands pull away from his grasp. I reach into the drawer and grapple for the knife.

But my fingers don't quite reach it. I am tired. So tired. Too tired to fight another case. I allow them to go limp. It will be easier to die. Last time I so wished I had. It's been so hard being alive without you, Zara. Sebastian is here, granting my wish. I don't resist any more. The knife moves closer. I see the look of satisfaction in his eyes.

157

'Police. Drop the knife.'

Sharp, sudden words ricochet into the air like bullets.

The knife doesn't move. His eyes are fixated on my neck. He is contemplating pushing it in. He must be. It hasn't moved. Sebastian, I am ready. Ready to die.

158

Sebastian

'Drop the knife or I'll shoot.'

Words shouted from nowhere. Plenty of time to slash her in the jugular before they shoot. We'll both be dead but I don't care. Death will bring peace. Death will bring love. My fingers tighten around the knife. Oh Zara I am getting my reward. Miranda looks so weak and scared. Is that how you looked my darling, before she killed you?

159

The knife clatters to the floor. I step back. I am trembling. I am faint. About to collapse. A slender policewoman with dark brown hair and almond eyes catches me in her arms. She guides me towards the sofa and I sink into it, body trembling.

Somewhere in the distance of my mind I see that Sebastian is cuffed, hands behind his back. Two officers are flanking him and removing him. My trembling is increasing. He so nearly killed me. I cannot believe I am not dead. I stroke my face with my hand. The skin of my face is warm and solid. I am still here, I tell myself. Still thinking. Still breathing. A siren pounds across my mind. They are taking him away. It is his turn to be incarcerated.

The dark, slender police officer sits next to me on the sofa and puts her arm around my shoulders.

'How did you know Sebastian was here?' I ask.

'Because of Theo. Your barrister.'

'I don't understand.' My whole body is shivering but I feel hot.

'Theo was very concerned about Sebastian Templeton. He'd done a lot of undercover work on him during your trial and he was very frightened he would attack you as soon as you came out.' There is a pause. 'He predicted this.'

Even though I am sitting down, the blood is rushing from my head and I fear I am about to faint. I bend over and put my head in my hands. 'I didn't,' I mutter. The blood rush calms. I take a deep breath. 'How did you know he was about to kill me?'

'CCTV surveillance. We had officers outside waiting. All arranged by Theo Gregson, your barrister.'

Theo. Thank God for Theo. The police officer continues explaining. Her words are fading out now. I'm not listening properly. I am thinking about Theo. She is droning on about psychological profiling. Trauma. Loss. Distress. And then somewhere in the mist of her words I hear: 'You need to make a statement.'

'Right now?' I ask.

'It's probably best while it's all fresh in your mind.'

'I wish it wasn't in my mind. I never wanted any of this.'

'It won't take long. It'll soon be over.'

'It will never be over. My mind will store it.'

The slender police officer's eyes are soft with concern. 'You'll move forwards. One day bad memories with be tangled with good ones.'

'I will never have good memories again,' I tell her.

She doesn't reply. Her face just looks soft and sad. She pulls her notepad and pen from her pocket. 'Come on, let's do this.' There is a pause. 'And then I'm afraid we will have to ask you to leave the flat. It is now a crime scene. Forensics need to come here tomorrow. The flat must not be disturbed.'

A crime scene. Again. My flat, a crime scene. My whole life has become a crime scene.

'Do you want me to contact your mother? Understandably you are very shell-shocked. Get her to come and get you?'

'No. I'd rather be alone.'

'I'll text Theo then, get him to come and take you to a hotel? How about that.'

'Thanks,' I say and smile limply. I can't cope with my mother's emotion right now.

'Let's get started.' She pauses and takes a deep breath. 'Please Miranda, tell me everything you can remember that happened from the second you returned to the flat.'

I close my eyes. I lean back in my chair. My mind is on replay. My words start to spill.

'The doorbell rang. It was Sebastian, to talk to me.'

As I repeat what happened to the police officer I see it all again. I hear his every word, so graphically, as if I have stepped inside a movie screen that is real. Now I am back at that moment when I first began to fear he was going to kill me. He was looking at me with such hate. Eyes and face like acid. I don't tell her the moment I thought about killing him. That bit is too painful. Too private, adding to my guilt. My words float through time until I am back at the end.

'*Let me do what Zara should have done*, he said.'

I saw the knife moving closer. I felt the start of the cut. The look of satisfaction in his eyes as the knife started to plunge.

'Police. Drop the knife.'

He didn't move.

'Drop the knife or I'll shoot.'

He loosened his grip. The knife fell to the floor.

'I stepped away. I lived,' I tell her, my voice suddenly louder. I stepped away. I lived.

Sitting here with the police officer, who is taking notes. Still trembling and shaking. My life thin and watery, as if I am only just moving along inside it. As if, at any moment, I will be pushed away and no longer exist. Sebastian's knife coming towards me again. His eyes turn into yours, Zara. His knife becomes yours. I should have stabbed him, not you. My life as I know it would still be over, but his would be too.

160

Sebastian

Something was wrong. I tried to tighten my fingers around the knife, and plunge it into her neck, but I dropped it. The shouting had startled me. The knife clattered to the floor. The pigs were on top of me. All around me. Before I realised what was happening I was cuffed. I was crying, because you are gone, Zara, and I will never have you back.

They arrested me. You know the spiel. Everyone knows the spiel; we've all seen it so many times on TV.

'You are charged with the attempted murder of Miranda Cunningham. You do not have to say . . .'

My mind blanked as a young female officer spouted the meaningless words. They bundled me into the back of a police car, attached with cuffs to the arm of a tall thin male officer. The young woman was the driver. Across Bristol to the custody suite. Late Friday night, people tipping out of the pubs. People with lives to live. Rowdy groups of drinkers. My tears had stopped now. I could no longer feel moisture on my face. But I was still crying. Crying inside. And now I am in a cell with no windows in the custody suite.

161

I have stepped outside the crime scene, which once upon a time was my flat, accompanied by the police officer. I have been allowed, under her supervision, to pack a small bag of clothes and toiletries. I am in such a state – goodness knows what's in it. Knickers. Toiletries. A photograph of you, Zara.

As soon as the police officer saw Theo Gregson here, walking towards me, she made herself scarce and left. Theo Gregson is beginning to push my fears away, filling my mind with his smile, with his shoulders, with his runny honey eyes. I move towards him. Our bodies touch. I clamp myself against him.

'Theo.'

His body is taut and muscular, hard and reassuring. Maybe there is some point in living.

'Thank you so much.'

He kisses the top of my head. I feel his lips on my hair, so gentle, so comforting. I cling to him more tightly.

'I was told you don't want to be with your mother tonight,' he almost whispers.

I look up at him. He holds my eyes in his.

'I really can't face her worry right now; I can hardly face my own,' I tell him.

'My flat is just over the road.'

'So close?'

His eyes dissolve into mine.

'So close, we could have almost met before.'

If only. If only I'd met him before I became so damaged. If only I had met him in another life.

'Before I became so full of problems?'

'I just meant we could have bumped into one another earlier and I still would have . . .' His words trip into one another and stop.

Still would have, what? I think but don't ask. He is looking uncomfortable. Embarrassed.

'Shall we go there for a bit while I book a hotel?' he continues. 'The Ibis is the closest.'

The Ibis Hotel. My stomach coagulates. The hotel I ran to the night Sebastian raped me. The night of my walk of shame. My body shudders.

'I can't face going there either.'

'So . . .' There is a pause. 'You're welcome to stay at my place?' Theo looks even more embarrassed than he did a few minutes ago. 'I mean, I can sleep on the sofa; you can sleep in my bed.'

'But Theo, I've caused you so much trouble.'

'That's not how I see it. I think it's Sebastian who's caused all the trouble.'

He puts his arm around my shoulders to comfort me as we step towards his flat. His arms around my shoulders feel so natural. So comfortable. The evening breeze hisses through the ferns and grasses planted at the edge of the ornate pathway that separates our two blocks of flats. The evening breeze caresses my skin reminding me, like the feel of Theo's body against

386

mine, that in some small ways even after everything that has happened it is good to be alive.

Good luck. Take care, Jane the listener said. Be patient. It will take time to pull your life back. Don't expect too much too quickly. I need to remember that.

Theo's flat is shiny and new like mine. Very similar to mine, in fact. White tiled floor, toffee sofas, toffee-coloured kitchen granite. Same builder. Same interior designer.

'Can I get you anything?' he asks.

I shake my head.

'A glass of water perhaps?' A pause. 'Or a glass of champagne, to celebrate the verdict?'

'Perhaps I could have a glass of champagne. It isn't every day I get out of prison. I need to try and relax.'

His face crumples with concern. He moves towards me, wraps his arms around me, and holds me against him again. The feel of him, the scent of him, reassures me.

'Miranda, you have been through so much,' he whispers. 'It's over now.'

We stand clamped together. I wish I could press a button and stand like this forever. But after a while he steps back, eyes molten.

'Let's have that champagne.'

He steps to the fridge, pulls out a bottle of Piper-Heidsieck, pops the cork, and pours us a glass each. He opens the patio doors and we step out onto his wide, wide balcony. I can see Harbourside and the SS *Great Britain*. I can see the Wills Memorial Building and the cathedral. We clink glasses.

'Miranda, here's to you. For surviving your ordeal.'

'Here's to you for rescuing me. For saving my life.'

We clink glasses again. We laugh. Then my eyes begin to fill with tears.

'Thank you Theo. Thank you so much.' I pause. 'How did you know what was going to happen?'

387

I take a sip of champagne. It slips down my throat like silk.

'The more I investigated Sebastian, the more worried I became about him.'

I am shivering again.

'Do you want to go inside?'

'No. I never want to go inside again.'

Theo laughs. He takes off his jacket and puts it around my shoulders.

'Did you know he was a twin?' he asks.

'No.'

'Yes. His twin brother Jude and his parents were killed in a car accident, nearly three years ago now. Sebastian was driving at the time. He was convicted for dangerous driving. After their deaths, he had two years off work before he could cope.'

'But . . . but . . .' I splutter, 'he pretended his parents were alive. They just seemed to be permanently away, on a cruise, on a holiday. What a weird way to behave. But then he is weird. Seriously strange.'

'He's a liar. A serial liar. I don't think he wanted to admit they were gone even to himself. I think he kept the house as a mausoleum to them. He couldn't bear to sell it. He couldn't bear to live in it full time, because of the memories.'

'Lying about his family. That makes sense. They always seemed so distant. So strange. Always away.' I pause. 'Were they even doctors like he said?'

'Yes. That much was true. PhD doctors. Well respected in their research area I gather.'

Something stirs in the distance of my memory. 'What did you say his brother was called?'

'Jude.'

And I step back in time.

'Good to meet you, Sis,' he says.

'Please call me Miranda,' I say with a smile.

'Of course, Miranda. Far more glamorous than Sis.'

'Not as glamorous as Sebastian.'

He grins. His grin is a major weapon in the artillery of his attractiveness.

'I suppose my name is a little flowery.' He pauses. 'Not as compact as Jude.'

'What has Jude got to do with it?' I ask.

'Nothing.' He grins again. 'Just the name of someone I once knew.'

The memory fades. I am back in the present, looking into Theo's eyes. Theo's eyes pushing Sebastian's eyes away.

'He was very close to his brother. Losing his brother seemed to affect him very seriously,' Theo says.

'I can understand that,' I say tears welling. 'I miss Zara, very, very, much.'

'He missed his brother terribly. He couldn't bear watching you two together reminding him of what he had lost, so he drove you apart.'

'How did you manage to figure that?'

'I had him followed.'

'That must have cost.'

'Worth every penny.'

'What did you find out?'

'He visited his brother's grave regularly to put flowers on it – he sobbed his heart out, every time. He visited his parents' graves too. They were all close together. But he always seemed even more upset by his brother's.'

'I suppose he did go home almost once a week. I never really thought about what he was doing.'

'A lot of my deductions about him were just guesswork. Educated guesswork. The hateful way he looked at you at the funeral. The way he lied about his family.' There is a pause. 'I guessed he was in denial about his parents, about his brother. I guessed that he was warped and wanted you two to be without each other. Why should you have what he hasn't?'

I shiver inside. I shake my head. 'Poor Sebastian.'

'Miranda, reserve your sympathy. Think what he's done to you. How you've lost Zara. How you have suffered for being responsible for her death. He has refused any help. He wouldn't have counselling. He slipped through society's support net.'

'But will he get help from now on?'

'Yes. He will get psychiatric help in prison.'

'When did you first realise how very dangerous he was?' I ask and then once again my mind steps back. Sitting in the Roebuck on a Saturday night.

'What I want to know,' he is saying as he sits down, 'my dearest twins, is if you had been on the *Titanic* as it went down, just how far would you have gone to protect one another?'

'Oh Sebastian, it's Saturday night. Can't we just have fun instead of dwelling on problems that don't exist?' I groan and take a large gulp of red wine.

Zara, you are leaning across the table and smiling at Sebastian, golden brown hair shimmering in the firelight. You turn to me. 'But Miranda, it's fun to contemplate different scenarios.'

'Until you met Sebastian I always thought it was implicit we'd go all the way to protect each other,' I almost snap. My voice sounds haughty. Harsh and robotic.

'Are you saying I've fragmented your relationship?' Sebastian asks holding my gaze for too long.

I shiver at the memory, and then my memory deepens.

'Please Sebastian. Please don't tell Zara about what happened between us.'

'You sound as if you're begging.'

'I am.'

'I like it when you beg.'

The cruelty. The way he tormented me.

'I like it when you beg.'

I pull myself away from my memories.

'Theo, when did you first realise he was dangerous?' I repeat.

'The way you reacted whenever I mentioned his name made me think he had hurt you. But when I was researching him I found two rape allegations against him, both of which were suddenly dropped. That's when I really knew something was very, very wrong.'

'You sorted it out.'

'I did.' He pauses to take a sip of his champagne. 'I traced the girls who had made the complaints and went to interview them. They dropped the cases because he had threatened them after raping them. But as you know, Caroline Holt, when she heard what you had gone through, agreed to be a witness for your case. A brave girl who didn't want him getting away with anything like this again.' Another gulp of his wine. 'Guesswork and intuition. Works every time.'

'Anything else you'd like to tell me, Theo? Anything else left to guess?'

He leans towards me and kisses me. At first I just let him kiss me and then I begin to kiss him back. Soft gentle kisses. He tastes celebratory. Of Piper-Heidsieck. Of happiness, of success. Gentle kisses so different from Sebastian's anger.

'I would like to try and guess whether, if I was very lucky, you would be interested in coming out for dinner with me, when you have recovered from tonight's ordeal?'

'I think it would be a fair bet to guess yes.'

'A fair bet?'

Another kiss – longer this time. Longer, firmer, greedier.

'More than a fair bet.' I pause and look into his eyes. I pull back. 'But there's one more thing I want you to know. Something I feel bad about.'

His eyes soften with concern.

'When Sebastian was tormenting me, after he had raped me, I used to dream, even fantasise about killing him.' My voice is stalling. Tears prickle in the corner of my eyes. 'Tonight, I almost stabbed him. I had my fingers in the drawer, fumbling for the carving knife.'

His eyes melt into mine and push Sebastian's eyes away. He pulls me against him and holds my head against his chest. 'Miranda, the man tormented you to hell and back. You didn't kill him. You didn't murder your sister. Your life will move forward from now on.'

We kiss again. His kiss pulls me in. I want him so much. He breaks away.

'Please Miranda, stop blaming yourself. None of this is your fault.'

162

Sebastian

In prison, I have had so much time to relive my nightmares. All of them. Not just in my sleep. They have haunted me day and night, reaching out to me as I try to carry out my prison job in the laundry. As I thrust wet clothes into the tumble dryer, or as I am ironing. Moving towards me as soon as I am alone in my cell for the evening – no one to talk to, nothing to do but read books, or watch TV.

First, I see your face, Jude. Then your crumpled body. Sometimes I see Mother and Father, as they once were. They come to me, young again. Holding hands, laughing, and smiling. Then I hear and feel the crash.

Sometimes I see you, Zara, running towards me on Hannover Quay, hair streaming like silk behind you. I reach out to try and stroke your face but as soon as I stretch my hand towards you, you disintegrate slowly, like a satellite TV picture losing transmission.

I see Miranda's face and feel the knife in my hand. I close my eyes and feel the urge I had to plunge it deep into her jugular. That desire rotates in the core of my stomach. Sometimes my nightmare tells me I did it. And then blood flows all over my hands, dank and sticky.

Zara, I'm so sorry. I was off my head on alcohol and drugs. I feel so guilty now. Like me and Jude, you and your sister have lost so much. I feel guilty for all I have done. Attempting to kill her. The anger. The rape. The psychotherapist is helping me. The grief counsellor. The sex therapist. I am on a programme to help with grief and anger. A programme that is reducing my pain.

163

EPILOGUE

Evening sunlight slips through our bedroom window, stroking my daughter's head, as I sit on our bed feeding her. She is latched to my breast. Like superglue. A rhythmic suction pump, sucking and pulling. The rhythm of the pull is calming, satisfying. I could sit like this for ever. A freeze-frame moment to be remembered, like the first time I felt her body move inside mine. Or maybe every time I felt the miracle of life inside me.

One girl. Not twins. I suppose somewhere deep inside I thought I might produce twins. Even though the medical profession assured us there was only one. Sometimes Theo and I would laugh about what we would do if we suddenly had to go and buy an extra set of everything.

Olivia. Golden. Like you, Zara. Like Mother. Golden skin. Golden hair. Golden eyes. Satisfied from her feed, her head drops back from my nipple, as she falls asleep. Never have I seen such bliss. Olivia asleep. Soft-limbed. Open-mouthed.

Cradling her in my arms, head in my right hand, as if she is precious treasure, I slip off my bed and tiptoe slowly towards her cot. Gently, carefully, I lower her towards the mattress. Gently, carefully, I lay her on her back and begin to move my hands away. She stretches her chubby arms above her head, opens her eyes, looks at me, and smiles. Six weeks old today. Her first real smile. My heart soars. Zara, it is your smile. A little part of you lives on. In my heart. In my daughter's smile.

I look across at Mother; here to help in my early weeks of motherhood, so exhausted she has fallen asleep in my nursing chair. She needs her sleep. I will not wake her now. Tomorrow she will see her other daughter's smile once again.

I think of you, Zara – your warmth. Your smile. Of how much you loved Sebastian. His psychotherapist has written to me, explaining at length how much he is improving in prison. How guilty he feels. Maybe one day he will be well enough to meet Olivia. Maybe Olivia's smile will help him to live.

Acknowledgements

I would like to thank four people in particular for their help with *Guilt*.

First, my agent Ger Nichol of The Book Bureau, for all her encouragement and support. And then, of course, my fantastic editor Phoebe Morgan of Avon HarperCollins, and her wonderful team. It was a lucky day for me when my work landed on Phoebe's desk. She is such a pleasure to work with. Next, my dear old friend, Charles Owens, a retired police inspector. Charles is my tireless police advisor. I don't think I would have got away with writing crime in the first place, if it wasn't for him. He continues to advise and support me. Last, but by no means least, my husband Richard, my long-suffering first reader. Thank you. Thank you. Thank you.

As to everyone else, close friends, family, my parents, Shirley and Peter, I think you know how much I appreciate you. Or you should by now. I want to thank my new friends too. Friends I have met through the crime writing community. You are such fun. Thanks for welcoming me. For allowing me to join in.

He's not your husband.
He's hers.

The number 1 bestseller.
Available in all good
bookshops now.

Read on for a sample of
Amanda's debut,
Obsession.

ONE
~ Carly ~

I am drunk; liquid-limbed, mind-pumping drunk, and so is my husband, Rob. Craggy features, softened by shadows, move towards me across the mosquito candle placed in the middle of the camping table, as he smiles at me and tops up my glass. I shiver a little and zip up my jacket. The low sky of this Breton night has brought the sort of chill that predicates frost. But although frost won't happen in July in the south of Brittany, during this camping holiday, I have not felt warm enough. Not once. Not at night, curled up beneath my inadequate blanket, or in the day when I'm supervising our children around the unheated swimming pool. The extra layer of body fat, cultivated after the arrival of our third child, is not protecting me from the cold.

Our children are asleep in the tent behind us. I feel their silence and the exhalation of their breath, deep rooted and satisfying. At least I don't have to watch their every movement until morning, as I do during the days. Holidays aren't holidays any more. We just take our children to a different place to look after them. A place that is harder work.

Everything about this camping holiday is exhausting. Standing by the pool for hour after hour, checking that they're not drowning. The boredom of watching and waiting for the occasional sight of a familiar head coming out from behind a plastic palm tree or poolside dolphin. Holding giggling toddlers as we are tossed down knotted plastic tubes, sliding along until we're spewed out into the water, the movement almost breaking our backs. The endless cooking of barbecues – washing burnt gunk off the griddle. As far as I am concerned this is the best part of the day; the children are in bed and I have Rob to myself.

For this is what I like. Rob to myself. We married just over ten years ago, so we were alone for several years before our children were born. We met at the training hospital when I was a trainee nurse and he was a junior doctor. I will never forget the sight of him walking down the ward towards me, that first cracked smile. No doubt someone looking in would consider our relationship argumentative. Some of our friends say that they never have a cross word. How do they achieve that? Why do we argue? My mother says it is because we care. Whatever. It isn't really a satisfactory day without the rumblings of a discussion.

Tonight, sitting opposite my husband, a surfeit of alcohol pounding through my veins, I am filled with a new kind of mischief.

'Who else would you go for, if you could?' I hear myself slur.

'No one,' he slurs back.

'I don't believe you. You tell me and I'll tell you,' I push. Rob sits in silence.

'Come on,' I say. 'Let's be really honest – to compound our relationship.'

He looks at me and puts his plastic wine glass on the metal table.

'But Carly, we don't need to compound our relationship.'

'I think we do.'

Green eyes burn to emerald.

'I don't want to know who you fantasise about.'

'But I want to know about you.'

A jawline held taut.

'I don't fantasise about anyone.'

'I don't believe you.' I pause. 'Anyway, I don't need to know who you fantasise about. We're just playing a game. Give me a name, someone you quite like.'

He shrugs his shoulders.

'I quite like Jenni.'

'Jenni?'

Jenni. NCT Jenni. Placid and peaceful with doe-like eyes. Endlessly, endlessly kind.

'What about you?'

I don't reply.

The camping holiday continues but it doesn't improve. Our two-day conjugal hangover doesn't help. The swimming pool and the weather are growing colder. Cloud gathers and hangs along the coastline, releasing a clinging sea mist which sticks to the headland, making our nightly walk along the cliff path to the nearest restaurant border on suicidal. The rain starts on Tuesday evening. On Wednesday morning I wake up and hear its soft drum beat still pounding against the canvas. At first the sound is comforting. A 'let's stay in bed and make love because it's cold and wet outside' sort of sound. I snuggle up to Rob and then reality hits me. Camping. Rain. Bored children about to wake up. I escape to the shower block.

By the time I reach the shower block I am so wet I'm not sure why I'm bothering to have a shower. The lukewarm dribble of water from the showerhead slightly raises my body temperature, but not my mood as I struggle to pull my clothing back across my damp skin and worry about my weight. I shouldn't have eaten pizza yesterday. Or chips the day before. And what about the beer? Soft and delicious and brimming with calories.

Forget about alcohol. It's the only thing I'm enjoying about this holiday.

At least I am not like Jenni, so thin after childbirth that her breasts have disappeared. I look at myself in the mirror, cup my breasts with my hands, think of her boyish figure, and laugh. Jenni.

Rob and Jenni. Who would have thought of that?

When I return to the tent it has come to life. Rob is starting to prepare breakfast and the children are playing a shouting game, or, as I listen harder, a roaring game. Our seven-year-old daughter, Pippa, is crawling on the floor on all fours, head back and growling. She's trying to frighten her younger brothers, Matt and John, shaking her long blonde hair and attacking them with fingernail claws. They are crawling away from her and laughing, too innocent to realise that if she could, she would hurt them. Rob, seemingly deaf to the noise, is putting cereal on the table.

As soon as I enter the tent, Rob's face lights up and he moves towards me, kisses me on the lips.

'Hey you. Do you want to play?' he asks.

'Mummy, Mummy,' Pippa roars. 'You can be a tiger.'

'A tiger that needs morning coffee before it can growl,' I say, planting myself firmly on a chair.

'The swimming pool closes when it rains. What are we going to do today?' Rob asks as the kettle whistles.

'Go home?' I suggest hopefully.

Being back home has many advantages, warmth being one of them, temperature control at the touch of a button preferable to the vagaries of weather. Regular sex without worrying that the children can hear is another positive. But the biggest advantage is sitting at the breakfast bar on Monday morning sipping coffee, waiting for my mother, knowing I have a child-free day in front of me.

My triangular-shaped mother, Heather, arrives, straight from her flat just around the corner. She steps into the hall, wearing her favourite floral dress and her M&S cardigan. Her shoulder-length curly hair looks as if it needs combing. It always looks as if it needs combing, but it's just the way her curls frizz. Some remaining brown hair peppers her grey like drizzled dirt. Mother, when are you going to improve your appearance? It doesn't seem to make any difference to how much our children love her. Pippa thunders down the stairs, two at a time, and falls into her grandmother's arms.

'Gwandma, Gwandma,' John shouts, bumbling downstairs in his Gruffalo pyjamas which Gwandma has bought him, launching himself into the hug. Before long Matt has joined the love-in too. I tip the rest of my coffee down the waste disposal, place my mug in the dishwasher and sidle towards the front door. I manage to kiss my mother as I pass her; the children have left a patch of skin on her cheek accessible.

'I hope you don't mind, but I'll be late tonight.'

'That's fine, dear. I won't be in any hurry to leave. Are you working late?'

'Going for a drink with Jenni.'

I close the front door and step into watery sunshine. My mother looks after the children for us three days a week, so that I can work for Rob in Riverside Surgery. Rob. The most popular GP in Stansfield. I hear it from our receptionists, from the school-gate mums, from the neighbours, and have no reason to doubt that it's true. Our surgery list is full. I can't compete with his popularity. Why would I want to? I'm just one of his practice nurses. All I do is give injections, take blood, and perform breast and gynae checks. Although aspects of my job are boring, I enjoy my three days at work more than my weekdays at home with the children. Weekends at home are fine because Rob is so very helpful. But my weekdays with the children are just plain hard work. Stopping fights, making too many peanut butter sandwiches (Matt's favourite), wading through burial mounds of laundry. The worst part is Pippa's school-gate pick-up. Mother seems to relish it, enjoys talking to the school-gate mafia. She fits in. But I don't. The school-gate mafia; women who are living through their children. Women who don't have anything else.

I walk towards the surgery. Left at the end of our road, along Stansfield High Street, past the Chinese restaurant, past the fish shop. I cross the road at the traffic lights and enter the surgery through the side door, away from the receptionists and the patients. I hang up my raincoat and open the door to the nurses' station. Sitting at my desk, I switch the computer on to check my patient list. Eight patients this morning. Two breast checks. Three blood tests. Three sets of travel injections. As I press the buzzer for my first patient, the shadow that started following me on holiday begins to darken.

The shadow is no lighter when I finish at the surgery and am on my way to meet you, Jenni. You are waiting for me after work at the coffee shop, by the bus stop in the centre of town. I see you through the window as I move past the bus queue – sending a text from your iPhone, your glossy hair tumbling across your face. As soon as I enter the coffee shop you look up and beam at me, as if seeing me is the most important part of your day. Jenni, you always try to make people feel like that. As if they are important. It is one of your tricks. I know that now. When we first met, I fell for it.

We knew each other at nursing college, didn't we, Jenni? But only from a distance. You weren't really my type. Christian

Union. No make-up. Didn't look men in the eye. Rumour had it you didn't go out on Saturday nights, stayed in to prepare your mind for the Lord on Sunday. Jenni. What were you like?

Our paths crossed again on a couples' night nearly six years ago at our local NCT co-ordinator's house, stranded together like beached whales on a low-slung sofa, so heavily pregnant that we could hardly change positions. Mark and John incubating inside us, almost ready to be born. I was the expert because I already had Pippa. You were stick thin except for your bump, which overwhelmed you, looking so worried as the NCT co-ordinator droned on about Braxton Hicks contractions and TENS machines and whether they worked. I looked at you as you listened, chocolate brown eyes closed in fear, and wanted to protect you. To hold you against me and tell you it's not as bad as it sounds. (Even though with Pippa it was far worse.)

At the end of the meeting we went to the pub, I can't remember which one of the four of us suggested it, but we all thought it was a good idea. We went to the White Swan, down by the river at the end of our road. A cold October night, sitting by the fire drinking orange juice and tonic water whilst the men cradled their pints. We were so engrossed in our own conversation, we didn't talk to them much. It took me so long to find you, Jenni, the first female friend I really cared about. All through school and university, men had been my companions. Women can be so bitchy, don't you think? So temperamental. Men are kinder. Simpler. I had up to this point socialised with them more as a rule. But then came the female-dominated world of pregnancy and early childhood that led me to you.

Today, with Mark and John at school, and another birth behind each of us, we hug clumsily across a small wooden table in the coffee shop opposite the surgery. Across the coffee you are already halfway through drinking. Across the crumbs of someone else's cake. I sit down on an uncomfortable wooden stool, which scrapes across the floor as I position it.

'How was your holiday?' you ask.

'Awful.'

'That wasn't what Rob said.'

Your words punch into me.

'When did you see Rob?' I ask.

'I didn't. He texted me.'

'Texted you?'

'Because he was worried about you.'

You wave and smile at the waitress, who starts to weave towards our table.

We order fresh coffee for you, and chocolate cake and cappuccino for me. The waitress presses our order into a small handheld machine and disappears to the next table.

'Why is Rob so worried about me?'

'He said you weren't yourself on holiday. You didn't seem to enjoy spending time with the children, apparently.'

'Well, did you when you were on holiday?'

Your toffee brown eyes widen as you look at me.

'Yes.'

Yes?

Jenni. You sanctimonious, husband-stealing bitch.